S0-BYK-088

ROSS THOMAS

AH, TREACHERY!

PRAISE FOR ROSS THOMAS AND
AH, TREACHERY!
A *NEW YORK TIMES* NOTABLE BOOK OF THE YEAR

"Mr. Thomas, a very skillful writer . . . unfolds his story in natural, free-flowing language laced with humor and sophisticated dialogue."

—*New York Times Book Review*

"Treacherously funny."　　　　　—*New York Daily News*

"The absolute master of the double-, triple-, and quadruple-cross . . . at the top of his antic form."

—*Boston Sunday Globe*

"Not merely is Thomas one of the most prolific writers of crime fiction, he's one of the best. . . . AH, TREACHERY! quickly spins into the controlled chaos that is Ross Thomas's stock in trade. Thomas knows how to make the incredible seem plausible, if not sensible, which is what he does here with his usual skill."

—*Washington Post Book World*

"Swift pacing . . . the plotting is intricate. . . . Thomas's yarn reaffirms his expertise at the black-humored political thriller."
—*Publishers Weekly* (starred review)

"Simply wonderful . . . another tale of gleeful greed, poisonous politics, and murder by people who like their work. . . . Another amazing accomplishment from the best there is; if you haven't yet discovered Ross Thomas, you've truly missed something."

—*Coast Book Review Service*

ROSS THOMAS

AH, TREACHERY!

THE MYSTERIOUS PRESS

Published by Warner Books

A Time Warner Company

To Laura Sereno

MYSTERIOUS PRESS EDITION

Copyright © 1994 by Ross E. Thomas, Inc.
All rights reserved.

Cover design by and illustration by Peter Thorpe

The Mysterious Press name and logo are registered trademarks of Warner Books, Inc.

 Mysterious Press Books are published by
Warner Books, Inc.
1271 Avenue of the Americas
New York, NY 10020

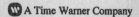 A Time Warner Company

Printed in the United States of America

Originally published in hardcover by The Mysterious Press.
First Printed in Paperback: November, 1995

10 9 8 7 6 5 4 3 2 1

He loved treachery but hated a traitor.
—*Plutarch on Romulus*

1

At 7:33 P.M. on Christmas Eve in 1992, the tall man with hair the color of pewter entered Wanda Lou's Weaponry in Sheridan, Wyoming, and pretended not to recognize Edd Partain, the cashiered Army Major turned gun store clerk.

Outside, which was exactly 21.8 miles south of the Montana line, the weather was cold and dry with both the humidity and the Fahrenheit down in the low teens. Yet the man with the short gray hair wore what some executive down in Denver or even Santa Fe might have worn—a lamb's-wool topcoat of springtime weight with raglan sleeves and a conservative houndstooth check. On his feet were a pair of black thin-soled loafers, well on their way to being ruined by Sheridan's two-foot accumulation of dirty snow.

Edd Partain let the gray-haired man look around for almost two minutes before offering a polite throat-clearing noise followed by an equally polite question: "Help you with something?"

The man nodded but still didn't look at Partain. "I need a last-minute gift or two," he said to a display of allegedly bulletproof vests. "Any suggestions?"

"Depends," Partain said. "For either Mom, the Mrs., or the girlfriend, you'd do well to consider the relatively rare and eminently collectible .25-caliber Walther PPK—the streamline 1913 vest pocket model, of course. For dear old Dad, perhaps a bespoke Purdy shotgun, which we can order from London, although we'll need a five-thousand-dollar deposit and delivery might take two, three, even four years. But old Dad'll appreciate your generosity and enjoy the years of anticipation."

The man turned from the bulletproof vests, walked slowly to the counter, leaned on its glass top with both hands and stared at the ex-Major with eyes whose color and warmth, Partain noticed, still resembled river ice just before the thaw.

"I wasn't absolutely sure it was you, Twodees," the man said. "Not till you opened your mouth and the crap flowed out."

"And I scarcely recognized you, Captain Millwed, what with all that new gray hair."

"*Colonel* Millwed."

"My God. The Army would never—but of course it would. And has. Congratulations."

Colonel Millwed ignored the suspect commendation and asked, "Wanda Lou around?"

"Wanda Lou, like Marley, has been dead these seven years. The Weaponry has passed on to Alice Ann Sutterfield, Wanda Lou's lovely daughter."

"She around?"

"Not until Boxing Day—Saturday."

The Colonel turned to give the gun store another quick inspection, then turned back to ask, "The lovely daughter pay anything?"

"Eight-sixty an hour," Partain said. "But since I usually work a sixty-hour week—with no time-and-a-half, I'm ashamed to admit—the pay's all right. For Wyoming. Besides, my wants are few and I serve them myself."

"Emerson on masturbation?"

"Or possibly Thoreau."

"So what did Alice Ann say after you told her about you and the Army and all?"

"She never asked and I never volunteered. But I knew they'd eventually send someone to tell her—maybe a freshly minted and slightly pompous second john who'd caught some colonel's eye. Or more likely, an overage-in-grade captain. That's why I wasn't surprised when you popped in, although I'm flattered they've sent a bird colonel to do the deed."

"Don't be flattered," Millwed said. "I volunteered."

"I should've guessed. But why now? Why not last year? The year before? Or even six months from now?"

"*The New York Times* get out here?"

"Yes, but I don't buy it. To keep au courant I rely on Sheridan's sprightly daily and the BBC world service."

"No TV?"

Partain frowned. "Really think I should buy a set?"

"Only if you're crazy about fires and jackknifed semis. Stick with the BBC. They'll have it soon enough."

Partain looked up at the old building's stamped tin ceiling, as if in search of a leak. "So it's all coming out," he said to the ceiling, then let his gaze resettle on Colonel Millwed. "But the sanitized version, I suppose, with some kind of respectable imprimatur."

"It'll come out in Spanish first, with the U.N.'s seal of approval," the Colonel said. "The U.N. believes—or pretends to anyway—that it's dug up all the real bad shit, but you and I, Twodees, we know better."

"And you come in the guise of what—a friendly warning?"

"Are warnings ever friendly?" the Colonel asked, obviously expecting no answer. "But if warnings give you the hives, think of my visit as the gentle nudge, which sure as shit's better than the hard shove."

Partain nodded thoughtfully, then brightened and gave Millwed a patently false smile. "Sure I can't sell you a little something now that you're here, my Colonel? Perhaps a nice cheap just-in-case throwdown?"

Millwed returned the false smile tooth for tooth, revealing his to be a peculiar off-white. Even his teeth are going gray, Partain thought as the Colonel said, "Just looking, Twodees. That's all. Just looking."

Only one customer dropped in after the Colonel left, but she bought nothing. At 9 P.M., Partain activated the alarm system; lowered the outside steel shutters; made sure the steel back door was locked and bolted; switched off the lights; locked the front door, and walked the three blocks to his one-room apartment atop his landlord's two-car garage.

Inside, Partain inspected and discarded his mail that included a Christmas card from a local bank where his checking account at last look was $319.41. He drank some bourbon and water, heated and ate a frozen Tex-Mex dinner, then sat up until midnight reading Freya Stark's *The Valleys of the Assassins* for the third time. He went to bed with the realization that, save for the Stark, this had been a virtual replay of all his Christmas Eves since 1989.

On Christmas morning the pounding on Partain's door awoke him at 7:02. He rose slowly, put on a shabby plaid robe, went to the door and said, "Who the hell're you?"

A woman shouted the reply. "It's me and you're fired."

Partain opened the door to reveal the too-thin, too-blond, 39-year-old Alice Ann Sutterfield. She stood shivering on the landing in the 11-degree temperature despite her gloves, sweater, flannel-lined jeans, boots and a heavy three-quarter length car coat. Her throat and mouth were hidden by a green and white wool scarf. Left exposed were crimson cheeks, glowing nose, squinty hazel eyes and dark brown eyebrows that betrayed the provenance of her butter-yellow hair.

She examined Partain warily, as if expecting some sort of violent reaction, but when he merely said, "And Merry Christmas to you, Alice Ann," she sniffed and brushed past him into the apartment.

After closing the door, Partain turned to find her, the scarf now loosened, standing slightly hipshot in the middle of the room. She was trying to glare at him with those squinty hazel eyes but her attempt only confirmed Partain's theory that squinty eyes, regardless of color, are incapable of really good glares.

"I don't want you in my store ever again, Edd, and I want my store keys right now."

Partain picked up the keys from the breakfast-dining-everything table and handed them over. "Been talking to the Colonel, have you?"

"That man sacrificed Christmas with his family to fly all the way out here and warn a poor widow woman of all that terrible stuff you did down there in—in, well, in Central America someplace."

"The Colonel has no family, Alice Ann, and you owe me one week's pay and two weeks' vacation."

"Think I don't know that? Think I didn't rush all over town last night, ruining my Christmas Eve, just to get the cash together and pay you every last cent you got coming? Here."

She thrust a white No.10 envelope at him. "Go on. Count it. It's all there."

"Then there's no need to count it," Partain said, accepting the envelope and shoving it into the pocket of his old robe.

"Well, I don't know, maybe you didn't do *everything* Colonel Milkweed says you—"

"Colonel Millwed."

"—everything he says you did, but I just can't take the chance of some, well, of some wildman loose among my guns. No telling what might happen."

"No telling," Partain agreed.

"I know you're gonna try and talk me out of it because you know what a softie I am. But this time I won't change my mind. So don't try and talk me out of it."

"Okay," Partain said. "I won't."

There wasn't much to pack. There were a few books, the small Sony shortwave, the clothing and toilet articles, some personal papers, a camera and one and a half bottles of fair whiskey—just enough to fill an Army duffel bag and most of the old Cape buffalo overnight bag he had bought cheaply in Florence years ago.

There were no dishes, glasses, cutlery, pots, pans, furniture or bedding. All that belonged to Neal, the landlord, who said he was sorry to lose Partain as a tenant and thought being fired on Christmas Day was one for the fucking books. Partain agreed, said goodbye over the phone, then called a number in Washington, D.C. that was answered on the third ring by a man's voice reciting the last four digits Partain had just dialed.

"It's Partain," he said. "They sent Millwed yesterday and I got fired this morning. My Christmas bonus."

"If you were Greek Orthodox like me, the true Christmas would still be two weeks away and your self-pity would be considerably lessened. Millwed, huh? Ralph Waldo Millwed, our jumped-up colonel now said to be a comer."

"Who says?"

"Rumor, of course."

"Any suggestions?" Partain said.

"As a matter of fact—and no little coincidence—there is a possibility. But it's more of a feeler than a definite offer."

"Let's hear it."

"A wealthy aged person of sixty-two years lies dying in Los Angeles. Needs bright aggressive go-getter to help solve one final problem. You interested?"

"What's the problem?"

"I don't know, but it pays one thousand a week and found."

"How many weeks?"

"Till death do you part, I suppose," the Greek said.

2

With his next-to-last $50 bill, Partain paid off the driver of the gypsy cab he had hailed and haggled with at LAX. As the cab sped away, he pocketed the $25 in change and turned to inspect the private hospital that was on the north side of Olympic Boulevard a few blocks east of Century City.

It was just past 6 P.M. and dark on the January Tuesday that was Twelfth Night. Partain found himself wondering whether the hospital had already taken down its holiday decorations or just hadn't bothered to put any up. He didn't care either way but regarded his mild curiosity as surprising, perhaps even encouraging.

As Partain studied the hospital, he began to suspect its architect had been enamored of long slabs of pale granite, and that its landscape designer had been equally smitten by drought-resistant plants—the expensive kind that still look thirsty even in a hard rain. Significant money also had gone into the hospital's outdoor security lighting system and Partain, who knew about such things, could find little fault with it.

He entered the hospital, carrying his Cape buffalo bag,

avoided the reception desk, rode an elevator to the top floor, the sixth, and slipped into a spacious corner room where the Greek had told him his prospective employer lay dying of some rare but undiagnosed ailment.

Partain found her sitting cross-legged on a hospital bed, wearing a Chinese-red silk robe decorated with numerous small gold dragons who were either yawning or roaring at each other. She had just finished a slice—the last slice, he noticed—of a small pizza, eating it out of the box it had been delivered in, and was now washing the last bite down with what little remained in a bottle of Beck's beer.

She lowered the bottle, stared at him for a moment with clever-looking, not quite gray eyes and said, "Edd-with-two-ds Partain, I hope and trust."

"They sometimes called me that—Twodees," he said. "In grade school mostly."

"Then I'd almost bet the Partains were Cajuns and probably in the oil bidness down around where—Opelousas? Lafayette?" She gave him a quick grin, showing off perfect teeth that Partain took to be perfectly capped. "Sorry," she said, "but I do like to make up tales about fellas I've just met."

"My folks moved from El Paso to Bakersfield right after the war," he said. "My old man was an over-the-road hauler and my mother ran a beauty shop out of their living room. I suspect the Partains were French Huguenots way back, but I never asked."

"Well, you already know I'm Millicent Altford or you wouldn't be here," she said, laying the empty beer bottle on its side in the empty pizza box. She then removed both box and bottle from her lap, placed them on the bed, slipped gracefully from her cross-legged perch to the floor and asked, "Want a beer?"

Partain said yes, thanks, and thought her come-and-go Red River Valley drawl must have originated at least 40 miles northeast of Dallas and not much less than 190 miles south of Oklahoma City. When the drawl went away, it was replaced by something cool and crisp out of Chicago, where, the Greek said, she had spent four years at Foote, Cone and Belding before signing on as a fund-raiser for the second Adlai Stevenson presidential campaign in 1956.

Altford glided barefoot to a small built-in bar that provided gin, Scotch and vodka but no bourbon. There were also some glasses, a tiny stainless-steel sink and, below that, a miniature refrigerator sheathed in a grainy brown Formica that looked nothing at all like walnut veneer.

Bending from the waist, she opened the refrigerator door and, with legs still straight and eyes now almost at knee level, peered inside and offered to fix Partain a real nice pastrami on rye with stuff the Stage Deli had sent over. Partain thanked her but said he had eaten on the plane.

She straightened as effortlessly as she had bent over—a bottle of Beck's in either hand—and turned to stare at him with an expression of what he assumed was sympathy. "You eat on planes?"

"An economy measure," he said, lowering his overnight bag to the floor.

"Well, we'll have to fix that, won't we?" she said and shut the refrigerator door with a backward kick of her bare left foot—a movement Partain suspected of being practiced and maybe even choreographed.

After crossing the room to hand him a beer, Millicent Altford turned and sank down onto a dark blue three-cushion couch, giving its center one a couple of invitational pats. Once both were seated, a cushion between them, Partain tasted his beer and said, "They told me you were dying. I assume they lied."

"I told 'em to lie. That way, if I didn't take to you right off, I could say: 'Sorry. Forget it. I'm just too busy dying.'"

"Since you're neither sick nor dying, it might be suspected you're hiding from something or somebody." He again looked around the large private corner room. "Although this has got to be one hell of an expensive place to hide."

"It'd cost anybody else or their insurance company at least two thousand a day—plus."

"Plus what?"

"Gourmet meals. The hospital went and hired itself a French chef with a yard-long menu, and now you can lie abed of a morning and spend an hour or so figuring out what you're gonna eat for the rest of the day and on into the night. But to me it's all free-gratis-for-nothing."

"Why?"

"Because when they first started planning this thing back in '83, they needed a million or so in seed money. I raised it in four days, didn't charge a dime for my services and now, well, now I've got myself sort of a permanent due bill."

"They actually cure anything here?"

"They're said to be hell on the clap."

To Partain she looked more like 52 than 62 despite the cap of thick short-cropped hair that had the color and sheen of old silver newly polished. Block out the hair, he thought, or dye it back to what must've been its original honey-blond, and she might, with the light behind her, pass for 41—your age.

Altford moved her legs around beneath the long red silk robe until they were back in their cross-legged position. She had a swallow of beer from the bottle and stared at Partain for a moment before she said, "Tell me about you and Nick Patrokis and all those renegade ex-spooks who call themselves BARF or VOMIT or some such."

Partain took his time before replying. "It began as Veterans of Military Intelligence, with VMI as its abbreviation. But when the Virginia Military Institute squawked, Nick and the rest of them thought up VOMI, which nobody liked. But because most of its members are fucked-over and otherwise disenchanted veterans of some kind of military intelligence, they decided, just for the hell of it, to call themselves Victims of Military Intelligence Treachery, which comes out VOMIT and makes an acronym nobody else'd want. It also got them some publicity, and that's the other reason they chose it."

"How long've you been a member?"

"I'm not anymore," Partain said. "I can't afford the dues."

"How much are they?"

"Twenty-five a year."

"Twenty-five *hundred*?"

"Twenty-five dollars."

She grinned. "You *are* broke."

"Or poor," he said. "I think there's a slight but significant difference." He had more of his beer, then asked, "How'd you hook up with Nick?"

"I have an old boyfriend who's a retired brigadier general?" she said, using the rising inflection indigenous to the Red River Valley and much of the South.

"Army or Marines?"

"Army. Truth is, he's the only general I've ever really known. But when he was my boyfriend back during the tail end of the Korea thing, he was a captain with funny politics."

"How funny?"

"He was a Stevenson Democrat."

"That's pretty funny from what I've read."

"A dozen years later, early Vietnam time, he was a colonel."

"And a fairly rapid riser."

"Goddamn brilliant, too. They sent him to Vietnam in '65 and made him a brigadier in '67. By then, he had his twenty years in. So in '68 he came out against the war and retired."

"In that order?"

She thought about it. "In that order."

"You still see him?"

"He's had two wives and I've had three husbands. But he and I still get it on now and then. After I started looking for somebody, I called and told him I needed to hire me some brains and brawn. He said they seldom came in the same box but, if they did, Nick Patrokis'd probably know where. So I called Nick and he called back with your name."

"Then you don't really know Nick?"

"Just over the phone. But I expect you know him pretty well."

"We met in Vietnam, where he had some rotten luck," Partain said and waited for her to ask what kind of rotten luck. When she didn't, his estimate of her rose a few degrees.

"Tell me about VOMIT," she said.

"It's really a one-man organization. Nick's a cofounder and executive director. He's also the publicist, fund-raiser, speakers' bureau, bookkeeper, gofer and editor of its now-and-again newsletter. He and VOMIT share an office with a skip-tracer on Connecticut Avenue a few blocks north of Dupont Circle—you know Washington?"

She nodded.

"Well, the office is above a Greek restaurant owned by Nick's uncle. Nick eats there free. The uncle also owns the building and doesn't charge VOMIT any rent. A few of the more crabby members, some sympathizers and even a groupie or two usually show up Saturday afternoons to carp and bitch and clean up and help with the mailings and such."

Altford nodded again, abruptly this time, signalling she now knew all she would ever need to know about VOMIT. "So how'd you get to be a victim of military intelligence treachery?" she said.

"I hit a superior officer and was permitted to resign my commission for the good of the service."

"How superior?"

"A colonel."

"And you were what?"

"A major."

"How hard you hit him?"

"I beat the shit out of him."

"Why?"

"You need a reason?"

"Yes, sir, I believe I do."

"He lied to me."

"All this happened where?"

"El Salvador."

"When?"

"Nineteen eighty-nine."

A silence followed that Millicent Altford ended before it bothered either of them. "You say you were also in Vietnam. You don't look old enough."

"From 1970 to '75."

"Right to the rotten end, huh?"

He nodded.

"I thought all you guys went home after '73."

"A few stayed on."

"Until '75?"

He nodded again.

"Then where'd you go?" she asked.

"Back to the States for a while, then to Germany for four years, stateside again, then to Tegucigalpa and on to El Salvador."

"Why there? I mean why you in particular?"

"I like to think it was because of my outstanding leadership qualities. Actually, it was because I speak Spanish."

"Learned where—El Paso?"

"From my mother. Her name was Sandoval. Beatriz Sandoval."

"How long were you in, all in all?"

"Nineteen years."

"No pension?"

"None."

"Where've you been working recently?"

"Until Christmas Day, I was a clerk at a gun store in Sheridan, Wyoming."

"What happened—the economy?"

"Irreconcilable differences with management."

Altford grinned, placed her now empty beer bottle on the blond coffee table and shifted around on the blue couch until, still cross-legged, she faced Partain.

"You wanta go to work for me?"

"Depends on what or who you're hiding from."

"Little Rock."

Because she seemed to be expecting or even needing some kind of reaction, Partain said, "No kidding?" and "Why?"

"Partly because they're real grateful for the two-point-six million in soft money I raised for the party. But shoot, that's what I hired on to do. What they're real, *real* grateful for is the two hundred and fifty-four thousand I bundled up for *them*, not the party, just three days after the New Hampshire primary. Check that *after*. And to do that I had to talk two hundred and fifty-four close personal friends into Fed Exing me checks for a thousand apiece made out to Little Rock's campaign. And you're damn right I delivered that bundle in person."

"So why all the hide-and-seek?"

"Because Little Rock wants to do something nice for me, and to them something nice might mean ambassador to Togo or some such and I'm just not cut out for stuff like that. But I didn't want to hurt their feelings, so I checked in here real sick and plan to stay that way 'til it all blows over and they forget about it, which I figure'll take another three days, maybe four."

"That's what you do, then—raise political money?"

"I'm a rainmaker and a good one. In odd years I sometimes go back to the plushbottoms I've hit up and try and put 'em together with a few solid guys I know who can make big bucks even bigger. When it works, I get a small percentage and the plushbottoms are so grateful they're almost happy to see me the next time I drop by to shake their money trees."

"Let's get to it," Partain said. "What d'you want with me?"

"One-point-two million in political funds have gone missing. Stolen, for sure. Maybe embezzled. I want it back."

"I wouldn't know where to start."

"Yeah, but I do," she said. "But while I'm doing it—and, O Sweet Jesus, I've just been dying to say this all day—I need somebody to ride shotgun."

Partain smiled. "I think I could handle that."

3

Once he made it to Wilshire Boulevard, Partain drove west in Millicent Altford's black Lexus coupe until he reached the apartment building that bore the name of either a failed British prime minister or the world's first garden.

The Eden was twenty-six stories of condominiums on the south side of the Wilshire corridor a dozen or so blocks east of UCLA. It had tinted windows and a façade of light brown stucco whose peculiar shade was called Jennifer after the late August tan of a 19-year-old beauty the architect had once met on Broad Beach in Malibu.

At 7:56 P.M., Partain made a left turn across traffic into a curved drive and stopped in front of the Eden's entrance. A uniformed doorman materialized on the driver's side, opened the door and said, "If you'll just leave the ignition key, Mr. Partain, I'll take care of the car."

Partain thanked him, grabbed the Cape buffalo bag and got out. The doorman handed him an electronic door key in the form of a plastic card with holes punched in it.

"This'll get you through the front door and into 1540, Ms. Altford's place," the doorman said. "When you need the car again, just press the asterisk on your Touch-Tone phone and ask for Jack."

"You're Jack?"

"I'm Jack."

The electronic key card worked nicely and the door to 1540 opened into a small formal foyer large enough for a burled elm wall table that could hold the mail, the keys and even a long shopping list. There was also room for a lyre-back occasional chair that looked as if nobody had yet found an occasion to sit on it.

A large mirror above the table was surrounded by an ornate gilt frame and both mirror and frame looked their age, which Partain guessed to be at least two hundred years. Opposite the mirror was a door that he assumed led to a coat closet. The foyer floor was covered with large black and white squares that his leather heels informed him were marble.

A few more steps and he was in an immense living room that boasted a Steinway baby grand and a real bar with lots of bottles and six comfortable-looking stools. There were more than enough couches and easy chairs, some covered in leather, some in fabric. There were also plenty, maybe even an excess, of tables and lamps. The floor itself was oak parquet and partially hidden by aging rugs woven in countries that were then called Persia and Mesopotamia. On the walls were a few large pictures, all representational oils, by painters whose names Partain thought he should recall but couldn't.

Beyond all this was the wall of glass that looked west toward the lights of Westwood, Brentwood and Santa Monica and beyond them to the blackness that was the ocean. It was a room, Partain decided, where it would cost you $1,000 for a glass of wine, a shrimp or two and the chance to chat up somebody who wanted to be your mayor, congresswoman, senator, governor—maybe even your President.

Partain, who had never missed voting absentee in every

presidential election since 1972, was wondering if he would ever vote again when the woman's voice behind him said "Don't move or I shoot."

Partain ignored the threat and spun counterclockwise with his right arm extended to give the old Cape buffalo bag added momentum. He let go the bag and watched it slam into the unarmed woman's stomach. After an explosive *whoof*, she stumbled back and down into an easy chair, somehow hanging onto the bag.

Six or seven deep recovery breaths later, staring at him all the while, she grinned and said, "I'd've shot you if I'd had a gun."

"You don't look that stupid."

She ignored him, lifted the bag from her lap, winced at its weight and dropped it on the floor with a clunk. "Christ, what's in there—the burglar tools?"

"Books and whiskey mostly."

"You're not the burglar?"

"No. Are you?"

"I'm Jessica Carver."

"Who used to be Jessica Altford."

"Wrong. I was always Jessica Carver, even if I do look like her. My mother."

"You're lucky to look like her."

"Am I?" she said, rose and went behind the bar, mixed Partain the bourbon and water he requested, then poured herself a glass of wine.

Partain now sat on one of the stools. After tasting his drink he said, "Your mother didn't call and tell you I was on the way?"

"Why would she? She doesn't even know I'm here."

"Since you're Jessica Carver, who's Mr. Carver?"

"My dad. Dr. Eldon Carver. He died in '69."

"Of what?"

"Of pain and an overdose of carefully self-administered

morphine. He had cancer of the pancreas, the inoperable kind, and didn't want to stick around. Nobody blamed him, certainly not Millie or me. He was her second husband."

"And her first one?"

"Why?"

"I like to know about people I work for."

"Well, her first was Harry Montague. They married in '57 and lived in Dallas until one Sunday afternoon in '59 when Harry took his old Stinson biplane up, did a couple of rolls, then tried an inside loop he didn't quite finish. A year later Millie married my dad and I came along in February of '61, which makes me almost thirty-two, if you forgot your calculator."

"Then came Mr. Altford, right?" Partain said.

She nodded and had another sip of wine.

"Who was he?"

"Slime."

"Any particular kind?"

"The all-purpose kind. Lawrence Demming Altford is sexy, smart and very rich. He's also a dedicated liar, a louse and a top-seeded paranoid. It lasted three years until Millie gave up and divorced him. But when she didn't ask for a property settlement or alimony, he sicced private detectives on her to find out what she was really up to."

"Why'd she keep his name?"

Jessica Carver shrugged. "Tired of changing it, I suppose. Or maybe she thought 'Millicent Altford' sounds kind of tony." She had another sip of the wine and asked, "What'd you say your name was?"

"I didn't. But it's Edd Partain."

"Spell it."

"Edd-with-two-ds P-a-r-t-a-i-n."

"What if I called Millie and asked if she's ever heard of any Edd-with-two-ds Partain?"

"I think you'd better."

She put her wine down, picked up a phone that was beneath the bar, tapped out 411, asked for the hospital's number, called it and requested Millicent Altford's room. After someone answered, she asked, "Ever hear of an Edd Partain, Ma?"

She listened for twenty seconds or so, staring at Partain as if he were some recent purchase she might return. "Well, this one's forty or forty-one, about six-two, maybe 175 pounds and wears an old blue suit, white shirt, striped red and blue tie that's way too narrow and honest-to-God black lace-ups."

She listened again, then said, "The hair's real dark with little gray streaks in it. The eyes are a funny-strange gray-green. Real white teeth. An okay chin, but it's only a chin. And he's quick, the way a cat's quick."

She again listened for several moments, looked at Partain and said in accented Spanish, "My mother wishes to know if you're willing to share the apartment, if not your bed, with her daughter?"

Partain replied in Spanish. "Any arrangement pleasing to her is pleasing to me."

"He'll go either way, Millie," Jessica Carver said, then listened some more and replied, "Christ, I don't know. Until I find work—like always." There were a few more seconds of listening before she said, "Right," broke the connection and put the phone away.

To Partain she said, "Can you cook?"

"Sure. Can you?"

"No. So first I'll show you your room, then you can show me your scrambled eggs."

The apartment had three bedrooms—one master and two regulars. Partain said the regular one facing Wilshire was fine. Because there was really nothing to unpack, he put the old overnight bag on the bed and told Jessica Carver her scrambled eggs would be ready in twenty-five or thirty minutes.

"Why so long?"

"You want biscuits, don't you?" Partain said.

* * *

Partain served it all at the same time—the scrambled eggs, the hot Bisquick biscuits, the double-thick, extra-lean bacon, and the sliced tomatoes that had come with little gold stickers boasting that they were organically grown.

They ate in a kitchen that, while not large, had virtually every appliance a small fancy restaurant would need. They ate at an old wooden table, a veteran of at least 25,000 breakfasts with the stains, scars and chipped yellow paint to prove it. They ate mostly in silence until Jessica Carver picked up her last slice of bacon, the one she may have been saving for dessert, ate it and said, "Millie grew up eating breakfast at this table, and when she was sixteen or seventeen decided she was going to eat breakfast at it for the rest of her life. My ma can be a little weird."

"She was born in Bonham, right?"

"She told you that?"

"No."

"Then how'd you know?"

"The same way I'd be willing to bet she moved to Dallas when she was eight or nine."

"Yeah, well, you could've guessed that from what I said about Harry and his Stinson."

"I'm just good at American accents," Partain said. "Your mother's comes and goes now, but it's pretty. If you go farther east along the Red River, they all start sounding like Perot."

"Which can cause nerve damage." Carver examined him curiously for several moments, then asked, "You travel a lot? Is that why you study accents?"

"I was in the Army a long time and it became a hobby."

"How long?"

"Nineteen years."

"What were you when you left?"

"A major."

"West Point? OCS? National Guard? ROTC?"

Partain shook his head. "I was in a long-range recon outfit in Vietnam that got wiped out except for me and two other guys—both short-timers. The Army panicked and thought it was in desperate need of an experienced second lieutenant to rebuild the platoon—except there weren't any experienced second lieutenants. There never are. So they made me one overnight."

"Where'd you learn your pretty Spanish?"

"From my mother. Where'd you learn your Mexican?"

"Mostly from a shit I lived with for a year in Guadalajara."

"Not a Mexican shit, though."

"Worse," she said. "An American one."

4

The Colonel and the Major General met at midnight in room 517 of the Mayflower Hotel in Washington. They met in a room registered to Jerome Able, which was Colonel Ralph Millwed's occasional nom de guerre and one he could document with a counterfeit Virginia driver's license, a real VISA card and a spurious Social Security number.

If more identification were needed, and it almost never was during normal commercial transactions, the Colonel would simply change his mind and walk away. Virtually all hotels, motels and car rental agencies readily accepted the VISA card. Once done with the rooms and cars, the Colonel paid for them with cash discreetly peeled from the $3,000 roll he always carried in $50 and $100 bills.

The $3,000 roll was replenished from a permanent cash hoard of $100,000 kept in the pseudonymous Jerome Able's safe-deposit box at a K Street branch of the Riggs National Bank. Whenever the hoard needed topping up, a fat wax-sealed brown envelope, stuffed with used hundreds and fifties, was delivered to the Colonel's apartment on Wisconsin Avenue just south of the National Cathedral. The delivery man was always the same silent morose cabdriver who seldom spoke and never asked for a receipt.

At first glance the 49-year-old Major General, Walker L. Hudson, seemed completely bald. But closer inspection revealed a faint gray-blond band of stubble that went up and over one ear, spread down to and across the nape of the neck, then climbed back up and over the other ear.

Tall and lean, almost skinny, the General was a wedgehead with a curiously small thin mouth that snapped itself shut into a short mean line after each utterance. At the end of the yard-long arms were huge hands that, even in repose, managed to look restless. The General sat quietly in the small room's only comfortable chair as his hands busied themselves with cigar, bourbon and water.

Neither the Colonel nor the General was in uniform. Instead, both wore dull suits, white shirts, muted ties and black shoes. Their topcoats were on the bed. Neither had worn a hat. After the General tasted his drink for the second time, he sighed and said, "Okay. Let's have it."

"He's in L.A.," Colonel Millwed said as he sat down on the room's lone bed and tasted his own drink.

"And?"

"Somebody hired him."

"Who?"

"Millicent Altford."

"Jesus," the General said. "What's she want with Twodees?"

"Guess."

Instead of guessing, the General said, "Draw me Twodees."

"Sure. For two years now he's been clerking in a gun store called Wanda Lou's Weaponry—"

"I gave you all that, for Christ sake."

"Yes, sir. I was merely setting the fucking scene."

"Let's stipulate it's Christmas Eve in Sheridan and the snow lies all about, cold and crisp and even. Poor Twodees, sad and lonely, is by himself in the gun shop when all of a sudden you waltz in. Then what?"

"I told him that some bad shit from our time together in El Salvador was due out from the U.N. in early spring. But it wasn't the really *bad* shit. Then I urged him to stay buttoned up and gave him a verbal nudge or two."

"How'd he take it?"

"Except for a crack about my being a colonel, he seemed indifferent. Even passive."

General Hudson grunted his disbelief. "Twodees is a bunch of things, but passive's not one of them. He's half Mexican and maybe even part Apache. If he's passive, so was Cochise."

"You want the rest of my Christmas carol?"

"Fast-forward it."

"After giving Twodees the hard nudge, I went calling on his boss, a lovely widow of thirty-nine summers by the name of Alice Ann Sutterfield."

"Slow it down a little."

"I told Alice Ann how unstable Twodees is and informed her of the horrible crimes against humanity he'd committed in El Salvador. Alice Ann somehow got it all mixed up with Nicaragua and Ollie North, who she still thinks is real cute. But after I sort of straightened that out, she asked me what she should do about Twodees."

"And you said?"

"I said that to protect not only herself but her community, she should fire Twodees first thing Christmas morning and pay him off in cash. She started bleating about how she couldn't fire him because it didn't seem fair and, besides, she owed him three weeks' pay, including two weeks' vacation."

"How much, all in all?"

"A gross of $1,548. Less Federal withholding and Social Security, a net of $1,022.30."

"What about state income tax?"

"Wyoming doesn't have any."

"I think I'll retire there," the General said and asked, "Then what?"

"Then she said there was no way in God's world she could come up with that much cash on Christmas Eve with the banks closed. So I told her that since this was, in essence, a matter of national security, it was also her beloved nation's responsibility. Whereupon—"

"By God, I do like the occasional 'whereupon,' " the General said.

"Whereupon, I gave her two thousand cash money, eased her back into her bedroom and fucked her cross-eyed."

The General chuckled. "And Twodees?"

"He'd cleared out of Sheridan by noon Christmas Day."

The General's expression went from merry to grim. "That, I don't like. He didn't set up a howl. He didn't lose his temper. He didn't even beat the shit out of you the way he did me that time. He just packed his bags and caught the noon bus."

"He flew out," Colonel Millwed said. "He flew to Denver and disappeared for about a week until he surfaced in L.A."

"How'd you find out Altford might've hired him?"

"Our guy in VOMIT."

"Ah," the General said contentedly, finished his drink, put the glass on a table and leaned forward, forearms on thighs, cigar now in his right hand. "What we need, Ralphie, is a direct line to Ms. Altford. Any notions?"

"Maybe."

"I don't want maybes, goddamnit. I want specificity and hope."

"It's better you don't know just yet. Sir."

"Since ignorance is not only bliss but also an alibi?"

The Colonel nodded.

"What else?"

"Comes now General Vernon Winfield. Class of '48. DSC from Korea. He was in Vietnam when you were."

"The deserter."

"He didn't desert."

"Might as well have," the General said. "The son of a bitch said it was a dumb war and unwinnable. He was right, of course, but he shouldn't have said it. Not then. Not in '68 with the whole fucking country about to explode. And who does he say it to? To that pissant wire service guy and zap, out it goes all over the world. Looking back, that's when I think we really lost it. Right then and there."

"It was lost in '54 at Dien Bien Phu."

"Shit, Ralphie, you weren't even born then." The General sighed, drew on his cigar, blew smoke at the ceiling and said, "So what about General Winfield?"

"He's close to Millicent Altford."

"How close is close?"

"They were sweeties back in the early fifties and I hear they still hold hands now and then—or whatever it is they do at sixty-five or thereabouts."

"I don't know about you, kid," General Hudson said, "but at sixty-five I plan to be fucking good-looking women."

"I'm sure you will be, sir."

"So what've we got on Winfield other than that he lost Vietnam and cofounded VOMIT?"

"Nothing."

"Another wrong answer."

"I can try to dig up something," Colonel Millwed said. "But if nothing's buried, I'll have to fabricate it and that can get expensive."

"Tell me something, Ralphie," the General said. "You really want that star by the time you're forty?"

The Colonel only nodded.

"And do you want to retire at fifty, like I'm planning to, with a nice little pension and maybe a useful contact or two in whatever's left by then of our military-industrial complex?"

"That very thought has occurred to me."

"Then you'd better listen carefully to your orders, Colonel.

One: You will remain on TDY until further notice. Two: You will get us some nasty on Vernon Winfield, even if you have to fabricate said nasty. Three: You will then coerce Winfield into using his liaison with Millicent Altford to feed us a running line on Twodees. And four, you will, at the appropriate time, fix Twodees."

"Why?"

"Why what?"

"Why fix him now? He was more of a threat to us last year than now."

"You apparently haven't yet noticed, Colonel, that in two weeks or so we'll have a new administration. In less than a year this new administration will find itself in deep political shit. New administrations always do. It will then cast about for a suitable diversion. What Twodees knows and possibly can prove could serve this new White House bunch as just such a diversion of the minor witch-hunt variety. Unfortunately, Colonel, it'll be you and me they burn at the stake."

After ten seconds of thought, the Colonel finally agreed with a reluctant nod.

"But with Twodees fixed," the General continued, "this new bunch need never hear of you or me except, of course, in a most salutary manner. And when it does find itself in need of a scapegoat or two, it can go hunt up somebody far more deserving."

There was a lengthy silence until Colonel Millwed said, "I think," then paused and began again. "I think I'll farm out the fix on Twodees."

5

The man with the clipboard and the manila envelope didn't look like a messenger to Edd Partain. But because of California's stubborn recession, Partain wasn't at all sure how Los Angeles messengers should look.

The few he occasionally had dealt with in Sheridan had all been old guys, World War Two vets mostly, with ancient pickups, raging thirsts and a desperate need to supplement their Social Security checks.

But the one who stood in the apartment doorway at 7:19 that morning seemed to regard himself as more emissary than messenger. He appeared to be 36 or so, topped Partain's six-two by a couple of inches and outweighed him by at least twenty pounds. Everything about him—his weathered good looks and size, his superior attitude and expensive clothes—irritated Partain and made him, at 41, feel old and jaundiced and secondhand shabby.

Partain was barefoot and wearing worn jeans and a ripped white T-shirt when he had opened the door to silence the chime-ringing. The smiling messenger stood there, resplendent in a navy-blue cashmere blazer with gold buttons, pale cream shirt, tan cavalry twill pants and, on sockless feet, cordovan loafers. But now the smile had vanished and the messenger wore an earnest, if puzzled, frown and beneath that an assortment of other lines and creases that Partain attributed to idleness, dissipation and too much time at the beach.

"I guess I haven't made myself clear," the messenger said in a friendly bass.

"Sure you have," Partain said. "You said she has to sign for the envelope. I said I won't wake her up but'll be glad to sign for it. You say that's against the rules. I'm about to say: Come back later."

"Who the fuck're you?"

"I'm the family's new best friend."

"Well, look, friend, I'm just trying to do my job and—"

"Like hell," Jessica Carver said as she entered the foyer. Partain turned to find her wearing only a very long white T-shirt she obviously had slept in.

"Claims he's a messenger," Partain said.

"He's Dave," she said. "Does Dave look like a messenger?"

"Goddamnit, Jessie. We have to talk."

"No, we don't," she said and turned to Partain. "Get rid of him."

"Could be messy," he said.

"So?" she said and vanished into the living room.

Partain was still watching her leave when he said, "Sorry, Dave," and turned around just as the false messenger cocked a big right fist and sent it toward Partain's heart. But because of the fist-cocking business, Partain easily slipped the blow, went in close and slammed the heel of his left palm against Dave's right eye.

Dave howled, dropped the clipboard, clapped his right hand over the eye, then covered that hand with his left one, leaving himself open to more damage. Partain instead placed a gentle hand on Dave's shoulder, steered him into the living room and eased him into a comfortable armchair.

"You won't lose the eye," Partain said.

"Fuck off," said Dave and bent over to hang his head between his knees, either to ease the pain or to keep from fainting. Only his right palm now covered the wounded eye and he was still in the bent-over position when Jessica Carver came into the living room, glanced at Dave and said, "What's his problem now?"

"A disagreement," Partain said.

"I see he won."

"I think not."

"He's inside, isn't he?" she said.

Because Jessica Carver had locked herself in her bedroom, refusing to have anything to do with Dave, it was Partain who taped a gauze pad over the bruised eye where the surrounding skin was beginning to hint of the bilious colors to come. Partain then fed the big man a Percodan and a beer after making sure he had arrived by taxi and would leave the same way.

They now sat at the living room bar, Partain sipping a breakfast beer and listening to the alcohol-and-Percodan-inspired monologue from the false messenger who confessed he was really David Laney, a 36-year-old UCLA graduate, class of '79, with a degree in political science even though he had never given a shit about politics but back then had figured it ought to be a good way to meet women and was, in fact, the way he'd met Jessie in '88 during the Dukakis campaign. And where the hell was Jessie, anyhow?

"Taking a nap," Partain said.

"Yeah, well, are you and she—you know?"

"I work for her mother."

"Doing what?"

"Security consultant."

"Rent-a-cop, huh?"

"If you like."

"Old Millie's something, isn't she? She'll hit on anyone. She even tried me one time."

"Jessica's mother?"

"Sure. Who else? There was this guy who wanted to be governor—Van de something. So Millie ran through her spiel and asked me to contribute a thousand to the guy's campaign. Well, Christ, the only income I've got is from this almost nothing trust fund, so I told her I'd do what I could and sent her a check for twenty-five bucks. That pissed her off so much she wouldn't speak to me for months."

"A trust fund sometimes must be more burden than comfort," Partain said.

"You know you're right?" Laney said. "Everybody thinks you're rolling in it, but two million's nowhere near what it used to be. Mine's handled out of a bank in Boston by some belt-and-suspender guys who still think six percent oughta draw money from the moon."

Partain decided it was time to send Laney on his way. "Want me to call a taxi?"

"Yeah, thanks, but let me ask you this." He touched his right eye. "How bad's the mouse going to be?"

"Bad enough."

"I still don't see why you had to pick my eye."

"To get your attention. If I'd wanted to do real damage, the eye'd've popped out and rolled around on the floor. But you're lucky in a way. If I'd been having one of my real black mood swings, I might've shoved your nosebone up into your brain and we wouldn't be sitting here over a couple of beers."

"What mood swings?"

"They started in Vietnam," Partain said, wondering where his embellishment would lead. "When I'm crossed, I'm sometimes subject to violent episodes. For example, if you try to bother Jessica again, I might go berserk and bite off your nose."

Laney's right hand went to his nose as he said, "You're shitting me, aren't you?"

"Am I?"

Laney studied Partain carefully with his one good eye for several moments, then nodded, as if reaching a decision. "I've met guys like you before. Lots of times. Guys who claim they eat lizards and fried red ants for breakfast and shit like that. I met a lot of 'em in Mexico."

"In Guadalajara?"

"There and La Paz and a bunch of other places. Guys who don't work and never have, but always have new cars and money and women. Fact is, I met one like that just before I flew up here. He came looking for Jessie, but she'd already gone. The guy wanted Jessie to tell her mother something."

"He have a name?" Partain said.

"Guys like him have as many names as they do women. Take your pick. But the one yesterday was calling himself Sid Solo."

"Is Ms. Altford supposed to know Mr. Solo?"

Laney started to shake his head no, thought better of it and said, "Nah. He was just the runner. Someone handed him maybe a hundred or two and told him to go find Jessie and tell her something."

"Tell her what?"

Laney frowned. "Will you tell her—Millie, I mean?"

"Sure."

"Okay," Laney said. "Sid Solo said for Jessie to tell her mother to call off the hunt. That's it and don't ask me what it means."

Partain smiled. "I misjudged you, Dave, and I apologize."

"For what?"

"You turned out to be a real messenger after all."

6

In the spring of 1971, a reporter for the now defunct *Washington Star* was roused from sleep by a phone call and a harsh deep voice that the reporter later wrote "sounded like the first cruel crack of doom."

The voice belonged to Emory Kite, a private investigator and skip-tracer, who warned the reporter to come up with a couple of past-due car payments or face unspecified consequences, which, the reporter imagined, would "begin with the rack, continue with the thumbscrew and end mercifully with a variation of the Asian bastinado."

The reporter borrowed money from his credit union, paid up and later that week went calling on Emory Kite at his rented desk in a divorce lawyer's office on the fourth floor of the old Bond Building at 14th and New York Avenue, N.W. The reporter discovered "a small man, somewhat larger than a big jockey, with the eyes of an amused hangman, the face of a young Mr. Punch and the sole proprietor of what sounds like hell's own official voice."

The byline feature ran fifteen column inches on an inside page under a three-column headline that read:

Want Deadbeats to Pay Up Fast?
Try Hell's Own Official Voice

The story gave only a sketchy account of Kite, noting that at 19 he had left Anniston, Alabama, in 1961 with only the vague promise of a patronage job as an elevator operator in the Capitol building. He arrived in Washington with one suit, a high school diploma and his frightener's voice, which he claimed to have acquired at 13 after being treated for strep throat with a home remedy tasting of turpentine.

Kite never got the elevator operator job, but he did find work with a collection agency that specialized in harassing Federal employees who fell behind on their installment loans. His voice soon made him the agency star and, after five and a half years, Kite acquired a private investigator's license. Soon after that, he quit the collection agency and, in his words, "went independent."

Since it was only a feature story, the *Washington Star* reporter saw no reason to dig more deeply and three months later quit the newspaper to teach journalism at the University of Nebraska at Lincoln. But on sheer hunch one of the story's readers did dig more deeply and discovered what he would later describe as "some very rich and nasty pay dirt."

The man who dug deeper was a young Army major just back from Vietnam. His assignment at the Pentagon was to devise a new and better way to track down Vietnam War deserters—most of them draftees. The Major had convinced his superiors to fund a small pilot program that would offer civilian bounty hunters $200 for each deserter they located. During Emory Kite's one and only visit to the Pentagon he asked Major Walker L. Hudson if, for the $200, "I gotta just find 'em, or both find 'em and bring 'em in, even if they don't wanta come?"

"You find, we fetch," Major Hudson said.

Kite began his hunt with an Army-supplied list of the names

and last known addresses of one hundred deserters. Within a week he had tracked down seventy-three of them by phone and, using only his voice from hell, convinced sixty-four of the seventy-three to stay put until either Federal marshals or the military police dropped by to pick them up.

Twenty-two years later the 51-year-old Emory Kite looked up from his Big Mac with those still-amused blue eyes and asked, "How come we gotta meet way the fuck out here in Silver Spring to eat hamburgers when we could be having something decent down at Zeibert's?"

"Because I don't know anybody who'd eat lunch at two forty-five in a McDonald's, especially a McDonald's in Silver Spring."

After that Colonel Ralph Millwed took his second and last bite of his Quarter Pounder and put it back on the tray, never to touch it again.

"So how's General Hudson doing?" Kite asked, his mouth full of hamburger and French fries.

Millwed looked away. "Fine."

"Been a while since I saw him."

"Three years, seven months and thirteen days," Millwed said, still glancing around the almost empty restaurant. He continued to look around until he thought the open-mouth mastication might have ended. He looked back, only to find Kite's hand poised over the Colonel's abandoned Quarter Pounder. "You gonna finish it?" Kite asked.

"No."

"I might as well, then," Kite said, picked up the remains, had a large bite and said, "Me and the General used to be real tight, you know."

The Colonel looked away again and said, "We go through this every time."

"I just want you to let him know I understand," said Kite. "Christ, a two-star general can't be buddy-buddy with a guy like me or something shitty might rub off on him. I know that. I bet when you get to be a general, Ralphie, you'll have yourself some tame major to eat lunch with me—probably out at the Roy Rogers in Hyattsville."

"Hyattsville does sound promising," the Colonel said.

Kite sucked up the last of his Coke with a straw, pushed away his tray, rested his elbows on the table and leaned toward Millwed. "What's up?"

"We want you to find us someone."

"Like the three I already found you? The one in Montana, the other one to hell and gone in Texas and the one with the ha-ha name way to fuck out in Wyoming? Twodees. Old Edd-with-two-ds Partain."

Kite cocked his head to one side to study Millwed. The Colonel thought it made the detective look rather like a reasonably intelligent rat terrier.

"You and the General," Kite was saying. "You and him must've made just one hell of a lot of enemies down there in Central America and wherever else the fuck you guys were."

"We made all the right enemies, Emory," said Millwed. "Which is as important as making all the right friends. The General and I think of you as a friend—although an expensive one."

"I'm not all that expensive. Fact is, I've been kind of cheap."

The Colonel reached into a pocket of his tweed jacket and brought out a slip of paper. After glancing at it, he said, "Since January of 1990, your fees and expenses have amounted to $231,373. All cash. And all, I trust, unreported to the IRS."

The Colonel produced an old Zippo and set fire to the slip of paper. He looked around for an ashtray, but finding none, dropped the burning slip into his coffee. Kite watched the paper burn, then drown and said, "If you guys think I cost too much, go take from somebody else."

"I like it when you pretend to have hurt feelings," Millwed said. "It always reminds me of a sensitive scorpion."

"The General and me used to kid back and forth like this," Kite said. "Before he got to be a general."

"You think I'm kidding?"

"I sure hope so, Ralphie," Kite said, smiled his thin wide smile and asked, "So who d'you want me to find this time?"

"Somebody to fix Partain."

Kite nodded judiciously, curling the corners of his wide mouth down into small hooks. "When?"

"We'll let you know."

"How much you willing to spend?"

"What's the going rate?"

"The going rate," Kite said, spacing the words. "Well, I didn't check the price list this morning, so I can't give you an exact figure. But it's sort of like asking, How much does a house cost? You see, Ralphie, when you hire somebody who's in the business of doing what you want done, you're dealing with the loose-wire crowd. It might be fifty thousand, five thousand or five hundred. Or the price can depend on if it rains or shines. Know what I'm saying?"

"You're saying you'll do it yourself for the right price."

Kite's eyebrows formed two surprised arcs above the blue eyes that remained cool and amused. "Never crossed my mind."

"Think about it," the Colonel said. "You've got two minutes."

"Your pal Twodees, huh?"

The Colonel nodded.

"He expecting it?"

"No."

"You want it done right, of course. I mean, you don't want some amateur job. You want it done by a pro who'll be in and out but not so fast he don't clean up after himself."

"You to a T, Emory," Colonel Millwed said.

"Maybe."

"How much?"

"Fifty thousand—plus expenses," Kite said. "Half in advance, half when it's done. That's the no-dicker price."

The Colonel stared at him before he finally asked, "How're things at VOMIT?"

"The usual."

"The usual what?"

"The usual 'Lordy, Lordy, look what they went and done now.'"

"Has Partain been back in touch with the Greek—Patrokis?"

"Nope."

"You're sure?"

"I'm there from nine to six, six days a week, practically sitting in Nick's lap. He's there from nine to nine, seven days a week. So what the fuck happens on Sunday I can't say. But far as I know, Nick's only talked to your friend Twodees twice since Christmas Day."

"You were there Christmas?"

"Sure. It's one of my best days. Maybe the very best. You call up Christmas morning around seven or eight and tell the guy you're on your way over for the pickup or the TV or the VCR or maybe even the stove and icebox, and that really puts the fear of God in him. He not only comes up with the cash, he even wants to bring it down to you." Kite smiled at the Colonel. "Twodees went to work for her, didn't he—out there in L.A.? For Millicent Altford?"

"Maybe."

"That why you want him fixed?"

"No."

"Old scores, huh?"

"You don't really need to know the why, Emory. Only the who."

"And the how much?"

"I can okay the price."

"So that just leaves the when, don't it?"

The Colonel rose. "I'll let you know."

7

Millicent Altford stared at the red carpet of her corner room for nearly a minute before she said, " 'Sid Solo said for Jessie to tell her mother to cancel the hunt.' "

The words had come out in the near monotone that some use for quoting or reading aloud. Altford now looked up at Edd Partain and asked in a normal voice, "Why isn't Jessie telling me this?"

"Because she wouldn't talk to Dave. So after some Percodan and beer, he told me."

"What'd he need Percodan for—that scrap you all had?"

Partain nodded.

"You on Percodan?"

"I had a root canal three months ago. The dentist gave me a prescription for twelve Percodans. I have ten left."

Altford nodded her approval of Partain's abstemious ways, then asked, "Could you please hand me my purse over there on the bed?"

Still on his feet after delivering his six-minute report, Partain crossed to the bed and picked up the large old brown Coach shoulder bag. After he handed it to the seated Altford, she removed a wallet, counted out twenty $100 bills, gave them to Partain and said, "Two weeks in advance."

He nodded, folded the money uncounted, stuck the bills down in his left hip pocket, buttoned the pocket carefully, then said, "What about expenses?"

"I'll want receipts for everything they give receipts for. But for the stuff nobody gives receipts for, I'll want a one-or two-word description such as, 'Bribes, $500.' Fair enough?"

Partain nodded again but Altford had already resumed her study of the red carpet. It was only then that he noticed she was wearing a different robe—a belted one of a light cream color that covered her from neck to ankles. Partain guessed it was cashmere and even hoped he was right.

After nearly forty seconds of utter concentration, Altford frowned, as if she had just reached a difficult decision, looked up at Partain again and asked, still frowning, "You like tamales?"

"Very much."

"Then why don't you go down and get the car and meet me out front in ten minutes and we'll drive up to Santa Paula and have us some tamales for lunch? Ever been to Santa Paula?"

"Not that I recall," Partain said.

It was a cool overcast day with the temperature down in the low sixties and Altford had dressed for it in a thick dark gray turtleneck sweater, tailored pale gray flannel pants and blue sneakers over bare feet. Partain stood beside the passenger door of the Lexus coupe, much as he would have stood if Altford had been a major and he a second lieutenant. Partain wore his blue suit, a fresh white shirt and his other tie. He opened the passenger door but she shook her head. "I'll drive," she said, went around the front of the car and slipped behind the wheel.

She was a quick assertive driver and took Olympic across

Lincoln Boulevard, then cut down to the Santa Monica Freeway, dived into the McClure tunnel and came out the other side on the Pacific Coast Highway that was also State Highway 1. Except for a few gaps, State Highway 1 went all the way to the Oregon line.

"We're taking the long-way-around scenic route," she said, making "route" rhyme with "out."

Partain nodded and they rode in silence until she stopped for a red light at Sunset Boulevard. "You like politics?" she asked.

"I like to vote."

"Why?"

"Probably because I never got to vote on anything in the Army. Sometimes, just to get a rise, I'd argue that officers and noncoms should be elected. Nearly everyone else argued that that'd lead to anarchy. When I asked them to define anarchy, they'd usually come up with a pretty fair definition of democracy."

"You voted in what—presidential elections?" she said.

"Never missed."

"When'd you start?"

"Seventy-two."

"Who for?"

"Nixon. Ford. Reagan twice. And Bush both times."

"Mind if I ask why?"

"I figured I was voting against a military coup."

She stared at him and kept on staring until the car behind her honked. She moved her right foot from the brake to the accelerator and the Lexus shot away. "You're not serious?" she said.

"There hasn't been a coup yet, has there?" Partain said. "Not a military one anyway."

Just past Oxnard, State Highway 1 merges with U.S. 101 for a stretch and it was then that Partain said, "Tell me about the missing one-point-two million and why you won't go to the cops and report it stolen or embezzled."

Altford slipped the car over into the far left fast lane and nudged it up to 73 miles per hour before she said, "You know how politics works?"

"I know how it works in the Army. You do favors for guys who, expecting more favors, do favors for you. Some call it politics. Others call it brownnosing. But it's how it works in the Army."

"And everywhere else," she said. "Except that in elective politics you make promises to get elected. And once you're elected, you promise even more things to get reelected. But promising isn't cheap—especially when you have to go on TV to outpromise your opponent. The entire political process requires God knows how much money and, like I told you, that's where I come in."

She looked at him, as though expecting some kind of rebuttal. Instead, Partain gave her what he hoped were a couple of wise nods.

"I suppose I best tell you about the damp money," she said with a small sigh.

"Is that money that went through the laundry but somebody forgot to fluff-dry it?"

"They didn't forget. They just thought I might sunshine it dry. Once damp money's dried out, it's just plain old money. The missing one-point-two million was sun-dried. By me."

"But still just a little bit damp?"

"Not enough to notice. Anyway, it made up a discretionary fund to be used only in emergencies."

"For example?"

She thought about it, then said, "I'll give you a sanitized for instance."

"Fine."

"A sixteen-year-old U.S. Senate page is about to go public with an accusation that a forty-seven-year-old U.S. senator is the father of her unborn child. The Senator is privately questioned and admits he might've had sex with the kid once or twice, maybe even three times or, maybe, after thinking about it, half a dozen times."

"Who asks him?"

"An intermediary or go-between of impeccable discretion, who's also a long way from being broke."

"Rich, huh?"

"Sort of."

"Does the go-between do much of this kind of thing?"

"Enough," she said. "Anyway, it's two weeks or ten days before the November election when the go-between pays a call on the girl to find out how much she thinks her silence is worth."

"How pregnant is she?"

"Two months."

"What about her parents?"

"They're back in Idaho, she's in Washington and, anyway, she thinks if they knew, they'd want a cut of whatever she gets."

"How much does she ask for?"

"She tells the go-between her silence is worth at least one hundred thousand. They bargain and the go-between knocks her price down to seventy-five. That's when he comes to me with his problem, which is money."

"And you decide if reelecting a U.S. senator who fucks sixteen-year-old girls is worth seventy-five thousand?"

"Right."

"Why not get the money from the Senator?"

"One, he'd claim he hasn't got it and, two, if he did have it, he'd be too tight to part with it. He'll take his chances instead and his defense will be that the girl's lying. If that doesn't work, he'll say he's not the only senator she fucked."

"Sounds like a prince," Partain said.

"Just average. So I ask the go-between to make sure the

girl's really pregnant and that the Senator's really the father. He does and they are. I ask him if there's a chance the girl will take the money and then talk her head off. He doesn't think so and is almost sure she'll have an abortion, then simply blow what's left of the money. Because I trust his judgment, I hand over the seventy-five thousand."

"What's his cut—the go-between's?"

"Zero."

"Must be a lot of altruism going around these days."

"I haven't noticed," she said. "Anyway, the girl vanishes after the payoff and the Senator never even asks what happened to her."

"And that's when you tell him what he owes you?"

She turned to glance at him with obvious wonder, then quickly went back to her driving. "If we told him we'd spent seventy-five thousand on her, he'd've laughed and said we were a couple of marks who got taken by a teenage con artist."

Partain thought that over, examining its weird logic, then asked, "Who gives you the okay to fork over that much money?"

"Nobody."

"Why not?"

"Because nobody wants to get their hands dirty."

"Ever get ripped off?"

"Twice."

"Where's the money come from?"

"You don't want to know."

"Okay. Then where did you keep it—the one-point-two million? Under the mattress? In a tin trunk? A safe-deposit box?"

"In a floor safe in my bedroom closet under a pile of suitcases."

"Good safe?"

"The best Diebold I could buy."

"Yesterday, you said it might have been embezzled."

"Since I'm the one entrusted with it," she said, "I have to be the prime suspect. There's only one other person who knows where I kept it but he doesn't have the combination. Still, since he did know where the safe was, that makes him a suspect—although I'm the most likely one."

"Your cotrustee and the go-between and your old boyfriend and the General, the one who got you in touch with VOMIT, they're all one and the same guy, right?"

"I thought I'd made that obvious."

"You did, but I had to be sure. Another question. Do you keep a set of books and, if so, when do you tot 'em up?"

"Every February first."

"Then you have about three weeks."

She said nothing and they rode in silence until Partain said, "When did you find out it was gone?"

"November the fourth—the day after the election. Most of the returns were in and I wanted to see how much we'd spent and how well we'd done." She paused. "I opened the safe and went into shock for three hours. I finally pulled myself together but there wasn't anyone I could call."

"Not even the retired Brigadier?"

"Especially not him."

"If you have to make an accounting to somebody or other on the first of February," Partain said, "what'll happen when you report that one-point-two million in off-the-books money disappeared last November, but you didn't see much point in bothering anybody until now?"

"That won't happen," she said.

"Why not?"

"Because on December seventh, Pearl Harbor Day, I replaced the entire one-point-two million," Altford said as she turned off U.S. 101 onto State 33 that led into Ojai, where it turned into State 150 that went up over the mountains and down into Santa Paula.

8

The Acropolis Restaurant on Connecticut Avenue occupied the ground floor of a sixty-six-year-old gray stone building that was only thirty feet wide. The building had no elevator but the retired Brigadier General walked up the four flights of stairs and arrived at the top-floor landing with no more loss of breath than if he had just completed a brisk stroll around nearby Dupont Circle.

He paused on the landing to remove his seventeen-year-old camel hair topcoat and drape it carefully over his left arm, which was encased in the sleeve of a fourteen-year-old tweed suit whose tailor had died at 83 two years ago in London.

After making sure his blue-and-maroon-striped tie nestled properly into the collar of his white shirt, the General removed the old light tan Borsalino—with its new dark brown grosgrain band—and transferred the hat to his left hand. He used his right hand to open the door whose upper half was mostly opaque pebbled glass. Painted on the glass in neat black letters were two signs. The top one read:

Victims of Military Intelligence Treachery
(V.O.M.I.T.)
Walk In!

The other sign read:

Emory Kite
Investigations

There was no reception area beyond the door, but to the right was a partitioned-off twelve-by-twenty-foot office with six-foot-high plastic walls whose top third was clear glass. The walls enclosed three bar-locked gray steel filing cabinets, a gray metal desk, a phone console, a personal computer, a fax machine, a photocopier and Emory Kite, licensed private investigator, who spun around in his swivel chair to wave at Vernon Winfield and give him a bass greeting of, "Hey, General, how's it going?"

Winfield paused, nodded formally to the small detective and said, "Very well, thank you, Mr. Kite." Winfield then turned toward the nerve center of VOMIT, which was a massive seventy-three-year-old golden oak flat-top desk jammed up against two windows that overlooked Connecticut Avenue. The top of the desk was nearly buried under piles of domestic and foreign newspapers, magazines and government reports—all of them with that plump, well-thumbed, well-read look.

Beyond the desk and against the building's south wall were overcrowded and unpainted pine bookcases that rose to the fourteen-foot ceiling and stretched thirty feet toward the alley. Close to the desk were a personal computer, a fax machine, a small Xerox copier and a very old, very large, wide-open safe with flanges that had been bolted to the floor so long ago that the bolts had rusted to a dull red.

Occupying, or perhaps filling, the golden oak swivel chair in front of the desk was Nicholas Patrokis, a huge half-bald man in his forties, who wore an enormous black mustache and a gold ring as big as a wedding band through his left ear. Patrokis's eyes were as black as human eyes ever get and above them a pair of dark hedges just failed to meet over a nose that hooked down toward the mustache.

A white scar formed a lightning bolt that began near the top of Patrokis's left ear, slashed across his mouth and chin and ended an inch or so below the right earlobe. A woman had once told him the scar made him look like an N. C. Wyeth illustration of a pirate in one of her childhood books. Patrokis liked the image so much that on days he judged too hot or too cold he wore a red bandana wrapped pirate fashion around his half-bald head.

Hunched over the desk now, a phone clamped to his left ear, Patrokis listened and scribbled notes on a gray legal pad. At the General's approach, he turned, phone still to his ear, and pointed with a ballpoint at a wooden armchair whose seat was occupied by a foot-high stack of *The Economist*. Patrokis used the worn jogging shoe on his left foot to kick the magazines to the floor, then went back to his listening and note-taking.

General Winfield settled into the chair and glanced around with the neutral expression of someone who knows all there is to know about waiting. From his seat next to the desk he had a fine view of the entire fourth floor and automatically began taking inventory of its contents.

About two-thirds of the fourth floor was devoted to what Patrokis liked to call the auditorium. This was an open space separated from the two offices by a divider railing much like those found in courtrooms. Beyond the railing were fifty folding metal chairs in two rows that were five wide and ten deep. Some of the chairs were gray, some brown, a few were black and all of them were old.

Beyond the chairs and near the alley end of the room was a long golden oak table placed parallel to the back wall. On top of it was a speaker's podium that faced the wrong way. Surrounding the table were fifteen more folding chairs used for board meetings, panel discussions and by those who dropped in on Saturday afternoons to clean up and help with mailings.

Against the exposed brick back wall was a five-gallon coffee urn that rested on a fifty-gallon steel drum. Next to the urn was a card table that held three gallon cans of Yuban coffee, six small cans of Pet milk and a ten-pound paper sack of C&H sugar. Six boxes of Styrofoam coffee cups were stored beneath the table.

The walls offered no posters, no slogans, no photographs. The only decoration was a huge American flag turned upside down in the traditional signal of distress. The General thought the upside-down flag was sophomoric and raised the issue at each board meeting. But his motion to right the flag always lost 7 to 6.

The General sat as he almost always sat, not quite at attention, knees nearly together, hands on thighs, topcoat folded over knees, hat on topcoat, back straight but not touching anything. Winfield had restless shiny blue eyes that were fine for distance but needed glasses for reading. They flicked around the big room, noting all changes—even a nearby recent copy of *El País*, airmailed from Madrid. He assumed Patrokis must have recently subscribed to it.

The General's gaze eventually landed on the back of Emory Kite's head. He noticed the private investigator wore earphones as he typed away at his computer. Winfield didn't care for Kite and had opposed renting him space. But the $1,100 monthly rent Kite had agreed to pay for a fourth-floor walkup office was such a godsend to the organization that the General had withdrawn his objection.

When Kite stopped typing to stretch, both hands high above his head, Winfield shifted his gaze back to the upside-down flag. Kite swivelled 180 degrees, noticed the General's fixed stare and used the opportunity to inspect him for signs of dissipation or dotage. He found only planes and angles that formed a resolute chin, an extra-bold nose, a rather stern mouth, a smart high forehead, a sagless throat and a lot of thick white hair, neither short nor long, that lay flat on the narrow head and looked as if it had been parted on the left at birth.

Kite was wondering how many men still wore real hats when Patrokis finally ended his phone call, turned to the General and asked, "You got any idea where we could lay our hands on five thousand dollars cash money?"

As Patrokis's raspy baritone came through Kite's earphones, he quickly turned back to his personal computer, switched on a concealed mini-recorder and slowly began typing "Now is the time for all good men to come to the aid of their party" over and over as he both recorded and listened to the conversation between the two founders of Victims of Military Intelligence Treachery.

It was a moment or two before General Winfield replied to Patrokis's question with a sigh and a question of his own. "Five thousand for what?"

"There's this Salvadoran ex-Army Captain, an illegal, holed up on Columbia Road who claims he has facts, figures and names concerning Langley money that went astray in 1989."

"What does he say 'astray' means?"

"That the money was passed by Langley to U.S. Army advisers who only passed half of it to the Salvadoran Army brass."

"Half of how much?"

"Two-point-four million dollars."

"How many of our people were involved?"

"Only two. A captain and a colonel."

"No names, of course."

"For five thousand we get names," Patrokis said.

"What do you think?" the General asked, then sighed again, as if he already knew the answer.

Patrokis shrugged. "If I had five thousand, I'd buy. But it's been three years since I saw that much cash all at one time."

"How much is in VOMIT's account?"

"Sixteen hundred and something, which'll just about take care of postage for the newsletter."

"You have enough paper? Envelopes?"

"Paper and envelopes I've got."

The General took out his checkbook and asked, "To cash, of course?"

"Of course," Patrokis said and offered his ballpoint pen.

As he wrote the check, Winfield asked, "Have you had lunch?"

"It's two forty-five. Of course I've had lunch."

"Well, I haven't," Winfield said, signed his name, tore out the check and put it away in a pocket. "If you have a tie, we'll go to the Madison, where I'm sure they'll feed me something. You can have dessert and listen."

"You don't need a tie to get into the Madison," Patrokis said.

"That's not the point, is it?"

Patrokis stared at the General for a second or two, then opened a desk drawer, closed it, opened another one and said, "I know there's a tie here somewhere."

After they left, Emory Kite rewound the taped conversation, played it, rewound it again and used a foot pedal to make it start and stop as he typed out a verbatim transcript on his PC. Kite was a fast accurate typist. When finished, he read the transcript over and made one minor correction.

He then rose, made a hard copy, and went to the fax machine, switched it on and sent the page and a half of double-spaced dialogue to a fax number listed under the name of

Jerome Able, the favorite of the three aliases used by Colonel Ralph Waldo Millwed.

After the "message received" signal, Kite returned to his swivel chair, sat down, leaned back, clasped his hands across his small still-hard belly and waited for his phone to ring, confident that it would be a short wait.

9

As General Winfield and Patrokis were leaving for their late lunch and dessert, Edd Partain was discovering that Santa Paula, a small agricultural city with a strong Mexican flavor, was just large enough and old enough to boast an historic district.

He would also discover that the tamales at El Charrito were even better than Millicent Altford had promised. He ordered the tamale plate lunch and ate three of the monsters, plus all the rice, refried beans and salad that came with it. Altford ate only half of one tamale, most of her salad, but ignored the rice and beans.

After the lunch, Partain leaned back in the booth, examined Altford for several moments, then asked, "You really replaced that missing one-point-two million with your own money?"

"Think I'm lying?"

He shook his head. "I just have a hard time dealing with the notion that anyone has that kind of money lying around."

"It wasn't just lying around. It was nearly all tax-deferred retirement money. I cashed in a Keogh plan. Liquidated six annuities. Closed out a money market fund, which wasn't paying a hell of a lot of interest anyway. I also cashed out all of my IRA mutual funds." Altford shook her head slightly, as if mourning the death of some old but slight acquaintance. Maybe the mailman, Partain thought.

"I knew there'd be a big tax bite," she continued. "But I didn't realize how godawful the penalties would be for cashing out my annuities early."

"How much?" Partain asked.

"About fifty-seven percent, including state and Federal taxes."

"Then you must've had to cash in what—about two-point-seven or -eight million to net one-point-two million?"

"Close," she said.

"How'd you do it? I mean, how'd you get your hands on the actual cash?"

"I put all proceeds into my regular checking account," she said. "Then I got certified checks, five of them for around $240,000 each. I used the certified checks to open regular checking accounts at banks in Santa Monica, Pasadena, West Hollywood, Culver City and Malibu. For six weeks after that I made irregular cash withdrawals from each of those accounts in odd amounts ranging from $8,500 to $9,500. At the end of six weeks, about the middle of December, I had the one-point-two million in cash. And because all the withdrawals were for less than ten thousand dollars, none of the banks had to report them to the IRS or the Treasury—or wherever they're reported."

"Who figured your tax bite for you?"

Altford stared at him coldly. "Why do you think I needed someone to figure it?"

"I would've."

"I went to the source," she said. "I went to the IRS office on Olympic just west of Sepulveda and talked to a real smart woman. I told her I was cashing in everything and needed to know exactly how much I'd owe the Federales and the state.

She was so shocked—well, surprised anyway—that I wasn't there to lie to her that we sat down and figured it all out in a couple of hours. She even found a way to save me close to thirty-two thousand."

"Where's the substitute one-point-two million now?" Partain said. "Not back in your safe, I hope."

"No."

"Where?"

"Here."

"In Santa Paula?"

She nodded. "Wanta go take a look at it?"

Partain thought about whether he did or not. "I don't know. You want me to?"

"I need a just-in-case witness."

"Just in case of what?"

"In case something happens to me."

Partain picked up the check. "Let's go."

As they drove toward the bank on Main Street, Partain noticed that a sign on the front door of a Santa Paula newspaper said, "Closed." On Main Street itself, at least nine stores stood vacant. A few optimistic entrepreneurs had rented other stores to try their luck at selling used furniture, secondhand books, Army surplus and palm readings.

Partain also noticed that while two Main Street banks had either failed or moved, the independent Farmers & Mechanics Bank was still in business. It had been founded in 1909 and Partain decided its plain granite façade and six fat round stone pillars were curiously reassuring. He was almost certain they had had a lot to do with the bank's survival.

The safe-deposit boxes were in the bank's basement. Millicent Altford and a young woman who was an assistant cashier used separate keys in the box's two locks. After the young woman left, Altford pulled at a big steel box-drawer that had a hinged lid. She had it halfway out when she looked at Partain and said, "Mind?"

"Not at all," he said, pulled the steel box the rest of the way out and carried it over to a semi-enclosed waist-high counter. He guessed the steel box itself weighed nine or ten pounds, but now contained something that made it weigh close to thirty-one or thirty-two pounds. Because it had once been his business to know how much U.S. currency weighed, Partain wasn't at all surprised by the box's weight. Nor was he surprised when Altford raised the box's lid to reveal what he assumed were 240 wrapper-bound packets of $100 bills, each packet containing fifty bills.

"Okay," he said. "I've seen it."

"Want to count it?"

"No."

After she closed the lid, Partain said, "Who else knows about it?"

"Nobody."

"Your daughter know?"

She shook her head.

Partain picked up the box and shoved it back into its slot. "What about your boyfriend and fellow trustee, the General?"

"I hope to God he doesn't," Altford said as she turned the key in the safe-deposit box lock.

The General cashed the $5,000 check at his bank and handed the money to Patrokis. They then drove to the Madison in the General's car, which he turned over to the hotel's doorman. In the Madison coffee shop, Winfield ordered the croque-monsieur and a bowl of potato and leek soup. Patrokis demanded and got a hot fudge sundae.

"So what's the report from the coast?" Patrokis asked after licking the last of the hot fudge from his spoon.

"Major Partain seems to be exactly what was needed."

"He's not a major anymore."

"Yes, well, I've looked into that a bit and, as far as I'm concerned, he's still Major Partain."

"But he's no sleuth, no private detective."

"She wasn't looking for one," the General said. "She was looking for someone to guard her back."

"At that he's good," Patrokis said, then paused and asked, "You really did check him out?"

"I made some superficial inquiries," Winfield said, ate the last of his ham and cheese sandwich, chewed, swallowed and said, "You two met in Vietnam." It wasn't a question.

"He pulled me out of a hole."

"Really? What sort of hole?"

"A mental one."

"Ah," the General said and looked at his watch. "What time is our meeting with the Salvadoran Captain?"

"Four-thirty."

"We'd best be on our way, then."

After the Madison doorman whistled up the General's new red BMW convertible, he was rewarded with a $10 tip. Once they were in the car and heading west on M Street toward Connecticut Avenue, Patrokis said, "You gave him ten bucks."

"No, I didn't."

"I saw you."

"The dollar is now worth twenty-three percent of what it was worth in 1965. So in effect, I gave him $2.30. In 1965, I probably would've tipped him $2 or, in today's money, $8.69. Therefore, instead of being too generous, I was, in fact, rather parsimonious."

"God, I hate money nuts," Patrokis said.

The General turned right at Connecticut and Columbia Road and drove until he found a parking lot within walking distance of Mintwood Place. He entrusted his car to a young Guatemalan who wore a strange derby of sorts that seemed three sizes too small.

The address on Mintwood Place was a typical three-story brick row house that had been converted into small apartments. The Salvadoran Captain's apartment was 321, which turned out to be at the rear of the third floor.

Patrokis knocked at the door twice before a man's voice from inside the apartment demanded in Spanish to know who was there.

"El Greco y un amigo," Patrokis said.

The door opened just enough to let one dark brown eye peer at them. It then opened wide enough to let them slip through and into the apartment. The Salvadoran Captain was not yet 30 and not very tall, no more than five-six, but he still had a military bearing even in T-shirt, jeans and running shoes, which, after all, the General decided, was the civilian uniform of the times.

The Captain didn't ask them to sit and looked embarrassed because of his rudeness. He looked embarrassed enough for Patrokis to ask, again in Spanish, "What's happening, friend?"

"I fear there has been a misunderstanding," the Captain replied in Spanish.

The General also used Spanish to ask, "Of what kind, please?"

The Captain stared at him and said, "You are called?"

"Winfield."

"He's the General I mentioned," Patrokis said.

The Captain came to attention and stayed that way even after Winfield said, "Retired."

"I regret what we discussed is no longer possible," the Captain said to Patrokis.

Patrokis nodded and took the roll of $5,000 in $100 bills from a pocket. There was now a rubber band around the roll and Patrokis snapped it absently. The Captain stared at the money.

"You are certain?" Patrokis asked.

"I am certain."

"May I ask why?"

"It is not possible," the Captain said again.

"But why is it not possible?"

"If a thing is not possible it is impossible."

"Perhaps the money is insufficient?" General Winfield asked.

"It is not a question of money."

"We need those two names," Patrokis said. "We will pay five thousand dollars for the names."

"There are no names," the Captain said.

"There were this morning."

"I was mistaken this morning."

"You don't look like a man who makes mistakes," the General said.

The Captain said nothing and looked away.

"Let's go," Patrokis said in English and turned toward the door.

"If you change your mind," the General said, "please telephone my friend."

"I will not be changing my mind, sir."

The General nodded his understanding and glanced around the room, noting the new television set and the old couch. He also noticed the picture of the Virgin and the dining table below it. Beyond the table was a small kitchen. To the left of the couch was a closed door that he assumed led to a bath and a bedroom. On the floor was an eight-by-ten rug of indeterminate age and color. There were two floor lamps, one of them next to the old couch, the other beside a worn easy chair that looked even older than the couch.

Winfield smiled at the Captain. "Goodbye, Captain."

"Goodbye, sir."

"Call me," Patrokis said in Spanish, opened the door and

waited for the Captain's response. When none came, Patrokis went through the door, followed by the General.

The Captain continued to stand almost at attention, staring at the just closed door. The bedroom door behind him opened and a young woman came out, followed by Emory Kite, who wore a too-long black topcoat, a smile and, in his right hand, a .25-caliber semiautomatic with a homemade silencer almost as long as the weapon itself.

"Were you harmed?" the Captain said to the young woman, who hurried to him.

"He did not harm me," she said and buried her face in his shoulder.

"You both were perfect," Emory Kite said in soft soothing English. "Both of you were absolutely perfect and I just hope you know how much that means to me."

Kite brought the silenced semiautomatic up and shot the young Captain in the back of the head, then scuttled around the falling body and shot the young woman in the left temple before she could scream, protest or pray.

10

It was Claudia Ransaw, a homicide detective sergeant with the Metropolitan Police, who called Nick Patrokis to ask whether he might be interested in the murder of an ex-Salvadoran Army captain and his wife. Ransaw, the forty-sixth person to join VOMIT, had been a first lieutenant in an Army CID unit until 1981, when she quietly announced she was a lesbian and was just as quietly separated from the service. "Only thing saved me from a DD was my black ass," she had once told Patrokis.

When Ransaw called him shortly after 6 P.M., she first asked if VOMIT was still "poking around in all that real bad shit in Central America?"

General Winfield had just risen to leave. Patrokis waved him back to the armchair and replied, "Sure. Why?"

"Because we've got us a dead Salvadoran ex-Army captain by the name of José Trigueros Chacón, age twenty-nine. And we've also got us Señora Trigueros, age twenty-six, who's just as dead. No passports and not much in the way of ID except for some of his old Army papers and her civilian stuff that gives an address in San Salvador."

"Where'd it happen?" Patrokis said.

"Over on Mintwood Place just off Columbia Road."

"What's it look like?"

"A pro hit. That's why I'm calling. One shot each. Little-bitty gun, no more'n a twenty-five, maybe even a twenty-two. Nobody saw nothing. Nobody heard nothing. He got it in the back of the head. She got it in the left temple. Been living there a week, maybe less, but the manager's not around so I can't even be sure of that."

"Did you get the wife's given names?"

"Rosa Alicia," Sergeant Ransaw said. "You learn anything about anything, you call me, hear?"

"I'll do that," Patrokis said, recradled the phone, turned to the General and said, "That was Detective Ransaw."

"So I gathered," Winfield said.

"She says our Captain and a woman, who Ransaw believes was his wife, were shot dead not long after we left."

"Who found them?"

"I didn't ask."

"How prudent," the General said and rose, his face now so pale a stranger might think him faint, although Patrokis knew him to be furious.

Winfield produced a small address book, looked up someone and said, "May I use the phone? I need to ask some questions I should've asked long before this."

The small two-story house was in the 3200 block on the north side of Volta Place just off Wisconsin Avenue in Georgetown. Because it had taken Winfield more than twenty minutes to find a parking place, it was nearly 7:15 P.M. when he rang the bell with his right thumb. In his left hand was a brown paper sack that contained a bottle of J&B whisky.

The door opened the length of its short chain and a tall slim pretty woman in her middle thirties stared at him with enormous gray eyes that seemed to be in mourning. Before

Winfield could say anything, the woman said, "He told me to tell you he's changed his mind. He told me to say he won't see you."

"How have you been, Shawnee?" Winfield said.

"Rotten. And you?"

"Not too bad. May I come in?"

"He won't see you."

"Perhaps I can change his mind."

She shrugged, closed the door long enough to unhook the chain, then reopened it. Winfield went into a very small, not quite square entry hall whose only decorations, other than the pretty woman in old jeans and a man's white shirt, were a brown metal hat rack that looked like government issue and an inscribed color photograph of Ronald Reagan. Winfield remembered that the inscription read, "To Hank Viar with gratitude and admiration."

Winfield removed his hat, handed the sack of liquor to the woman he called Shawnee, then took off his camel hair coat and hung it and the Borsalino on the borrowed or stolen hat rack. Just beyond it were steep narrow stairs that led up to what he remembered were two bedrooms and a bath. For some reason—age, he suspected—the stairs looked steeper than when he had last seen them seven years ago.

Winfield turned back to the woman, who now held the sack of liquor down at her left side, almost as if she had forgotten it. "How's—uh—your husband, Shawnee?" Winfield asked, recalling the face, if not the name, of a large young man with strangely gentle features and a mass of dark curly hair.

"He got AIDS and died," she said.

Instead of offering words of sorrow and commiseration, Winfield gently placed his right hand on her left shoulder. She looked down at the hand with what seemed to be surprise, then up at Winfield. "He thinks I've got it now," she said.

"Hank?"

She nodded. "He thinks AIDS is part of God's special curse

on the parents of certain boomers. The rest of the curse is that these boomers will dwell in the house of their parents forever. So I get myself tested every month and the results are always negative. But he says the test results look like forgeries to him and makes me use one cup, one glass, one plate and one knife, fork and spoon. He's really kind of nutty now."

She gave her head two abrupt shakes, as if to clear her mind. The shakes made her long auburn hair swirl and almost writhe. Winfield patted her shoulder and removed his hand just as she said, "Well, fuck Daddy dear. You wait in the living room and I'll tell him you won't leave till he comes down."

"He's not in bed, is he?"

"No, but he spends a lot of time upstairs in the front bedroom, keeping an eye on the street. I don't know who he's expecting. Maybe a delegation of those Kurds he helped fuck over years ago."

She handed back the sack of liquor and started slowly up the stairs. The General watched her for a moment, then turned and headed for the living room, wondering whether it was still stuffed with the relics and leavings of the past four decades.

11

The living room offered five reminders of plain Danish modern from the 1960s. A wealth of chrome, glass and leather represented the '70s, and the '80s were remarked by three flexible floor lamps that hovered over easy chairs, as if about to pounce. The only artifact from the 1990s was a new 32-inch Sony television set. On the nearby VCR were four gaudily packaged rental videos, all of them pornographic. Winfield was reading their titles when Henry Viar entered the room and said, "You want ice?"

"Not really," said Winfield as he turned to examine Viar—all six-foot-four of him—who now appeared to weigh less than 160 pounds. He noticed Viar had lost more than weight. He also had lost much of his hair and the loss made the long, long face look even longer. Yet, it remained a tight, closed-up face, the kind that belongs to someone who no longer goes out much, orders most of his food and drink by phone and speaks only in monosyllables to those who deliver it.

"You look awful," Winfield said.

"I know how I look," Viar said. "But that doesn't mean I give a shit." He pointed his big chin at the sack of Scotch that rested on a chrome and glass coffee table. "You ever gonna uncap that?"

Winfield removed the bottle from the sack, the cap from the bottle and asked, "Should we use glasses?"

"You want ice, too?"

"You already asked that and I said no. But I would like some water."

Viar turned, hurried through the dining room and into the kitchen. He was back moments later, carrying a glass pitcher of water in one hand and two mismatched tumblers in the other. After he set everything down, he watched carefully as the General poured generous measures into both glasses and added water to one of them.

"We going to drink or just sip?" Viar said.

Winfield added another ounce or so to his host's glass. The tall man bent over, picked it up, drank nearly half of the straight Scotch, came close to smacking his lips, but instead lit an unfiltered Pall Mall with a kitchen match. He then lowered himself into an easy chair (circa 1967, Winfield thought), put his feet up on its ottoman and said, "No lectures."

"No lectures," Winfield agreed, sat down on a cat-clawed couch that needed slipcovers and resumed his inspection of Viar, noting the frayed button-down blue shirt, chino pants and brown loafers. The pants and shirt, neither clean nor soiled, looked as if they might have been slept in. The loafers looked expensive but neglected.

Winfield's inspection seemed to amuse Viar, who smiled and said, "Some days I don't get dressed at all—just sit around in my underdrawers. Disgusting, isn't it?"

Instead of agreeing or disagreeing, the General said, "Let's talk about 1989."

"Why not 1968? That was another swell year."

"I prefer '89."

"What if I say go fuck yourself?"

"Then I'll use blackmail."

"That same old Panama crap? I don't think so."

"It might not land you in Leavenworth, Hank, but it'll certainly end your pension."

Viar thought for a moment, then smiled sourly and said, "I've wondered why you and that wacko outfit of yours hadn't already used it. The Panama stuff. Then I figured it out. It's because of Shawnee. You don't wanta do anything that'd hurt Violet's kid."

"She's also yours."

"You always had a yen for Violet, didn't you?" Viar said, then leered and asked, "Ever get anywhere?"

The General rose, feeling both ridiculous and determined. "You want to keep your pension or not?"

"Sit down, goddamnit."

The General resumed his seat on the couch, picked up his drink, tasted it, put it back down, examined Viar for a few seconds and said, "Toward the end of 1989, during the month of November, you were in El Salvador."

"So?"

"Doing what?"

"I was agency liaison with Salvadoran intelligence—with the DNI or, *auf Englisch*, the National Intelligence Directorate. What I was really doing was loafing my way toward the end of a long and distinguished career, my last role being that of an aging GS-16 bagman."

"Was there a large payoff during the first two weeks of November?"

Viar smiled. "So that's it?"

"That's it," Winfield said. "Was there?"

"Maybe."

"Who got it?"

"Like I said, I was merely liaison to Salvadoran intelligence."

"Who got the money, Hank?"

"The fucking Atlacatl battalion eventually got it, who else?"

"You handed over the money to U.S. Army advisers, who then gave it to the Atlacatl battalion?"

Viar only nodded and drank more whisky.

"How much?" the general asked.

"The battalion wanted five million but we gave 'em less than half, which is about what they expected. Two-point-four million dollars."

"For the time, was that a large, medium or small amount?"

"Well, since Washington had already sunk about four billion into that mess, it wasn't significant money—except to those who divvied it up."

"What were the mechanics of the transfer?"

"Be more specific," Viar said and drank the rest of his whisky.

"What was the money actually carried in?"

"A great big old gray Deutsche Post mailbag. A real monster. Sealed."

"How was it sealed?"

"With a quarter-inch wire cable and a big glob of solder. The seal itself was a steel engraving of Mickey Mouse pressed into the solder. A generous nation's little joke."

Winfield picked up the Scotch bottle, went over to Viar and poured him another ounce or so. Once back on the couch, the General asked, "Why a German mailbag?"

"Because if it fell off a truck, we could blame it on the Krauts." He smiled slightly. "Another joke. The bag was just handy. That's all."

"You picked up the money where?"

"The embassy. Where else could Langley pouch it to?"

"Then?"

"Then I went to see our Army guys, the advisers who'd make the payoff to the Atlacatl brass."

"Who were our Army guys?"

"A colonel and a captain."

"You gave them the money?"

Viar nodded.

"Then what?"

"Then the three of us counted it."

"And after that?"

"After that they call in a major—a guy with good Spanish—who'll make the delivery. They tell him what they want him to do and he says swell. Then he asks how much is in the bag and they say two-point-four million. He says fine, let's count it. The Colonel tells him it's already counted. Not in my presence, the Major says, then respectfully requests, in the interest of what he calls fairness and accuracy, that we count the fucking money again. So we did. The four of us."

"Then what?"

"Then we put it back in the German mailbag and seal it back up with wire, solder and Mickey Mouse. After that, we watch the Colonel tuck it away for the night in his big safe—all this in the presence of Major Doubting Thomas."

"Go on," Winfield said.

"The next morning the Colonel and the Captain open the safe and hand the bag over to the Major, who checks the seal, then delivers the money to his contact, a young captain in the Atlacatl battalion."

"You remember the date of the delivery?"

"November sixth."

"Go on."

"Well, the Atlacatl Captain delivers the bag to his Colonel. Together, they open it up. Guess what? Half the money—one-point-two million's gone south. But to make the bag feel and weigh right, somebody's added a lot of carefully cut-up packets of newspapers, all nicely wrapped with rubber bands. The Colonel goes ape shit, of course, and screams and yells at the Captain, who's a real little guy. Then the Colonel beats up on him for a while, gets tired of that and demands the name of the piece of American shit who gave the Captain the money. The Captain names our American Major."

"What happened then?"

"What happened then was I get a call from a friend of mine in the DNI—"

"Their intelligence outfit."

"The same. And he's really pissed off. The little Salvadoran Captain's with him, pretty banged up by now, and my friend's demanding the name, rank and serial numbers of all the North Americans involved. So I name names. Then I call the American Colonel and say I want a crash meeting with him, the Major and the Captain. But I won't say why."

"What a duplicitous mind you have," the General said.

Viar nodded in happy agreement. "Just covering my ass." He paused to light another cigarette and drink more whisky before continuing. "Well, when I arrive, they're all three there—the Colonel, the Major and the Captain. So I deliver what I like to think of as a terse, factual report on how half the money's been stolen. Then I sit back and watch."

"Who exploded first?" Winfield said.

"The Colonel. He blames it all on the Major, accuses him of stealing the money and calls him names that'd make motherfucker sound like an endearment. The Major just sits there and listens till the Colonel runs down. Then he denies it. No yells. No shouts. Just that one cold flat denial. The Colonel starts in on him again. The Major takes it for about two minutes, maybe more, then hits the Colonel three times and damn near kills him."

Viar drank a little more of his whisky, almost a reflective sip, and said, "I was sitting right there and if I'd blinked I'd've missed it. He was that fucking fast."

"What happened to him—the Major?"

"What d'you think happened? They arrested him and tossed him into the guardhouse, or what passed for one. It was more like a real small motel with barred windows and metal doors. The charge was striking a superior officer. That's when I did a little snooping and, after that, went to see him. The Major."

"Why?" Winfield said. "Surely not to offer comfort and consolation."

Viar stared into his half-empty glass. "Ever notice Mickey Mouse has only three fingers?"

"I was five when I first noticed it. Maybe six."

Viar looked up at Winfield. "Well, the Mickey Mouse seal on the mailbag the four of us tucked into the Colonel's safe had three fingers on each hand. But the Mickey Mouse on the seal of the bag the little Captain delivered to his Colonel had four fingers. On each hand."

"How do you know?"

"My pal in the Salvadoran DNI somehow got hold of the mailbag and the broken seal. I noticed the four fingers. He didn't, of course, and I saw no reason to mention it."

"But you said the American Major checked the seal when he took delivery."

"He checked to see if it was broken. He didn't count fingers. Who would?"

"You would."

"Yeah, but that's my trade. Or was."

"Then it was a purposely clumsy forgery, which, if necessary, could be blamed on the Major?"

"Uh-huh," Viar said. "Well, I checked with the home office first and let them mull it over. After they got back to me was when I went to see the Major and tell him he'd been shortchanged by his fellow Americans, the Colonel and the Captain."

"You were acting under orders at the time?"

"My orders were to smooth things over."

"I see."

"I tell the Major he was deliberately provoked into striking his superior officer. I also tell him that's exactly what the Colonel and the Captain were counting on. Then I ask him if he'd noticed the four-fingered mouse seal before he handed the mailbag over to the little Salvadoran Captain."

"And his reply?"

"He closed his eyes for maybe fifteen or twenty seconds, then opened them. That was his reply. So then I tell him the best deal he can cut is to resign his commission and forget about the Army. The last thing I tell him is that Langley's sending the Atlacatl battalion another one-point-two million to replace what's been stolen and that the whole thing'll be forgotten—even the fact that he beat the shit out of his superior officer."

"His comment—if any?" Winfield said.

"Not one fucking word."

"Then what?"

"They let him resign his commission."

"Was that the end of it?"

"Almost—except for the little Salvadoran Captain, who sneaks by to tell me he's thinking of deserting because his superiors are convinced he got a cut of the stolen money but didn't share it with anybody. What he wants from me are the names of the American Colonel and Captain."

"Did you give him the names?"

"What d'you think?"

"You gave him the names," the General said.

Viar smiled. "But I also suggested he might go pay a courtesy call on the by then ex-Major."

"Who was where?"

"After he resigned his commission, they let him out of the guardhouse-motel and checked him into some fleabag in San Salvador to wait for his flight back to the States. And that's where the ex-American Major and the almost ex-Salvadoran Captain met and talked. And right after that the Major calls me."

"Why?"

"To let me know I have a loose end flapping around in the form of the little Captain who's hell-bent on revenge. The now ex-Major suggests I whisk the little Captain out of the country before he kills somebody."

"Did you?"

"Sure. It was no big deal. I had the Captain and his wife flown to Mexico City, where a couple of our guys met 'em, gave 'em a few bucks and waved goodbye. After I make sure they're really gone, I go see the American Colonel and Captain and tell 'em what I've done."

"Their reaction?"

"Well, they couldn't exactly tell me they were grateful, could they? So they just said it was a wise decision."

"This American Colonel and Captain," Winfield said, then paused, as if to think about what should come next. "It only took them three years."

"For what?"

"For Walker Laney Hudson to go from bird colonel to major general, and for Ralph Waldo Millwed to go from captain to colonel. Neither served in the Gulf, which makes their rapid promotions rather curious."

"Well, you'd know more about that than I would."

"I doubt that," Winfield said. "Still, I do know that in times past certain general officers have promoted those who could either harm or embarrass them. Some think of it as closing ranks. Others regard it as blackmail. As for Hudson and Millwed, I have a theory about their sudden promotions. Care to hear it?"

"As long as it's a theory and not a lecture," Viar said.

The General nodded and smiled a promise. "Let's assume that there's this turbulent priest we wish to be rid of—"

"Who's we?" Viar asked.

"Who knows?"

"I see."

"At any rate, this priest is rector of the University of Central America, which has the reputation of being sympathetic to the cause of the Salvadoran rebels, who, as you know, call themselves the Farabundo Martí National Liberation Front or the FMLN."

"It's a lecture after all," Viar said.

"Bear with me," the General said. "On November 16, 1989, our turbulent priest, Ignacio Ellacuria, is shot dead along with five other priests, their cook and her daughter. Sounds rather like the title of a French film, doesn't it? 'Six Priests, Their Cook and Her Daughter.'"

"I don't go to French films because, like your lectures, I don't think they'll ever end."

"Patience," the General said. "I have only a few more points to make and a question or two. From several sources I've learned that a CIA officer was at the scene of the priestly murders by 0800 the next morning. I need to know if that CIA officer was you."

"He was a Latino," Viar said. "Do I look like a Latino?"

The General studied him briefly, as if trying to decide, then said, "Back to the sudden promotions of General Hudson and Colonel Millwed. It's fairly common knowledge these days that commandos from the Atlacatl battalion murdered the priests and the two women. But it was only a week or ten days before these murders that you, acting for the CIA, entrusted Hudson, then a colonel, and Millwed, then a captain, with two million four hundred thousand dollars, which they were to turn over to this same battalion. My question is: Was that the price the battalion had put on the head of our turbulent priest?"

"How should I know? I was just the bagman."

"Yet when half the money was stolen, the blame for its theft fell on a luckless U.S. Army major. And almost immediately, more CIA money was dispatched to the battalion. The murders of the priests and the unfortunate women then took place, apparently on schedule. Meanwhile, some person or persons are one million two hundred thousand dollars richer."

The General looked slowly around the living room. "It would seem, Hank, that you're not one of those persons."

"Afraid not."

"After the murders, Colonel Hudson quickly—very, very quickly—rises to major general and Captain Millwed makes it to major and then full colonel, skipping over lieutenant colonel. I can't help but wonder if their silence about the murders was bought by their meteoric rise in rank and the one-point-two million they were permitted, maybe even encouraged, to steal?"

"Beats me," Viar said.

"The name of that unfortunate Major. Was it Partain by any chance?"

"Edd-with-two-ds Partain."

"Any idea of where he is now?"

"None."

"Too bad," the General said and rose. "Well, I do thank you for your time and patience."

"Why'd you really come?" Viar said, not rising. "You already knew everything before you got here."

"Some, but not all," the General said. "You confirmed a couple of points and supplied some interesting, even amusing, verisimilitude. The Deutsche Post mailbag, for instance, and that four-fingered Mickey Mouse seal. I rather enjoyed them."

Viar, still seated, grinned up at the General. "Then you won't mind if I give General Hudson a ring and tell him you've been here, nosing around?"

"Mind?" Winfield said. "Good Lord, Hank, that was the entire purpose of my visit."

12

At 9:23 P.M., EST, General Winfield, wearing his Borsalino and camel hair topcoat, its collar turned up against the 36-degree chill, closed the front door of the small house on Volta Place, and began to walk to his car. Five minutes later, at 6:28 P.M., PST, Edd Partain braked the Lexus coupe to a stop on the curved drive in front of the Eden on Wilshire Boulevard.

Jack, the doorman, appeared as Partain got out of the car, leaving the key in the ignition. "He came back," Jack said after Partain shut the not-quite-closed door with a hip to silence the insistent you-left-the-key-in-the-ignition chime.

"Who?"

"This morning's false messenger. Except this time he was totally immersed in his new role of David Laney, bibulous man about town."

Partain studied the doorman for a moment, noting the almost too regular and still-young features, the slight tan and the interested gray-blue eyes. "You an actor?" Partain said.

"From five P.M. to one A.M., I'm Jack, an obsequious doorman. The rest of the time I'm Jack Thomson, without the usual 'p,' a sometime actor." He smiled then, a wry, carefully crooked smile that displayed wonderful teeth. "Except it's not supposed to show."

"It's mostly the voice," Partain said. "There's no trace of regional accent."

"Yeah, well, the one I'm using now is my standard American. Upon demand, I can do Deep South, Jersey low-life, west Texas, Scandinavian-tinged Minnesota, fair Cajun and an almost featureless Omaha, where a lot of 800-number companies are now locating because of all those white-bread voices."

"You get much work?"

Thomson shook his head. "A TV commercial voice-over once in a while and some radio spots. They say my looks are too second-leadish for films. That's why I almost hoped Laney was shitfaced enough to take a poke at me and maybe break my nose, leaving me with a slight but memorable flaw."

"How'd you hear about Laney playing messenger boy?"

"From Tom, the day man. We share whatever gossip there is at the shift change. Normally, we don't have a lot to talk about. But Laney and his false-messenger dodge was a choice morsel."

"How shitfaced was he this afternoon?"

"His diction was good although his eyes were sort of waltzing around. He also had a nice mouse under the right one. No staggers, though. No goofy smile. But he must have gargled a quart of Scope."

"I suppose he wanted to go back up to the Altford place."

"Insisted on it. I called Jessie Carver from the outside phone and she said no, not now, not ever. But by then Laney was through the front doors, into the elevator and on his way up."

"I thought those doors were always locked," Partain said.

"They are, but he had somebody's key card. I stopped his elevator between floors, took the other one up, coaxed him out and walked him down six flights of stairs. He kind of tripped over my foot and fell the last few steps, but bounced right up and promised to be back after I got off."

"You take the key card away from him?" Partain asked.

"That's not in my job description."

"You get off at one A.M., right?"

The doorman nodded with a faint smile.

"Then I'll wait up for him," Partain said.

The faint smile was still in place when Jack Thomson said, "I thought you might."

Jessica Carver served herself a second helping of the corned beef hash from the old iron skillet that Partain had placed on the heirloom kitchen table. To the left of the skillet was a yellow ceramic mixing bowl that held a tossed salad of tomatoes, two kinds of lettuce and a thinly sliced sweet onion, allegedly from Vidalia, Georgia. The salad dressing was the only one Partain ever used: nine parts olive oil; one part red wine vinegar; vinegar-soaked salt; ground black pepper, and more garlic than most people liked. Jessica Carver also had more of the salad.

They ate in silence until Carver finished her hash, leaned back in her chair and said, "You really like to cook?"

"No."

"Then why bother?"

"Because it's cheaper than eating out."

"That poor-boy act of yours. Is it inspired by poverty or parsimony?"

"A little of both."

"What'd you do in the Army for fun, when you weren't soldiering?"

"I read a lot."

"What?"

"European history. When I got to World War One I always stopped."

"Why?"

"Because I already knew how it'd end in 1945."

"That was the end of World War Two, not One."

"Was it?" Partain said and smiled to take the edge off his answer. He was still smiling slightly when he said, "Tell me about you and Dave Laney."

"I already told you. He's a shit I lived with in Mexico."

"Where'd you meet him?"

"God, I hate that question," she said. " 'Where did you two meet?' It's as if everyone's expecting something cute—like in the movies. So for a while I'd give them cute: 'A bellhop at the Biltmore sent me up to his room.' "

"Dave says you met during the Dukakis campaign in '88."

"He lied. We met in November of '91 at a Beverly Hills wedding reception my mother'd dragged me to. I don't know why Dave was there because he didn't seem to know the bride or groom. Millie was working the room like a coyote. I stood in a corner, drinking the free Dom Pérignon and wearing something I'd got at the Nordstrom Rack in the Valley for ninety-six bucks that looked like nine hundred and sixty. That's why Dave made his move. He thought I looked like money."

"You do," Partain said.

"Almost any woman who stays out of the sun, is under forty and doesn't have a weight problem can look like money in this town. But for some reason, men can't fake it. Money, I mean. Dave sure as hell can't."

"Why?"

"Take those clothes he wears. He looks like some real tan guy who walks into Carroll and Company on Rodeo and says, 'Sell me some stuff that'll make me look rich.' And that's what they do: sell him stuff that'll make him look like a guy who wants to look rich but isn't."

"Then Dave's what—medium rich?"

She studied him for a second or two, smiled a small superior smile and said, "He told you about his trust funds, didn't he?"

"In passing."

"The two one-million-dollar funds that're managed by the stuffy old bankers back in Boston?"

Partain nodded.

"Well, it's not two one-million-dollar trust funds. It's a hundred-thousand-dollar one at the Bank of America, which isn't exactly giving Dave's money its undivided attention. They stuck it away in some money market account, for God's sake. When we went down to Mexico it was paying close to four or five percent. I forget which. When he came back it was below three percent. The main reason I came back is I got sick of Dave. The other reason is I'd run out of money."

"Where's it come from?" Partain said. "Your money?"

"You sure ask delicate questions."

"I see no reason for delicacy."

"Well, this may come as a shock but, except for food, I'm almost as much of a miser as you are. Where food's concerned, I don't want to buy it, prepare it, cook it or clean up after it. And even though I know I can buy a spring fryer at Vons for maybe $3.98, I'd rather pay thirty-two bucks at Chez Delano's for the *poulet à la Memphis.*"

"None of that answers my question."

"About where my money comes from. Okay. I earn a lot and save most of it. The only thing that gives me a bigger rush than saving money is sex. When I work, my money's parted out like this: about forty-eight percent for Social Security, state and Federal taxes. After you hit fifty-five thousand, most of the Social Security bite stops. Overall, I pay about forty-three percent in taxes. I live on forty percent of my take-home pay and save the rest. No stocks. No bonds. No mutual funds. Just a regular savings account in a too-big-to-fail bank that still gives out those little passbooks and records every deposit along with the picayune interest."

"You must be in the top bracket."

"Next to the top."

"Doing what?"

"I write advertising copy. TV, radio and print. Freelance. I even do billboards. One time I had three of them down on the Sunset Strip—big mothers—all at the same time. Real bust-eye stuff."

"You're good, then?"

"The best."

"Since it takes a certain amount of cunning to sell anything, I don't quite understand—"

She interrupted. "About me and Dave Laney."

Partain nodded.

"Sex," she said. "He's awfully good at it."

Partain gave her another nod, which he hoped said, "That explains everything." She apparently interpreted it to mean, "Please continue."

"What you're still wondering," Carver said, "if she's so shrewd and cunning, why didn't she spot Dave Laney for the rat he is. The sad answer is I did—from the moment he first opened his mouth and started in on his trust funds. People with trust funds don't talk about them. And people from fine old California families don't brag about how old and fine they are right after they've told you about their trust funds. The Laneys, this is Dave's version now, sailed around the Horn in either 1849 or '50 and made their first fortune off the miners. Every generation after that made another fortune off something or other—real estate, oil, insurance, agriculture, wars. The last big Laney fortune was made in real estate in the late '70s and early '80s. Dave says they bailed out because they saw it coming. The crash."

"It'd be more interesting if they hadn't," Partain said.

She nodded her agreement.

"Anyway, the Laneys performed all these wonderful economic tricks when they weren't serving their country in every war since the one between the states, as Dave calls it, when some of the Laneys fought for the Confederacy and some for the Union. He told me all this ten minutes after we met. Well, maybe fifteen. He even threw in an uncle who's recently been promoted to Army general."

"What year was this?" Partain said.

"When we met? Ninety-one."

"Who's the General?"

"General Laney, I suppose. Ever hear of him?"

Partain's reply was delayed and, when it came, it was a question. "Does your mother have a *Who's Who*?"

"Every volume since '52."

"Where?"

"In her study."

"Let's take a look."

They couldn't find any Laney who was a general under the Ls, but Partain did find one under the Hs. He was Major General Walker Laney Hudson, USA, b. Pasadena, May 19, 1943; grad. U.S. Military Academy, 1964.

After she closed the big red L to Z volume and put it back on the shelf, Jessica Carver said, "You know him, don't you— this General Walker Laney Hudson?"

"We've met," Partain said.

13

They had dined at a card table on salad and spanakopita, the Greek spinach and cheese pie that was a specialty of the uncle's ground-floor restaurant. For dessert, there was a far too rich baklava that General Winfield politely declined. Nick Patrokis ate both portions, then wrapped up the paper napkins, plastic plates and plastic cutlery in the *Washington Post* that had served as a tablecloth and dumped it all into a big brown plastic garbage can. The General folded the card table and stored it away.

It was just after 9 P.M. when they moved to the golden oak desk for the Greek coffee that Patrokis poured from a Thermos into a pair of small cups. After finishing one cup, Patrokis poured himself another and said, "Sounds like a nice job of mind-fucking to me."

The General winced slightly, then shook his head. "You have to understand that Henry Viar simply doesn't care anymore. He spends much of his time in the upstairs front bedroom, sipping whiskey, smoking Pall Malls, watching the street and, I suspect, fantasizing about the farther shores of Might've Been."

"I sailed there a time or two," Patrokis said, "but always sailed back as soon as possible."

"Most of us do. But Viar still regards himself as the ultimate realist. You've heard the phrase 'tough-minded'? It was popular during the Kennedy administration."

"Still is."

"Well, back then Viar always claimed it was the Kennedyites' unconscious euphemism for 'hopelessly romantic.' The only truly tough-minded people Viar claims he ever knew were pimps, double agents and golf hustlers."

"Sounds like you guys were friends."

"We knew each other well, too well, probably, but we were never friends. And yet I introduced him to his wife, you know. To Violet."

"I didn't."

"A mistake I still regret. She was young and fairly well off. He was young and terribly ambitious. To her it was love. To him it was a career move. She came to see me years later. It was shortly after I retired in '68. You know my living room."

It wasn't a question but Patrokis nodded anyway.

"She sat on one side of the fireplace and I on the other. I served coffee and, at first, made all the proper social noises. She made no response. None. So we sat there for almost an hour in silence until she rose and said, 'Thank you, Vernon, you've been a great comfort.' Then she went home and shot herself. Their daughter, Shawnee, who was eight or nine at the time, came home from school and found the body."

"Sorry."

Winfield nodded and a silence began that Patrokis eventually ended with a false cough followed by a question. "Which way d'you think Viar'll bounce?"

Winfield gave it some thought. "He'll study his options with the aid of a few more drinks, then choose the one he believes will do him the least harm." He glanced at his watch.

"That means he'll have called General Hudson by now and made a full report on my visit."

"And Hudson?"

"He's called Colonel Millwed and they'll've met, or could even be meeting now in some room at the Mayflower."

Patrokis reached for his Rolodex, found a number and called it. When it was answered, he said, "Mr. Jerome Able's room, please."

He listened as the Mayflower Hotel operator rang the room, finally gave up, told him there was no answer and asked if he'd like to leave a message. Patrokis said he'd try again, thanked her and ended the call.

Winfield rose and reached for his hat and coat. "You didn't really expect them to answer?"

"No, I just want them to wonder who the hell's calling Jerome Able."

"The Odyssean mind never rests. Well, I'm going home and to bed. I suggest you do the same."

Patrokis glanced around the big empty VOMIT headquarters and shrugged. "I'm already home."

Their room at the Mayflower Hotel was much like their previous room except this one was on the fourth floor instead of the fifth. Their topcoats again were on the bed. Colonel Ralph Millwed sat on the edge of it. General Walker Hudson and his rank again occupied the room's only comfortable chair. Neither had wanted anything to drink and the General had just lighted a cigar without apology.

He blew the smoke to his left and away from Millwed before he said, "That phone call," but didn't bother to complete his sentence.

"It could have been a simple mistake. Some guest, direct-dialing another room, could've hit a four instead of a five." There was no conviction in Millwed's tone.

"Well, it'd be smart of Jerome Able to empty out his safe-deposit box at the Riggs Bank, cancel his VISA card and join the ranks of the disappeared."

"Able disappears tomorrow," the Colonel said, "replaced by Gordon C. Beale."

"What's the 'C' for?"

"Collin," Millwed said, then asked, "How'd he sound when he called—Hank Viar?"

"Neutral. But he was born neutral and'll stay that way as long as he's on our payroll at—I forget how much."

"Two thousand a month. Cash."

"Viar claims he didn't tell Winfield anything the old crock didn't already know. And certainly nothing Twodees can't tell him, if he hasn't already."

"Viar drinks too much," Millwed said.

"Does he, now? But we knew that, didn't we, when we gathered him into the fold by offering him just enough cash money to keep him in booze and happy pills? We're his supply line now and, drunk or sober, Hank Viar'll never endanger it."

"I don't trust drunks," Millwed said. "Especially old ones. The closer they get to the end, the more they start thinking about redemption."

"That's your religious drunk," the General said. "But your bedrock atheist drunk like Viar has a belief in the Great Oblivion that's as devout as any Christian drunk's belief in the Great Hereafter."

"It's your call, of course, but since you raised the question of life after death, how soon does Twodees find out if there is one?"

"The sooner the better," the General said. "How much did Emory Kite charge us for the Captain and his wife?"

"Fifty thousand for them and twenty-five more for a rush job well done."

"You pay him?"

"Not yet."

"Pay him and then give him the fix on Twodees."

"He'll try to double his price."

"Don't haggle with him," the General said.

"That's extortion."

The General chuckled. After a moment, Millwed smiled and said, "How do you really want to handle it?"

The General examined his cigar, then put it back in his mouth, puffed a few times, drew in a large mouthful of smoke and blew four fat smoke rings at the ceiling. He watched the rings dissolve, turned to the Colonel and said, "Pay Emory some up-front money for Twodees. When he's done the fix and comes around for the rest of his fee, we'll have to decide what should be done about Emory himself."

"And your nephew," Millwed said, "out in L.A.?"

The General frowned, looked up at the ceiling and sighed.

14

Millicent Altford awoke after midnight in her hospital room to find a doctor bending over her. She knew he was a doctor because of the surgical mask, shirt jacket and hair cap, all pale blue, and the no-color surgical gloves he wore over hands that held a fat pillow only a foot or so from her face.

The pillow erased his medical degree and made Altford scream although it was more yell than scream. She went on yelling as she rolled over twice to her left and fell off the bed. After landing on the floor with her eyes squeezed shut, Altford continued to yell and even swear so loudly she didn't hear the false doctor leave. She was still making a racket when someone slapped her face. Altford shut up, opened her eyes and found Liz Ball, the night nurse, kneeling beside her and wearing that half-concerned, half-irritated expression that's taught at nursing school.

"You just slap me?" Altford asked, knowing the answer.

"Damn right," Ball said. "You were having a nightmare and cussing your head off. Come on. Let's get you back into bed."

"I fell out of bed?"

"Fell or jumped, you're on the floor."

"Maybe you ought to get that big doctor to help," Altford said, not proud of her slyness, but unable to think of anything better.

"What big doctor?".

"Well, maybe he was just an orderly—a real big guy who sorta popped in on me."

"White or black?"

"White."

"We haven't got any white orderlies on this floor," Ball said. "Fact is, we haven't got any orderlies at all. It's the shift change and one orderly left early and the other one's late. And at this time of night, we sure as hell don't have any doctors up here, big or little, white or black. Now let's get you back into bed."

Using the nurse's strength, Altford rose slowly and carefully to make sure nothing had been sprained or broken. After she was back in bed, the nurse asked if she'd like something to help her sleep.

"I'd like a big glass of ice, please, Liz. And after you get that, I'd be ever so grateful if you'd pour in one of those miniatures of gin and let it sort of percolate down?"

The nurse left Altford propped up in bed on pillows, her hands wrapped around a tumbler of iced gin. Altford had two large swallows, put the glass on the bedside table, placed the nearby telephone on her lap and tapped out a number that was answered halfway through the second ring by Edd Partain.

"How long's it gonna take you to get over here?" she said.

Millicent Altford let Partain drive this time and noticed he was a timer who hit most of the traffic lights on the green or yellow. She liked the way he drove and also the way he listened to her tale of the failed smothering.

When Partain was sure she had finished, or at least run down, he said, "The guy waited for the shift change."

"Obviously."

"Would you recognize him again?"

"In a second—providing he wore a blue mask, coat, hair cap and see-through plastic gloves."

"You said he was big. How big?"

"Six-four at least."

"What about his eyes?"

"You mean were they the cruel eyes of some crazed proctologist who'd rather kill than cure?"

"Just their color."

"I don't remember."

"Too bad," Partain said.

"Would you remember their color if a pillow was about to cancel your breathing?"

"Yes, but that's what I do. Or did. Notice things. Like how many fingers has Mickey Mouse got?"

"You're asking me?"

Partain nodded.

"Three," she said. "Because it's easier and cheaper to draw three than four."

"Then you do notice stuff."

"Yeah, when guys aren't trying to smother me."

Partain nodded his understanding.

"Fact is, I closed my eyes," she said. "That's a lie. After that first look at him, I squeezed them shut, just like a little kid."

"A little kid wouldn't have rolled off the bed," he said.

"I reckon I also yelled and cussed a lot."

"Even better," Partain said, then asked, "He say anything?"

"Not a word."

"If he'd said something, maybe you'd recognize his voice, if you ever heard it again."

"Maybe," Millicent Altford said.

* * *

It was just after 1 A.M. when Partain stopped the Lexus in
front of the Eden's glass doors, switched off the engine and
turned to Altford. "Don't get out till I open your door. I'll
see you up to your place, then come back down and put the
car away."

"You think he'll try again?" she said, sounding more interested than frightened.

"I don't know what he'll do," Partain said, got out, went
around the car's rear and opened the right-hand door. As
Altford stepped out, a dark brown windowless van with no
license plate stopped on Wilshire Boulevard, shifted into
reverse and backed quickly into the Eden's concrete drive
until it was no more than thirty or thirty-five feet from the
Lexus. By then, Partain had slammed the passenger door shut
and forced Altford to kneel beside the right front wheel where
it and the car's V-8 engine would provide some protection
should the shooting start.

But there were no shots. Instead, Partain heard, but didn't
see, the van's back door open, then close. In between the
opening and closing was the sound of something landing on
the concrete drive. It made that peculiar sound of something
that doesn't mind being dropped. Huge sacks of flour or rice
don't mind, Partain thought, and neither do dead or unconscious bodies.

After he heard the dark brown van speed off, heading west
on Wilshire, probably toward a freeway, Partain rose, hurried
around the nose of the Lexus, went another seven or eight
quick strides, stopped and stared down at the dead man who
wore a lot of light blue clothing.

Altford called to him from behind the Lexus. "What is it?"

"I think it's your fake doctor."

She rose slowly and even more slowly joined Partain. The
body lay on its right side, facing the street. The blue hair cap
was still in place. So was the blue shirt jacket, but the surgical

mask was gone. The one hand they could see, the left one, still wore a transparent surgical glove. The pants and shoes were the only clothing that wasn't blue. The shoes were sockless cordovan leather loafers and the pants were tan cavalry twill, now badly soiled.

"Let's make sure," Partain said as he moved around the body.

"Of what?"

"That he's dead," Partain said.

"He's dead all right," she said, joining Partain in his inspection of the man's face, which belonged to Dave Laney, late of Guadalajara. Laney's eyes were open. So was his mouth, and something other than his tongue was sticking out of it.

Partain removed the car keys from his pocket and gave them to Altford. "Call 911 on your car phone."

She absently accepted the keys, still gazing down at the dead man. "Dave tried to kill me," she said, giving each word equal emphasis so that her sentence was neither accusation nor question but merely a statement of fact.

"Go make the call," Partain said. Altford nodded, still staring at Laney until she turned and hurried toward the car.

Partain knelt to remove the thing that had been protruding from Laney's mouth. It was a plastic key card that Partain was almost sure would unlock the front doors of the Eden and also the door to apartment 1540, the residence of Millicent Altford, her daughter and their temporary live-in bodyguard.

15

The stay-behind LAPD homicide detective sergeant, Ovid Knox, reminded Partain of certain Special Forces types he had known in the Army. Not the dumb ones, who liked to boast of their membership in a chosen elite, but the smart ones, who scoffed at elitism even though they devoutly, if secretly, had believed in it since they were four years old or maybe even three.

After Millicent Altford's 911 call, a swarm of plainclothes detectives, uniformed police and technical staff, most of them from the Westside Division, had quickly arrived and slowly departed, taking with them the late Dave Laney. But Ovid Knox had lingered on because of what he said were a couple of minor items he needed to check with Ms. Altford, her daughter and Mr. Partain.

Knox was closer to 40 than 30 and still had a lot of tousled sun-streaked blond hair that complemented his easy manner and lazy smile. Partain suspected the smile and manner of being a mask for the contempt that lay just behind a pair of sardonically amused blue eyes.

At 2:44 A.M., the four of them sat drinking coffee in the

significant-money salon, which was how Partain now thought of Millicent Altford's huge living room. She still wore the gray pants and sweater. Her daughter wore baggy dark green shorts, a white T-shirt and laceless white jogging shoes. Partain wore the blue suit, white shirt and the same carefully knotted tie. Of the four, Ovid Knox seemed most at ease, perhaps because he was the law and also the most elegantly dressed in his sand-colored suede jacket, chocolate-brown gabardine pants, tieless off-white shirt and the plain loafers whose leather resembled carefully polished black walnut. It was an outfit whose retail price, Partain guessed, would top $2,000. But Partain also guessed that Knox never paid retail for anything over $100.

The detective's first question had dealt with what he called Jessica Carver's "relationship" with the late David Laney ("We lived together for a year in Mexico"), and also with Laney's futile attempt to meet with her yesterday morning ("Mr. Partain convinced Dave I didn't want to talk to him, so he left").

It was then that Partain asked Knox, "Mind if I ask you a question?"

If Knox minded, neither his voice nor his expression did. "Not at all."

"What killed him?" Partain said. "There weren't any obvious bullet or stab wounds, no signs of strangulation or massive blows. That leaves lots of other stuff of course—ice pick, hot shot injection, poison, even a heart attack."

"Maybe he was smothered."

Partain nodded and said, "Now why didn't I think of that?"

"Probably because big guys like Laney are hard to smother. But that's why we do autopsies—to find out what killed our customers." He examined Partain briefly, then added, "I assume you saw some dead folks in the service."

Partain nodded.

"Where'd you serve—all over?"

"Pretty much," Partain said. "First with the infantry in Vietnam, then the States, then Germany and then Central America."

"Still with the infantry in Central America?"

"Army intelligence."

"Was your Army intelligence experience why Ms. Altford hired you—or am I hopping to a conclusion?"

Millicent Altford supplied an answer. "He was recommended by an old friend of mine, a retired Army general."

Knox looked only slightly interested. "To do what, Ms. Altford?"

"I've been told or warned—unofficially, of course—that I'm being considered for an appointive job in the new administration, one that'll require a full field FBI investigation. I retained Mr. Partain to poke around in my past and see if there's anything that'd upset anybody."

Knox looked at Partain. "That the kind of stuff you did in the Army, Major?"

"Did I say I was a major?"

"No, but we live in the age of fax, phone and computerized files," Knox said, smiled apologetically and then asked, "How long were you in?"

"Nineteen years."

"If you'd stuck it another year, you'd've had your pension."

"Plus PX privileges. I chose to resign instead."

"Where were you in Central America?"

"El Salvador mostly."

"Got a little hairy there, didn't it?"

"Not for an observer—a cautious one."

Knox had a sip of coffee, put his cup down and, without looking at her, asked, "How's your health, Ms. Altford?"

"Just fine."

Knox turned to look at her with that quick practiced gaze that both policemen and doctors use. "You were in the hospital for what, if you don't mind my asking?"

"For observation," she said.

"No bad news, I hope."

"None."

"You checked out at a little past midnight this morning. Kind of an odd time to check out, isn't it?"

"I didn't check out. I simply left because I was fed up and my stay there was giving me nightmares. That's why I called Mr. Partain and asked him to come fetch me."

"You have any visitors last night?"

"None—except for those in my nightmare."

"Mr. Partain drove you home in your car—a Lexus, isn't it?"

She nodded.

"Like it?"

"Very much."

"He got out first, went around the car and opened your door. Is that when you saw the brown van—after you got out?"

"I never saw the van," she said. "Almost before I knew it, Mr. Partain had me down on my hands and knees beside the right front wheel."

Knox looked at Partain. "Why'd you expect trouble?"

"A van stops on Wilshire, backs into the driveway and doesn't have a rear license plate. I took routine precautionary measures, that's all."

"You saw its rear door open?"

"By then I was down beside Ms. Altford."

"Then you didn't see who threw Laney out?"

"No."

"But you heard him land?"

Partain nodded.

"You know what a dead body sounds like when it hits concrete?"

Partain again nodded.

"Then what?"

"I heard the rear door close and the van drive off."

"East or west?"

"West."

"So it was your ears and not your eyes that told you it turned west?"

"My ears are pretty good."

"What'd you do then?"

"I got up, saw the body and decided to take a closer look."

"Could you tell it was Laney?"

"No. He was lying on his side, facing the street. As soon as we saw it was Laney, I asked Ms. Altford to call 911 on her car phone."

Knox smiled contentedly, leaned back in his chair and, still smiling, inspected Jessica Carver first, then Partain and, finally, Millicent Altford. He stopped smiling and asked, "Why d'you think Dave was all dressed up like a doctor, Millie?"

The use of the diminutive was a routine interrogative ploy that Partain had never cared for, especially in Latin America, where it was usually counterproductive. Still, he was curious how Altford would react.

She smiled sweetly at Knox and said, "No idea."

The detective nodded, turned to Jessica Carver and, once again smiling a little, asked her, "Who wanted Dave dead, Jessie?"

"I did sometimes and don't call me Jessie. Now then. Back to Dave. I sometimes wanted him dead because he was a liar and a cheat but much better at cheating than lying."

"Then why'd you stay with him?"

Partain kept his eyes on the detective, waiting for his reaction to Carver's reply. She cocked her head a little to one side, studied Knox for a moment or two, then said, "Because he was the best fuck in six states, maybe seven."

Partain heard Millicent Altford's sigh as he watched Knox

give Jessica Carver a cold stare before he said, "But even so, you left him. Why?"

"I ran out of money."

"Didn't Laney have money?"

"At first he did, then he didn't, then suddenly he did but claimed he didn't and even though I knew he was lying, we spent mine. When that ran out after the first of the year, I told him I was going back to L.A. and find some work."

"You were in Mexico then?"

"Guadalajara."

"How'd Dave react when you told him you were splitting?"

"We had a long loud argument that didn't change my mind. Then, the day before my plane left, he came home and dumped a whole bunch of money on the bed and begged me to stay."

"How much is a whole bunch?" Knox said.

"Lots."

"Twenty thousand? Fifty?"

"More."

"What happened then?"

"We celebrated," she said. "And after he passed out, I packed my bag, called a taxi, went to the airport and took the first flight I could get to L.A."

16

After coming across what might turn out to be a money trail, Ovid Knox's interest in the late Dave Laney's sudden wealth increased sharply. "How much cash did he dump on the bed, Miss Carver?"

"I don't know."

"Come on. Dave's passed out. The money's just lying there. He's snoring. You're all packed. The cab's on the way. But there's plenty of time for a fast count. So how much was there, Miss Carver?"

"Fifty-four thousand and I prefer 'Hey, you' to Miss Carver."

"What'd Dave call you?"

"Jessie, honey or bitch—depending on his mood."

"How much did he owe you?"

"Around four thousand dollars."

"And you didn't collect any? I would've."

"That could be because you're not into conceptual thinking. Let's say Dave was given the money to make a dope buy. His reputation won't suffer if I reveal he did that now and then. And let's say the dope buy's for sixty thousand, but

Dave's already blown six. If I'd 'collected,' as you call it, what he owed me, four thousand bucks, that would've left him ten thousand short, which is a lot of money in Mexico. And if you short a Mexican dope *jefe* that much, you can get yourself killed. That's why I neither collected nor stole any of Dave's money, if it was his, which I very much doubt."

"That was a nice little self-exculpatory talk based on supposition," Knox said. "What I want are details. I don't care how trivial."

"Okay. Trivial details. The taxi came. A Volkswagen. I gave the kid who drove me to the airport twelve American dollars, which is about two-thirds of what he said his usual daily take is. When I got to LAX I had thirty-four bucks left. I blew twenty-four on a cab. My net worth is now four dollars and change and I'd appreciate it very much, fella, if you'd get the fuck off my back."

Knox's face went still. Nothing moved. His color remained the same light tan and Partain diagnosed the utter stillness as anger, certainly not embarrassment. The amusement in Knox's blue eyes had either died or gone away as he leaned toward Jessica Carver and perhaps would have yelled something at her, a threat or a warning, if Partain hadn't said, "I'd like to ask her a couple of questions."

Knox leaned back, his face again relaxed as the amusement in his eyes rekindled itself. "Sure," he said. "Why not?"

Partain arranged himself into a nonthreatening posture by resting his right elbow on a walnut side table and cupping his chin in his right palm. It made him look both slightly interested and slightly bored.

"You took a morning flight out of Guadalajara," he said, making it sound more like an offhand statement than a question.

She nodded.

"Long flight?"

"Three hours and something."

"You arrived at LAX around one or two?"

She nodded again.

"Who was on the door downstairs, Tom?"

"Yes."

"He let you in?"

"Sure. And offered to carry my bag up."

"You let him?"

"It was heavy and I was tired."

"You tip him?"

"Five dollars—which is why I'm down to four dollars and change."

"Then what?"

"You mean after Tom left? Well, I dumped the bag on the bed, poured a double vodka on the rocks and drank it while the tub filled. I don't remember how long my bath was. Maybe forty-five minutes. Maybe more. Then I took a long, long nap, woke up hungry and was heading for the kitchen when you materialized in the living room and threw your bag at me."

"What bag?" Knox said.

"I told Mr. Partain not to move or I'd shoot. He spun around like a top and let go his leather carry-on. It hit me in the stomach and knocked the breath out of me."

"What about the gun?" Knox said.

"There wasn't any gun," Carver said. "I lied."

"What'd Partain do then?"

"He cooked us dinner," Jessica Carver said.

It was 3:32 A.M. when Ovid Knox finally left and nearly 4 A.M. when Jessica Carver rose, yawned, and said she was going to bed.

After she left, Millicent Altford said, "You outwaited her."

"I have to ask some questions," Partain said.

"I can't sleep anyhow so go ahead and ask."

"This may sound personal but it's not. What's your birthday?"

"That's sure no secret. July 17, 1930."

"You know your Social Security number?"

She rattled it off. "Four-four-eight—eighteen—thirty-four twenty-five."

"A hundred dollars says the combination to your safe is either seven seventeen thirty or forty-four eight eighteen."

"No bet," she said.

"Which one?"

"My birthday. Seven right, seventeen left, nineteen right, thirty left. I changed the combination after the horse was stolen, but I haven't memorized the new numbers because there's not much point."

"That money you showed me in Santa Paula," Partain said.

"What about it?"

"I was sitting here, half listening to Knox, when it occurred to me that what you showed me could've been a flash bundle. One-hundred-dollar bills on top of bound packets of plain paper. Or maybe even dollar bills underneath, if you wanted to run the de luxe model by me."

"I offered to let you count it."

"What if I said let's go back up there tomorrow and count it together?"

"Swell. Let's go. Now do I get to ask what the hell you're getting at?"

"I'm getting at the 'just in case,'" he said. "That was your reason for taking me up to Santa Paula: in case something happened to you, there'd be somebody who knew about the damp money."

"It's damn well bone-dry by now."

"But it was almost as if you had a premonition that some-body'd try to kill you. Or was it more than premonition— say a real honest-to-God threat, which is why you hired me in the first place?"

"No premonition. No threat. Just logic. Somebody stole one-point-two million dollars of nonexistent invisible money. Money I couldn't even report stolen. I believe the thief knew that. In fact, nobody to this day knows it was stolen except you, me and the thief. Or thieves. That's why I decided I needed a just-in-case witness—somebody who'd go after both the money and the thief if something happened to me like being smothered to death with a pillow."

"You have a will made out?" Partain said.

"Everything goes to Jessie."

"And Jessie's broke."

She frowned at him, although it was really more glower than frown, but then a merry grin erased it and she said, "Nice try. Hell, it wasn't just nice, it was almost elegant. Jessie and Dave are broke in Guadalajara, right?"

Partain nodded, barely smiling.

"Dave wakes up one morning with his usual hangover and asks Jessie how much her mama's worth, and Jessie says she doesn't know exactly, but maybe a million or two. So Dave says, Honey, why don't we run up to L.A. and kill Mama and make it look like somebody else did it? Well, Jessie thinks inheriting all of Mama's money right away is a real fine idea. So they fly up here, but not together, and Jessie finds you in residence."

"I got here after she did," Partain said.

"Details," Altford said. "Meantime, Dave gets a bit smashed, develops a case of cold feet and needs to talk to Jessie. But you're in the way. Then you and I traipse off to Santa Paula to admire the invisible money while Jessie and Dave plot and plan. How's that sound?"

"Slick," Partain said.

"Okay. Dave gets hold of some doctor clothes, sneaks into my hospital room and tries to smother me but botches the job. He calls Jessie from a pay phone on the corner and she says, 'Don't worry, darlin', just wait right there on the corner and some friends of mine in a brown van'll come by and pick you up.' Sure enough, the van arrives, Dave hops in, they dump him out dead in my driveway and poor Jessie's net worth is still only four bucks and change."

Partain grinned. "I like it—even if it didn't happen."

"The part about Dave happened. The part where he died."

"Let's go back to the safe's combination. Who else knew it?"

"Just Jessie and me."

"Did she write it down or memorize it?"

Altford frowned, trying to remember. "She wrote it down on something—I remember now, on her driver's license so she wouldn't lose it."

"Your birthday?"

"Who remembers Mama's birthday?"

"Then Dave could've accidentally run across it."

"It wouldn't have been an accident."

"Probably not," Partain said, paused, then asked, "You discovered the money was missing the day after the election."

She nodded. "November fourth."

"Where were you the evening and night of the election?"

"After wandering for twelve years in the political wilderness? Out celebrating."

"Had a drink or two, I imagine."

"Five or six."

"Get home late?"

"Very late. About three A.M."

"Fall into bed?"

"Managed to get my clothes off first."

"Then Dave could've flown in that afternoon or evening, opened the safe anytime after one A.M. when Jack, the night man, got off, then been back in Guadalajara by midmorning, noon at the latest, before anyone knew he was gone."

"Then where's my one-point-two million?"

"What's five percent of that?" Partain said.

The number came first, followed instantly by rage. "Sixty thousand dollars—just about what he dumped on Jessie's bed. The son of a bitch stole my money on commission, then mooched off my daughter. What a piece of shit."

Partain merely nodded and said, "You ever give Jessie a key card to the building and your place here?"

"When I first moved in. Sometimes she'd stay a weekend or even a month, if she was between jobs. But three or four months ago she wrote she'd lost it and told me to get the locks changed or whatever they do when a key card's lost. I just never got around to it."

Partain reached into his pocket and brought out the key card he'd removed from the dead Dave Laney's mouth. Altford stared at it for a moment, then asked, "Where'd you get that?"

"Somebody stuck it in Dave's mouth."

"What's it supposed to be—a threat? A warning? A curse?"

"It's supposed to make you worry about what it is."

"What I need to know is who the fuck put Dave up to it? Who talked him into stealing one million two hundred thousand dollars for a lousy five percent commission?"

"Someone who wanted the money, knew about it and had a total lock on Dave."

"Okay. You're my security wizard. What do I do now?"

"Call in reinforcements."

"Aw, hell, Partain. Who?"

"Your old flame, General Winfield."

"Why? I mean, why him?"

"Because he's a preeminent authority on Major General Walker Hudson."

"What's a serving Army general got to do with me and my money?"

"For one thing, he's Dave's uncle. For another, he's the guy I beat the shit out of down in El Salvador."

17

The century-old red brick house was a tiny two-story affair in the 400 block of Fourth Street, Southeast, and a pleasant stroll from the Library of Congress, the Supreme Court, the Capitol building and the birthplace of J. Edgar Hoover.

It was owned free and clear by Emory Kite, the private investigator, who sat on a red plush couch as old as the house itself, counting $50,000 in $100 bills onto a marble-top table with carved griffin legs that clutched glass balls in their claws.

It was 7:14 A.M. and Kite was still wearing a much too long green velvet bathrobe or dressing gown that Colonel Ralph Millwed thought made him look like one of the more unsavory Disney dwarfs. Grumpy, the Colonel decided, running through the seven names as he watched Kite count the money quickly, even expertly, licking his right forefinger after every tenth bill.

Once he reached the five hundredth bill, Kite replaced the ten banded packets in the big brown paper Safeway bag they had arrived in and folded the sack's top over three times, securing it with an enormous blue plastic paper clip.

Now cradling the bag, he wriggled backward on the couch

until his short legs almost stuck straight out beneath the green robe. Kite gave the money a pat that was almost a caress and said, "When?"

"You have seventy-two hours," the Colonel said.

"Not enough. Not near enough."

"Make do," the Colonel said.

"L.A.'s one big town, Ralphie. I gotta get situated, do some tracking, run the routes, figure the percentages. It all takes time."

"Do it within three days and you get another fifty thousand. If it takes more time than that, you get just what's in the sack."

"How about expenses?"

"You get expenses no matter what."

Kite turned the corners of his wide mouth down, forming the twin hooks that Millwed had come to despise because they often meant the little shit had just thought up something elaborate, expensive and probably too good to turn down.

"How'd you like the way my Mexican friends out there handled that rush-rush order?" Kite said.

"I didn't know they were Mexicans."

"Yeah, well, they're actually Mexican-Americans, but how d'you think they handled it—the nephew thing?"

"They did what they were paid to do," the Colonel said, smiled slightly, then asked, "Do they need a letter of reference?"

"No, but while I'm there, I thought I might use 'em as backup out of my own pocket."

"Emory," the Colonel said, his voice nearly toneless but full of warning.

Kite widened his eyes until they were brimming with feigned innocence. "What?"

"You will not under any circumstances subcontract this thing. Understood?"

"Never crossed my mind. I'm talking backup—contingency

stuff. The General wants a custom job and I'll do it just the way he likes. Set your objective, he used to tell me, then ram straight toward it. That's the way he likes a job done and the Captain and Mrs. Central America are a good example of it. So's the General's nephew. And you gotta admire the General for that because I can't even imagine what it must've cost him. I don't mean money. I mean the way it must've made him feel."

"He felt nothing," the Colonel said.

"I can't believe that, Ralphie," Kite said, obviously believing every word. "His own nephew."

"General Hudson long ago decided that remorse and regret are counterproductive emotions. Once he decided that, he had his removed."

Kite chuckled. "That's a good one. But you know what I hear? I hear that before he went to Vietnam, way back when he was a lieutenant or captain, he had his appendix out even though it wasn't bothering him. He must've figured coming down with appendicitis way out in the boonies would've been sort of, like you say, counterproductive. So maybe while they were taking out his appendix, they also cut out his remorse and regret glands. What d'you think?"

"I think you'd better get to the point, if there is one."

"The point is Twodees."

"He bothers you?"

"Him? Nah. But after he's fixed, I figure he'll be the last one—the last you guys'll have to worry about anyway. Then it'll only be me, you and the General who know what happened to those two kids from El Salvador, the nephew and Twodees."

"Get to it, Emory."

"Well, I've been thinking—and I'd like your advice on this—but what I've been thinking is maybe I oughta take out some insurance."

"What kind?" the Colonel said.

"The usual kind. Find myself a lawyer and hand him one

of those to-be-opened-only-if-something-nasty-happens-to-me letters."

Colonel Millwed leaned forward, rested his elbows on his knees, clasped his hands together and studied Kite with icy gray eyes that never seemed to thaw.

"Do what you please, Emory. But should something bad ever happen to me, something equally bad will happen to you and General Hudson. I can only assume that General Hudson has made similar arrangements."

Kite nodded contentedly several times and said, "That's good news, Ralphie. Each of us looking out for himself means that we're all looking out for each other. Like the three musketeers. Sort of."

"Sort of," the Colonel agreed and leaned back in his chair.

Kite wriggled off the couch and rose, clutching the money bag to his chest. "Look. I better go call my travel agent at home and see if she can get me on that ten o'clock flight to L.A. You got any problem with me in first class?"

"None."

"You gonna stick around till I find out about the flight?"

"I thought I might."

"Yeah," Kite said. "So did I." He turned and left the room, the money bag still clasped to his chest, the hem of his long green velvet dressing gown trailing after him.

Colonel Millwed rose and wandered around the parlor that took up half of the ground floor and was stuffed with furniture, photographs, paintings and souvenirs that dated from the 1900s to the mid-1930s. None of them had been supplied by Kite, who had bought the house and its contents from the great-great-grandniece of the woman who first lived there in 1903 as a 21-year-old bride. When her husband died in 1937, she lived in the house alone until her death in 1980. A year later, her only heir, the great-great-grandniece, who lived in Oregon, sold everything to Kite.

Millwed had once asked Kite if living in the old place

wasn't like living in a museum. "Maybe," Kite had said. "But it's my museum."

The Colonel turned from his inspection of a corner whatnot stand as Kite reentered the room, wearing a Raiders sweatshirt, faded jeans, scuffed white Reeboks and on his big head a blue Dodgers baseball cap.

"That should make you invisible," Millwed said.

"Think so?" Kite said. "I just checked the Weather Channel and it's gonna be sunny and about seventy-six out there. Maybe I'll go to the beach this afternoon."

"And Twodees?"

Kite seemed to give Partain some thought. "Well, maybe I'll fix Twodees first, then go to the beach."

18

General Vernon Winfield was the last to board the German-made shuttle bus that ferried passengers to and from their planes at Dulles International. The shuttle started off smoothly enough but one of the standing passengers wasn't quite prepared and stumbled against the General, forcing him to step back and onto the toe of a seated passenger.

Winfield turned to apologize and was surprised to find himself staring down at the equally surprised and upturned face of Emory Kite. The General recovered first. "Well, Mr. Kite. I *am* sorry."

"S'all right, General. Going to L.A., huh?"

"A brief vacation. And you?"

"Business. You in first class?"

The General shook his head. "Afraid not."

"Too bad," Kite said. "I thought if you were, maybe we could switch seats with somebody and sit together."

"That would've been pleasant," the General lied just as the shuttle veered left, giving him an excuse to turn away, grab a vertical pole and avoid Kite for the rest of the flight.

* * *

All the first-class passengers except Emory Kite were gone by the time General Winfield made his way from far back in the 747's crowded economy section to the LAX arrival-departure area. He noticed Kite still hanging around or perhaps even loitering with intent. Winfield wasn't sure what the loitering phrase meant precisely, but it sounded as though Kite would be good at it.

The General then saw the white shirtboard sign with the neat black Magic Marker lettering that read: "Winfield." The sign was displayed with no trace of self-consciousness by a man in his early forties who wore a blue suit, white shirt and tie.

Winfield shifted his carry-on bag to his left hand, walked over and said, "Major Partain?"

" 'Partain' will do, General."

The General smiled, offering his hand. "Do you mind 'Two-dees'?"

" 'Twodees' is fine," Partain said and ended the handshake just as Emory Kite, still wearing his Dodgers cap and Raiders sweatshirt, sidled up to Winfield and said, "Need a lift into town?"

"Thank you, Mr. Kite, but I have a ride."

Kite examined Partain. "You a limo driver?"

Partain shook his head.

"Mr. Partain is a friend of a friend," the General said.

Kite stuck out his hand. "Emory Kite. I do investigations outta Washington."

After a brief handshake, Partain said, "Federal?"

"Private," Kite said. "You live in L.A.?"

"I grew up in California."

"Yeah? Then maybe you could recommend a nice hotel."

"They say the Peninsula's a nice hotel."

"What's a room go for?"

"I'd guess two-eighty, three hundred. Around in there."

Kite nodded neutrally. "Sounds about right. Where's it at?"

"Beverly Hills."

Kite seemed to like the location, too, because he smiled up at the General and said, "When you get some free time, gimme a call and we'll have a drink and some lunch. My treat."

"Thank you," Winfield said. "I'll see how my schedule works out."

"I'll be at the Peninsula," Kite said, smiled his goodbye, turned and walked away.

Before Partain could ask, Winfield said, "He shares office space with us at VOMIT."

"You and Nick must really need the money."

"Yes," the General said. "We really do."

They were in the Lexus coupe, heading north on the 405, when the General said, "Perhaps you could recommend a hotel more moderately priced than the Peninsula."

"Mrs. Altford would like you to stay at her place."

"That's very kind of her, but—"

Partain didn't let him finish. "She thinks her daughter and I need a chaperone."

"I've never in my life been a chaperone."

"And I've never needed one. But she said if that argument didn't work, I should try the second and more compelling one. The room's free. Or as she put it, free-gratis-for-nothing."

"There really is a room?"

"You get the master bedroom. It has its own bath. Jessica Carver and I share a bath."

"How is Jessie?"

"Broke and looking for work. Or thinking about looking for it."

"How'd she take the death of her—what? Boyfriend?"

"Try lover," Partain said. "She took it okay. She even may've been a little relieved."

"When you called me late last night or, I suppose, very early this morning, you said you were virtually sure David Laney was a nephew of General Walker Hudson."

"Now I'm absolutely sure," Partain said. "The Laneys and Hudsons are two old California families who sometimes intermarried. Dave's mother was Ruth Ellen Hudson. She married Gerald Laney. General Walker Laney Hudson is Ruth Ellen's brother. General Hudson got Laney as a middle name because his father and the father of Gerald Laney—Dave's dad— were best friends."

"How'd you discover all that?"

"I didn't. I set Jessie down in front of her mother's computer and turned her loose. An hour later she had it all wrapped up. Jessie likes stuff like that. Says it reminds her of market research."

"How was Laney killed?"

"I don't know," Partain said. "I saw his body just after they dumped it out on Mrs. Altford's driveway. The cops say they won't know what killed him until after the autopsy."

The General nodded thoughtfully, waited a few moments, then asked, "Ever know a young captain in Salvadoran intelligence called Trigueros?"

"José Trigueros Chacón," Partain said. "What about him?"

"He and his wife were shot dead in Washington yesterday afternoon. A professional job, I'm told."

"Who told you?"

"The police."

"Why would the cops tell you how Trigueros was killed?"

"Because the investigating homicide detective is a member of VOMIT."

"He tell you why the Captain was killed?"

"The detective's a she and she didn't know why," Winfield said. "But earlier yesterday the Captain offered us—Nick really—the names of some Americans who were connected to the murder of those six Salvadoran priests, their cook and her daughter. The Captain claimed he had proof of the connection and wanted five thousand dollars for it."

"But got killed before you could raise the money and make the buy."

"That's not at all how it happened. We raised the money and then went to see the Captain. Nick and I. But when we offered the money he said it was no longer possible to sell us the proof. I thought he looked, well, terrified. So did Nick. Less than an hour after we left, Trigueros and his wife were murdered."

They rode in silence for half a mile before Partain said, "I'm sorry they're dead. He was a nice kid, if not overly bright."

After another lengthy silence, Winfield asked, "Does it seem either likely or possible that they could all be connected somehow—the murder of Trigueros in Washington, Laney's murder here and the attempt on Millie Altford's life?"

"Something that wires them all together?"

"I'd settle for a common thread."

A mile later Partain said, "Well, there's me. I'm a common thread. But that's only if you're looking for a person. Some inanimate common threads might be money, greed, politics, revenge or treachery."

"Ah, treachery!" the General murmured, his voice soft yet curiously orotund. "One of history's favorite shortcuts."

"Right up there with assassination."

"You may be right about yourself," the General said. "By chance or choice you know or have met most of the players— General Hudson, of course; Colonel Millwed; the late Captain Trigueros; the equally late David Laney and his lover, Jessica Carver—and her mother, Millicent Altford. You know Nick Patrokis, of course, and now me. You even know the former resident CIA bagman in El Salvador, Henry Viar."

"I haven't thought of Viar in months," Partain said.

"Why would you? But now I've almost convinced myself

that you and the aforementioned treachery are the most likely common threads that run through everything."

"Well, you could yank on the thread and see what unravels," Partain said. "But there's a surer way to find out if I'm the guy."

"What?"

"Wait till somebody tries to kill me."

"Or succeeds," the General said.

19

Late that same January afternoon, Millicent Altford sat cross-legged on the high hospital bed, wearing her red silk robe with the small golden dragons and watching a C-Span rerun of a call-in show that featured three Washington-based reporters. The reporters were listening with barely concealed dismay to a call from a retired Army master sergeant in Flagstaff, who was pressing them on whether the Trilateral Commission would exert as much evil influence on the incoming administration as it had on the outgoing one.

Altford missed the reporters' response because Liz Ball, the night nurse, entered the corner room and asked, "You wanta talk to some sixteen-year-old college professor who claims he sits at the right hand of your guy in Little Rock?"

"He offer any proof?"

Ball shrugged. "What he showed me looks okay."

"Send him in."

Marvin Gipson was about what Altford expected: Medium height. Thirty or thirty-one. A runner's lean frame. Tortoise-shell-rimmed glasses over smart blue eyes. Stubborn mouth beneath a know-it-all nose. Bony chin atop a long, long neck and lots of light brown hair. He came wrapped in a tweed jacket, white button-down shirt, chinos, a tie that looked borrowed and penny loafers with a fresh shine, which, she suspected, he had sat still for when he changed planes at Stapleton International in Denver and found himself with time to kill.

Gipson smiled at her with his generation's perfect teeth and said, "I'm Marvin Gipson, Ms. Altford, and probably your greatest fan."

"Thank you kindly, Marvin, and would you please be good enough to hand me that phone over there?"

Gipson handed her the phone and she tapped out eleven numbers from memory. Once her call was answered, she said, "It's Millie. Have you guys sent me a Marvin Gipson?" She listened to the reply, then asked, "What's he look like?"

Staring at Gipson, she said "uh-huh" several times as the description came over the phone. Gipson at first stuck his hands in his pants pockets and jingled some keys. But after a frown from Altford, he removed his hands and, following a moment's indecision, clasped them behind his back. They were still there when Altford said, "Thanks, Phil, just checking," hung up the phone, examined Gipson thoughtfully, then slipped off the bed and glided toward the mini-refrigerator. Over her shoulder she asked, "Want a beer, Marvin?"

"A Diet Coke, if there is one," he said.

Altford took a bottle of beer and a can of Diet Coke from the small refrigerator, handed him the soft drink and said, "Let's sit over here."

Once they were seated, he in an armchair, she on the dark blue couch, Altford drank beer from the bottle, leaned back and waited for Gipson to say what they had told him to say.

He dutifully swallowed some Coke first, placed the can on the coffee table, cleared his throat, smiled deferentially and said, "You've had such a long and varied career, I was wondering whether—"

Altford interrupted. "Phil tells me you teach at Sewanee. What d'you teach?"

"Political science and economics."

"You on leave?"

"A year's sabbatical. But the reason I'm here—"

"I know why you're here, Marvin. You're here because somebody dumped a dead body on my driveway and that's got Little Rock worried. Not terrified. Just worried. You're here to find out how bad it might be. If you decide it stinks out loud, you'll fly back and recommend that they move my name to the bottom of the true-blue-and-faithful list, or maybe strike it off altogether."

"They're primarily concerned about your health, Ms. Altford. All of us are."

"That's bullshit. If they were really worried about my health, they'd've called Draper Haere here in L.A. and asked him to drop by and see whether I'm dying or playing possum. So it's not my health they're worried about. It's about that dead guy on my driveway who was shacked up down in Mexico for a year with my daughter."

"A Mr. Laney, I believe," Gipson said.

"Dave Laney."

"Yes, well, I suppose if there is anything about Mr. Laney's past activities that could somehow, you know—"

"Pose a problem?" Altford said.

Gipson gave her a grateful nod. "Exactly."

"*I* didn't shack up with Laney, my daughter did. Or is her mistake reason enough for Little Rock to dispatch a member of its watch-and-ward squad?"

"Mr. Laney's reputation does trouble us," Gipson said. "It makes us wonder whether he somehow could've been involved in your fund-raising activities last year."

"He sent me a check once."

Gipson leaned forward. "For how much?"

"Twenty-five bucks, I think. But that was about four years ago, not last year."

Gipson leaned back, more disappointed than relieved. "Then he wasn't involved in your fund-raising in any way?"

"He was in Mexico, for Christ sake. In Guadalajara. Why would you guys even think I'd let him handle anything—especially money?"

"I didn't say that, Ms. Altford."

She drank from the green bottle again, gave him a long stare and said, "You think he might've been my Mexican laundry, don't you?"

"We really don't know what to think."

"Then think about this: I raised a lot of money for Little Rock—a whole hell of a lot—and Little Rock was ever so grateful and said so. After the election, the mentioners started mentioning my name for some kind of appointive job. Nothing grand, of course. Maybe ambassador to Togo. Assistant Secretary of Commerce. Crappy jobs like that. But still it was kind of flattering even though nobody's ever asked me if I'd accept anything. If they had asked, I'd've said no thanks. So here's what you tell 'em when you get back to Little Rock, Professor."

She placed the beer bottle on the coffee table and rose. Gipson started to rise but noticed her grim expression and decided to remain seated. She stared down at him for a moment or two before she spoke.

"One," she said. "Tell 'em Millie's not interested in any government job so don't bother to offer her one. Two. Tell 'em Millie insists that Little Rock stop poking around in her personal affairs. And three, tell 'em Millie still knows all the plot numbers by heart."

"Plot numbers?" Gipson said.

"At the political cemetery," she said, as if explaining to a slow-witted child. "Where they bury the dead bodies."

"Aw, hell," Gipson said, then rose with a regretful sigh. "We've been a little clumsy, haven't we?"

"About average," said Millicent Altford.

General Winfield stood almost at attention that evening in the condominium living room as the cashiered Army Major circled him slowly, picked a microscopic bit of lint from the right shoulder of Winfield's midnight-blue suit, then held it under the General's nose for inspection before flicking it away.

"New suit?" Partain asked.

"Nine years old. What I buy lasts."

Jessica Carver looked up from an ad-fat Paris *Vogue* and asked, "Where'd you and Ma decide to go?"

"She made a reservation at a place called Morton's," Winfield said. "I'd suggested Chasen's but she informs me that that's where all the ghosts dine."

"Morton's is noisy," Jessica Carver said. "But the food's okay."

Winfield looked at his watch, then at Partain. "Anything I should know about the car?"

"It drives itself," Partain said. "Jack the doorman's bringing it up from the garage. If you have any questions, ask him."

"He's the actor?"

"Right. Tom, the day doorman, is the surfer."

Winfield turned to Jessica Carver. "Are you sure you two won't join us?"

"For God's sake, Vernon," she said. "You're heading for a hot date, not a family reunion."

Partain escorted the General to the foyer, then reentered the living room to find Jessica Carver at the big window, staring out at the lights. Without turning, she said, "What's on the menu tonight—Salisbury steak?"

"We're going out," he said.

"No kidding? Where?"

"Westwood."

"Want me to call a cab?"

"We'll walk," Partain said.

"*Walk?*" she said, turning from the window.

"Why not?"

"Ever hear of drive-by shootings? Don't misunderstand me. I like to walk. But I don't want to be a slow-moving target for some teenage crackhead."

"We'll walk to Westwood and take a cab back."

"Who's buying?" she said.

"I am."

"The meal *and* the cab?"

Partain stared at her without expression.

"Sorry," she said. "I must've spent a year too long with Dave."

As he and Jessica Carver came out of the Eden's front entrance, Partain noticed the shimmer in the air near the exhaust of the black stretched Lincoln limousine. It was parked at the curb across Wilshire Boulevard in front of a twenty-one-story condominium building someone had named the Castillian.

Partain turned to Jack the doorman and asked, "How long's the limo been there?"

"Maybe forty-five minutes. An hour."

"With its engine running?"

"It's cold out."

"It's fifty-five, maybe even sixty."

"That's cold," Jack said.

"Why don't they park it in the Castillian's drive?"

"Maybe because it's a long wait and the driver doesn't want to block the driveway. Some limo drivers are thoughtful that way. Maybe one out of a hundred."

"Don't the cops bother them?"

"The cops've got other stuff to do. Besides, what if the limo's waiting for the girlfriend of the indy prod at Paramount who's almost promised to look at the TV series treatment the cop wrote?"

"Could you call us a cab?" Partain said.

"Sure," Jack said and turned away as Jessica Carver gave Partain a questioning look.

"Let's wait inside," Partain said and took Carver by her left elbow as Jack headed for the outside phone. Just before they reached the Eden's glass doors, Partain glanced back at the limousine and noticed a lowered rear window and the dull glint of something metallic. He gave Jessica Carver a hard shove that sent her sprawling to his right. Partain dropped to the concrete, rolling from there to his left.

The gunshot came then and Partain automatically classified the weapon as a .30-caliber sporting rifle, possibly an old Schultz & Larsen M 65. He tried to press himself to the concrete as he waited for the second bullet's impact—or for someone's groan or cry. He fully expected the second shot but hoped desperately for the sound of the limo's revving engine and the getaway screech of its rear tires clawing at the pavement.

But he heard nothing and, after a moment, sat up and looked across the street. The limousine was gone. He looked then for Jessica Carver and found her crouched six feet away in almost a caricature of a sprinter's starting stance. Her mouth was open, her eyes were wide and her head was turned toward Partain. But she was staring at something beyond him.

Partain turned to find Jack the doorman lying faceup near the outside phone in death's familiar position of a rag doll, carelessly dropped. Jack's eyes and mouth were open. Partain decided it had been either a head shot, expertly aimed, or a shot gone wild. The relief came then, flooding through him and drowning the brief guilt he had always felt whenever it had been he who lived and someone else who died.

* * *

The black limousine turned right off Wilshire and eventually chose Santa Monica Boulevard as its path to the southbound 405 freeway. It was not until the limousine was in the freeway's number three lane and rolling south at a sedate 59 miles per hour that the Latino driver spoke to his passenger in the rear.

"You missed," he said, his accent making it sound something like, "Chew meesed."

"Did I?" said Emory Kite from the backseat.

20

They stood in front of Jack Thomson, the dead doorman, until the first black-and-white arrived. They stood side by side, Partain in a mildly threatening "at ease" military stance, Jessica Carver with arms folded across her chest.

A small crowd had gathered and wanted to know if the guy was dead and if they had killed him and if anybody had called the cops. Partain answered only the last question.

After the black-and-white arrived, Partain and Carver abandoned their guard duty, answered a uniformed sergeant's questions and agreed to wait upstairs until homicide talked to them which, the Sergeant warned, it sure as shit would.

They took the elevator to the fifteenth floor without speaking and entered the apartment. Carver went silently to her room and locked the door. Partain retired to the kitchen and began cutting up two plump fryers that were in a bag of groceries General Winfield had insisted on buying during the drive from the airport.

An hour later Partain knocked on Carver's door and said, "Dinner's ready."

"I don't want any," she said, her voice muffled by the door.

"Fried chicken. Mashed potatoes. Cream gravy. A three-lettuce salad. Corn bread."

After a moment she asked, "Real corn bread?"

"From scratch."

Five seconds later the bedroom door opened and Jessica Carver, her eyes swollen and bloodshot, gave him a sad tired smile and said, "Well, I reckon we have to eat."

"It's on the table," Partain said as the corridor door chimes rang.

"I'll get it," he told her. "You go ahead and start."

Partain opened the door and wasn't surprised to find that the caller was the fashion-plate homicide Detective Sergeant, Ovid Knox. Before Knox could say anything, Partain said, "You eat yet?"

Knox didn't try to hide his surprise. "Why?"

"Because dinner's on the table. Fried chicken. Salad. Mashed potatoes. Cream gravy. Corn bread. You're invited. We eat in the kitchen."

"Who's we?"

"Jessica Carver, me and now you. But if you don't want to eat, you can watch."

"I'm not much of a voyeur," Knox said.

They ate everything but the bones and the beak. And because Jessica Carver and Ovid Knox still seemed hungry, Partain found some Sara Lee brownies in the freezer and served them with the coffee. Carver had two brownies, Knox, three, and Partain, none.

After his third brownie and final cup of coffee, Knox pushed the cup and saucer aside, rested his elbows on the table, leaned forward slightly and said, "Who shot him?"

"At least two guys in a black stretch Lincoln limo," Partain said. "One drove. The other was the backseat shooter."

"Any description?"

"It was night. The windows were tinted. They were at least fifty yards away."

"Tell me about the dead guy—Jack Thomson with no 'p.'"

"He was the night doorman and a sometime actor."

Knox turned to Jessica Carver. "How long've you known him?"

"Three years. Maybe three and a half. He came with the building."

"Then he was here when your mother moved in."

She nodded.

"Nice guy?"

"Yeah, he was nice. He'd get you a taxi, carry your groceries up, get your car washed, tell creeps you weren't in when you were. He was just a nice accommodating guy. Ma always tipped him for doing stuff and gave him two hundred dollars at Christmas."

"He ever offer to sell you any dope?"

"No. But then I never asked him, did I?"

"He ever ask you to go out with him?"

"No. But if he had, I might've."

Knox turned back to Partain. "How'd he strike you?"

"He could do voices, or maybe I should say accents. He was very good at it. He also told me he was too second-leadish for films but got work in commercials—radio and TV, I suppose. I never saw him on TV but that might be because he said he did mostly voice-overs and also because I seldom watch television."

Turning to Carver again, Knox said, "He was the night doorman?"

She nodded.

"Then he wasn't on duty when Dave Laney paid you that early morning call."

"Tom was on duty. The day doorman."

"Did poor dead Jack know poor dead Dave?"

"Sure," she said. "I stayed here a while before I went to

Mexico with Dave, who was one of the creeps I sometimes told Jack to get rid of. They knew each other all right, but not socially."

Knox rose, went to the sink, found a glass, ran the cold water, filled the glass and sipped it. All this gave Partain the opportunity to assess Knox's outfit. That night he was wearing a double-breasted brown jacket with worsted slacks so dark green they might have been black. His shirt was the palest of yellows with a long-pointed collar. There was no tie and the collar was buttoned. Partain remembered when only hicks and rubes wore their shirts buttoned to the top like that. But if there was no tie, there was a dark green handkerchief that peeped out of the jacket's breast pocket. Partain leaned back so he could see the shoes and was almost disappointed to discover they were the same gleaming black walnut loafers Knox had worn before.

Knox turned from the sink, had another sip of tap water, peered into the glass instead of at Partain and Carver and asked, "What happened tonight—from the beginning?"

Jessica Carver made the reply. "We were going to dinner. We were going to walk to Westwood."

"Walk?"

She indicated Partain with a nod. "His idea. Walk there, cab back. We came out of the lobby. He asked Jack how long the limo had been parked across the street. Jack said about an hour or forty—"

Knox interrupted. "Let him take it from there, Ms. Carver."

Jessica shrugged and Partain said, "He said forty-five minutes or an hour. I asked him why the cops hadn't tagged it. Jack said the cops were too busy—and what if the limo was waiting for the girlfriend of some indy prod at Paramount who'd halfway promised to read the cop's treatment for a TV show. What's an indy prod?"

"Independent producer," Knox said. "What happened next?"

"I asked Jack to call us a cab, took Jessica by the arm and suggested we wait inside."

"Why'd you change your mind about walking to Westwood?"

"Because I don't like it when cars park out in front of where I live for an hour or forty-five minutes with their engines running."

"It was parked across the street—not out front."

"That bothered me even more."

Knox sighed. "Okay. Then what?"

"We were heading for the building's front door. I glanced back, saw the limo's rear window'd been lowered and thought I saw something metallic inside the limo. Something that, well, glinted."

"Glinted?"

"Glinted. I shoved Jessica to the right and I dropped and rolled left. Then I heard the shot."

"And then?"

"I waited for the second shot."

"Thought they were shooting at you, did you?"

"I knew they were shooting at somebody. So I lay there, hoping that what I heard next would be the limo's getaway. But I didn't hear anything. Then I looked at Jessica. She was on her hands and knees like a sprinter at the starting blocks. But she was also staring at something. I looked where she was looking and saw Jack, the dead doorman."

Knox nodded thoughtfully and turned to Jessica Carver. "You were on your hands and knees?"

She said yes.

"Facing the street?" he said.

"Facing the street."

"What'd you see?"

"I saw that the limo's back window was about three-quarters of the way down. Something was poking out of the window— something dark. The light caught it once. Bounced off it. Then

I saw a red flash and heard the bang. I looked at Partain, who was trying to imitate a pancake. When I looked back at the limo, it was already pulling away—not fast, not slow, just normally."

Knox sat back down at the old kitchen table. "It's 149 feet from the driver's side of the limo to Jack the doorman. It's night but there's still lots of artificial light. The single round hit Jack in the center of the back of his head and blew away a lot of his brains. You were Army, Mr. Partain. What kind of shooting would you call that?"

"Expert—providing the shooter hit what he was supposed to hit."

"From what we could figure out," Knox said, "poor Jack was moving toward the outside phone when he got it. You shoved Ms. Carver, then dropped and rolled to a point about eight feet away from Jack. Ms. Carver was sort of kneeling five or six feet away from you, looking at a limo, a driver, a shooter in the backseat and a nice slow getaway. What does all that tell you?"

"That it was a professional job."

"Back up," Jessica Carver said. "That limo'd been parked there with its engine running for forty-five minutes or an hour. They could've shot Jack anytime. But they waited till they had an audience." She looked at Partain. "You and me."

Knox leaned an inch or two toward Partain. "That makes a weird kind of sense to me, Partain. It make any sense to you?"

"None at all," Partain said.

21

After her trout and his lamb at Morton's, Millicent Altford and Vernon Winfield declined dessert but ordered espresso and cognac. During dinner, a producer, a director, an agent and three actresses had stopped by separately to gloat over the imminent change at the White House; tell a really nasty Bush joke; find out how well Altford knew the President-elect, and ask whether she would be joining his administration.

Altford introduced the General to each of them; grinned at the Bush joke; claimed to have known the President-elect for seven or eight years, and said she wasn't at all keen about going to Washington. During the drop-bys, the General had half risen six times for the introductions, smiled agreeably but otherwise kept his mouth shut.

Altford had a sip of her after-dinner cognac and said, "Two of those guys who stopped by voted for Bush, the agent for Perot and the women all went with the winner."

"How do you know how they voted?"

She smiled. "I know."

The General finished his cognac, examined the tablecloth for a time, then looked up and asked, "I ever tell you how big-city machine politics enabled me to dodge the draft during World War Two?"

She smiled and shook her head slightly. "No, I think I'd've remembered that one."

Seconds went by as the General seemed to gaze across her left shoulder at a past that went back almost fifty years. "From age fourteen," he said, "I was a hell-raiser. Something to do with hormones and puberty, I imagine. I got into one jam after another and my father always got me out of them with a single phone call. He was a lawyer who got rich off Chicago politics. But you knew that."

"You don't talk about him much."

"No, I suppose not. This time, the time I'm talking about, was a particularly bad jam. It was the spring of '44 and I was about to graduate from the university high school."

"What kind of jam?"

"Drunken driving and a wreck in which no one was hurt. Inexcusable, of course, but my father fixed it and a week later announced he'd arranged for me to go to West Point. A senatorial appointment. To me it sounded like a jail sentence and I told him that if I had to go to college, I'd rather go to Slippery Rock than West Point. At the time, I believed Slippery Rock to be in either Arkansas or Missouri."

"It's in Pennsylvania," she said.

"I know. But then I didn't. My father said okay, I could hang around until I was drafted and then go to any goddamned college I wanted to after the war on the GI Bill—providing I survived."

"This was 1944?"

The General nodded. "I was seventeen, about to turn eighteen when I'd have to register for the draft. It was also about a month before D-Day in Europe and they were drafting all the warm bodies they could find and shipping them off to infantry replacement training camps for eighteen weeks, then straight on to Europe or the Pacific. A lot of the replacements were killed or wounded during their first few days on the line. I regarded all this as a most unpleasant prospect but thought that West Point, in its way, would be almost as bad. I had no desire to be a soldier of any kind."

"Not too patriotic, huh?"

"Not enough to die for my country, if I could avoid it. I still regard that as a sensible attitude. Sometimes, of course, the dying is unavoidable."

"So what happened?"

"I went to see my godfather, a Chicago alderman, who'd been on the receiving end of all those phone calls my father'd made on my behalf. The alderman kept me waiting in his reception room for three hours."

"I don't blame him."

"Neither do I because I must've been insufferable. When finally admitted to his presence, I told him I didn't want to go to West Point, didn't want to be drafted and asked if he had any suggestions. He merely nodded and said, 'Well, kiddo'—and I'm paraphrasing here, of course—'well, kiddo, you got three choices. You can go join the Merchant Marine, go to West Point or go tell your draft board you're queer. That's what my nephew did, but then the little shit really is queer.'"

"So you went to West Point," she said.

"No, I went to see the Merchant Marine recruiter at the post office downtown. He was an ancient mariner of forty-two or -three who said he'd be happy to sign me on but was obliged to warn me they were drafting guys out of the Merchant Marine straight into the infantry."

"So on to West Point," she said.

He nodded. "Where I sat out the war and often thought of my godfather, the alderman, who'd given me sound sensible advice devoid of patriotic claptrap. I felt curiously indebted to him, which is exactly how he wanted me to feel. I even thought of it as an example of how politics really worked, not only in Chicago but everywhere. And of course it was—providing you were a rich man's son."

"Then on to Korea," she said, "where somebody finally managed to shoot you and somebody else gave you a DSC."

"Yes, but I was mentally prepared for it by then—the wound, not the medal."

"I've often wondered why you stayed in," she said.

"Because I'd learned a trade by then and was really quite good at it."

"You ever see the alderman again?"

"No, but I think I managed to repay my debt to him."

"How?"

"By voting the straight Democratic ticket since 1948," General Winfield said.

Millicent Altford was driving when they left Morton's. They had gone only a few blocks when the General, staring into his side mirror, said, "I think we're being followed."

After glancing into her own mirror, she said, "Let's make sure."

Altford started zigzagging her way toward Olympic Boulevard, turning left and right at random. She even circled a couple of blocks but the car behind followed at an almost measured fifty feet.

"If it's still back there when we get to the hospital, I'll alert the security people," she said.

"You mean wake them up?"

"Let's hope not."

They reached the hospital and turned into its curved drive. The following car also made the turn, closed the distance, then stopped, switched off its lights and Edd Partain got out. He looked around carefully before approaching the Lexus on the driver's side. Altford lowered the window.

"What's wrong?" she said.

"Jack the doorman was shot dead in front of the Eden

earlier this evening. Jessica and I saw it. After we talked to the cops, I rented a car and drove to Morton's just in time to see you leave." He inspected the hospital grounds again and said, "You'd better get inside."

Up in Altford's hospital room, she and the General sat on the blue couch, Partain in an armchair. She and Winfield finally had run out of questions, hers being mostly about her daughter, Winfield's about the shooting itself and the marksmanship of the gunman.

They also wondered briefly why anyone would want to kill Jack the doorman, but such talk led nowhere and, after a brief silence, Partain asked Winfield, "Who else besides Nick Patrokis knows you and I are in Los Angeles?"

"No one," the General said. "And what a curious question. It implies that either you or Jessica was the target, and that the shooter was incompetent."

"Does it?" Partain said.

Something flitted across the General's face, either regret or inspiration. Whichever it was made him look uncomfortable as he said, "I misspoke."

"When?" Partain said.

Instead of answering, the General turned to Millicent Altford and said, "Could you make a reservation for lunch tomorrow for me and two guests at some place that film people frequent?"

"Sure—if I can ask why?"

"I want to invite someone to lunch and I need to offer an inducement."

"This someone a star-fucker?"

"I can only presume so."

"Then I'll call Le Dôme," she said, rose, went to the phone, made the call and returned to the couch. "One o'clock tomorrow. Le Dôme's on Sunset. You'll have what they call a preferred table."

"Thank you," the General said, rose, went to the phone, dialed information, got the number of the Peninsula Hotel, called it and said, "Mr. Emory Kite's room, please."

After the call went through, Winfield said, "Mr. Kite? Vernon Winfield. Sorry to call you so late but I wonder if you could possibly join me at one tomorrow for a business lunch at Le Dôme on Sunset Boulevard?"

The General listened, then said, "Yes, I understand film people do eat there."

After more listening, he said, "I need your professional advice about a fatal shooting a friend of mine witnessed earlier this evening."

Winfield listened just long enough for Kite to ask a brief question, then said, "You met him at the airport today." Another pause. "That's right. Mr. Partain. He'll be joining us for lunch." One final pause and, after that, the General said, "Good. Tomorrow at one, then."

After Winfield returned to the couch, looking content, if not quite smug, Altford asked Partain, "Who the hell's Mr. Kite?"

"A real short guy from Washington who's the only person except you and Patrokis who knows I'm out here with the General."

"What else is Kite?" she asked.

"He rents space from us at VOMIT," the General said. "By trade, he's a skip-tracer turned detective."

Partain rested his elbows on his knees, leaned toward the General and said, "You forgot to mention why I'd want to consult with Kite about a dead doorman."

"I didn't forget," Winfield said. "You're Millicent Altford's security consultant and fairly new to the trade. You need to know who the doorman really was—his background, job history, friends and criminal record, if any. But what you especially want to know is if there's anything about Jack that might further embarrass Ms. Altford, who's already been politically embarrassed by a dead body being dumped on her driveway—the body of a young man romantically involved with her daughter in Mexico."

"I don't think romance had a whole lot to do with it," Altford said.

"Who's going to pay Kite if he says yes?" Partain asked.

"I will," the General said.

"Is Kite licensed in California?"

"Not to my knowledge."

"What if he turns me down?"

"We should feel relieved," the General said.

"And if he accepts?"

"Then," Winfield said, "we begin our reassessment of Emory Kite."

A long silence began that was ended by a question from Altford to the General. "You don't like him much, do you, your Mr. Kite?"

"Is it that obvious?"

She nodded. "Maybe you should wear a disguise tomorrow."

"A disguise?"

"You know," she said. "A smile."

22

It was almost midnight when Partain stopped the rented Taurus in front of the Eden and noticed Tom, the day doorman, talking to a uniformed policeman. Tom excused himself and hurried around the front of the car as Partain opened the door and got out.

Instead of saying hello or good evening, Tom said, "They say you guys were right here when it happened—you and Jessica."

"That's right."

"Jack was one helluva guy," Tom said, paused for two seconds, then asked, "Rented a Taurus, huh? How d'you like it?"

"Nice car," Partain said, handing over the keys. "You knew Jack pretty well?"

"It's like I told the cops. We weren't exactly buddies but we got along fine. He was into acting. I'm into surfing. I work days. He worked nights. That left him free for his auditions and acting jobs, except he didn't get a lot of either. When the cops asked how come I knew how many acting jobs he got,

I asked them how many actors with steady work did night doorman as a hobby?"

"You two ever trade off?" Partain said.

"Yeah. Once in a while—mostly when Jack got himself invited to a screening where he could bump noses and smell assholes with anyone who might do him some good. Or if the surf was way up, we might trade. Jack was real nice about that."

"Jack interested in politics?"

"Why?"

"Well, he and Ms. Altford seemed to hit it off. And if they had this mutual interest, I thought Jack might've traded with you on, say, election night so he could stay home and watch the returns."

Although the question sounded lame to Partain, it didn't seem to bother Tom. "You mean in November?"

Partain nodded.

"What day?"

"The third."

"I mean what day of the week?"

"It's usually on a Tuesday."

"Nah. I'd've remembered that if we had. Traded. I don't vote much and Jack said he was voting for Perot. When I ask him why, he says it'd be a vote against typecasting." Tom frowned, now obviously puzzled, then smiled. "I get it. You wanta know if Jack and me had regular trade-off days. And if today was one of 'em and we called it off, then it should've been me who got zapped instead of Jack." He frowned again, more puzzled than ever. "But who the fuck'd wanta shoot me?"

"Or Jack?" Partain said.

"Yeah. Him either?"

Even after Tom vouched for Partain, the uniformed Los Angeles cop still demanded ID, checked the Wyoming driver's license against a list of names, then nodded and let Partain use his key card to enter the Eden.

He let himself into 1540 and found Jessica Carver waiting in the apartment's foyer. "You find them?" she asked.

He nodded. "I followed them from Morton's to the hospital. Your mother didn't know who was following her, tried to lose me and almost did."

"How'd she take it?"

"She was more concerned about you than Jack."

"That's nice," she said, studied him for a moment or two, then asked, "Like a drink?"

Again, Partain nodded. "Very much."

From behind the living room bar, Jessica Carver set a generous measure of iced Scotch in front of Partain and asked, "Where's the General?"

"Still at the hospital."

She glanced at her watch, saw it was almost midnight and said, "That means he'll spend the night. It happens four or five times a year either here or in Washington. It's got to be one of the most enduring bicoastal liaisons on record."

"I assume it went on while they were both married to somebody else."

"Sure. Why not?"

"They have my blessing," he said and drank some of his whisky.

"You ever married?" she said after tasting her own drink.

"Once. For fifteen months."

"What happened?"

"She disappeared."

"You mean she split."

"No. She just—disappeared."

"Where?"

"San Salvador."

She waited for him to continue, but when he didn't she

slapped the bar with her palm and used a loud voice to say, "Wake up, Partain!"

He stared at her. "I'm awake."

"You sure you don't suffer from seizures of the eyes-wide-open kind? Or is it just too, too painful to talk about? When you start something, finish it. Even if it's the saddest of all sad tales."

"You're curious," he said, sounding surprised.

"That's quick of you."

"Why?"

"You mean why am I curious? Because I'm normal and have a lot of respect for beginnings, middles and endings. You did pretty good with the beginning. 'She just—disappeared.' Why don't you just go on from—"

He interrupted her. "You're a good mimic, aren't you? You had my intonation and pause down pat. Even my featureless California accent. Okay. The rest of the story. She was Salvadoran and eleven years younger than me. Or I, if you're a grammarian. We were living in San Salvador. One morning she went out to buy stationery. She liked the thick creamy stuff, which was hard to find. She'd heard of a small shop nearby where she might buy some. She'd walked exactly forty-two meters up our street when a black 1989 SEL 450 sedan stopped and three guys got out. Maybe they wore masks. Maybe they didn't. Witnesses differ. They forced her into the backseat. The driver stayed behind the wheel. The car drove off and she disappeared."

Her eyes now as wide as they could go, Jessica Carver gave her head a small hard side-to-side shake, as if to dispel the image of the abduction. "That's awful," she said. "God, that's awful."

Partain nodded.

"You never found any trace of—"

"No trace," he said. "No body. Nothing."

"Any chance she's still—" Carver read the answer in Partain's expression and said, "No. I suppose not. What about the four guys—"

Again, he didn't let her finish. "They were never identified. It was apparently a political abduction but she was totally without politics. The only political crime she ever committed was marrying me. If she'd been of the right or the left, somebody might've done something. Retaliated, if nothing else, or even tracked down the guys who kidnapped her. But the apolitical have no headquarters, no chairman, no cadre, no money, no muscle. So nobody did anything."

"What'd you do?" she asked.

"Offered a reward. Had three thousand posters printed. Paid kids to put them up everywhere. Then I had to give up."

"Why?"

"Because she disappeared just nineteen days before I beat up the Colonel."

"You think he—"

Partain again didn't let her finish. "No, I don't think that. If I thought that, he'd've never made general."

The slight noise awoke Partain. It lasted only a few seconds, just long enough for him to identify it as the sound of leather heels and soles on the foyer's black and white marble floor. The General, he thought and looked at his watch—squinted at it really because of what he diagnosed as a medium hangover. It was 5:22 A.M. and he guessed that the General had left the hospital at 5 A.M. and, with little traffic, had made it to the Eden in less than twenty minutes.

There was another sound. It was a long sigh and Partain turned to look at the sleeping Jessica Carver. After their second drink, she had come around the bar to sit on a stool next to him. A drink or so later he had kissed her and she had kissed back and they had stayed there for a time, doing all the things a pair of overly experienced teenagers might have done, until by mutual consent they came down off the barstools and headed for the nearest bedroom, which happened to be his. There they had shucked off each other's clothes, giggled over a condom and fallen into bed.

She was experienced, creative and eager. He was experienced, creative and overeager. That was the first time. The second time had been like sex between old lovers too long apart. Nothing had gone wrong. Nothing he could remember anyway.

He heard yet another sound, this time from the kitchen. It was the unmistakable, if faint, clink of a china cup being placed in a saucer. Partain rose, pulled on his pants and the old plaid robe and headed barefoot for the kitchen, where he found General Winfield in pants, shirt and socks. The General already had the Braun coffeemaker primed and was conducting a search for the coffee itself.

"She keeps it down here," Partain said, knelt and opened a cabinet door beneath the sink.

"What a perfectly illogical place," the General said, accepting the can of coffee. "Did I wake you?"

"You tempted me," Partain said and rose. "The sound of a cup and saucer means coffee."

The General studied him for a moment. "Pleasant night?"

"Not too bad. And you?"

"Not too bad at all," the General said as he spooned coffee into the machine.

23

The Safeway was the one on Wisconsin Avenue in Georgetown and, after a forty-two-minute wait, Colonel Ralph Millwed's vigil was rewarded with the gray six-year-old Volvo station wagon that entered the parking lot and nosed into a space only one row up and four cars to his left.

The driver of the Volvo continued to sit in the car for a minute or so before she slowly got out, as if either stiff or tired, and headed for the Safeway's entrance. She wore a denim skirt, a man's white shirt and black leather speed-lace boots that didn't quite reach mid-calf. The right boot even had a small snap-close pocket for a jackknife. For warmth, she wore an obviously old double-breasted navy-blue coat that would've had six ivory buttons if one of them hadn't been missing. She wore the coat over her shoulders like a cape.

Shawnee Viar Lewis, only child of a CIA pensioner and widow of an AIDS victim, was halfway to the supermarket entrance when she turned, went back to the Volvo and locked it. The Colonel waited until she was well inside the Safeway before he got out of his rented black Mustang convertible.

Millwed wore what he'd always regarded as standard casual dress: a tweed jacket, tieless white shirt, sleeveless black cashmere sweater and twill pants of that peculiar shade once called officer's pinks. On his feet were black cashmere socks and old but well-cared-for brown loafers.

They met at the frozen pizzas. Her shopping cart contained milk, a carton of Pall Malls, bread, butter, eggs, bacon, salad stuff and a matched pair of Idaho potatoes. The Colonel's cart contained far more wholesome fare of nonfat milk, broccoli, three kinds of fruit, oatmeal and a small roasting chicken.

Shawnee Viar was reading the label on a twelve-inch pepperoni pizza when the Colonel said, "It's none of my business, but if you're going to eat that crap, you might as well eat the best. Here."

He handed her a pizza that bore the name of Wolfgang Puck, a West Coast restaurateur who skillfully marketed not only his frozen pizzas but himself. Shawnee Viar put the pepperoni pizza back, accepted the one offered by the Colonel, examined it dubiously and said, "What's so great about these?"

"They're almost like the real thing."

"Well, that's about as close as I ever get," she said, dropped the Puck pizza into her cart, gave his cart a quick inspection, looked up and said, "What happens when you come down with an acute attack of the munchies?"

"I drink a little gin or whiskey."

"Then you're no purist?"

"Purity's pretty boring."

She smiled slightly. "You're trying to pick me up, aren't you?"

"I'm inviting you to have a drink."

"Where?"

"Know the Last Call way out on Wisconsin?"

"Damn near to Bethesda?"

He nodded.

"Afraid somebody'll see us?"

The Colonel shrugged. "I'm not sure how broad-minded your husband is."

"He's dead. What about your wife?"

"When last heard from, she was still living in Tulsa."

After two drinks at the Last Call, they drove in her car to the Sunrise Motel in Rockville, Maryland, where the Colonel registered them as Mr. and Mrs. F. Pierce and handed the room clerk $200 in lieu of a credit card. He also made up a license number for the Mustang, invented an address (741 N. Locust Street), a town (Mt. Morrison, Iowa) and used his own birthday, 71154, for a zip code. The room clerk scarcely glanced at any of it.

The motel room was neither larger nor smaller, cleaner nor dirtier than most motel rooms. It had a bathroom with a molded plastic tub and shower. The bed was queen-size. A sign on the big new Sony TV set offered free HBO but warned that the salacious-movie channel cost $8.00.

Shawnee Viar was sitting in the chair that went with the kneehole desk when the Colonel returned with two cans of Diet 7-Up and a bucket of ice. He placed them on the desk next to a bottle of Absolut vodka. After he mixed two drinks and handed her one, she tasted it, looked up at him and said, "This is almost like a real assignation, isn't it?"

"Why almost?"

"Well, assignations are usually made up of people who know each other."

"You're thinking of trysts."

"Am I? I thought they were the same." She drank more of the vodka, inspected the room, then looked up at the Colonel again. "What do we do now, take off our clothes and hop into bed?"

"If that's what you want. But I thought you might want to

talk a little and make sure you haven't hooked up with some weirdo."

"I don't mind weirdos."

"Know many?"

"Well, I'm back living with my father and on a weirdo scale of one to ten, he'd rate a nine. Maybe a ten. My late husband was only a four, maybe even a three, and I, well, I'm maybe a ten. Some days even a ten-plus."

"What's so weird about you?"

"The fact that I'm sitting here drinking your booze and it's not yet noon. That's weird for me. And the fact that ten or fifteen minutes from now I'll probably rip off my clothes, jump into bed and, with any luck, do stuff I never did with my husband, who believed there was some law that said people can only fuck Saturday nights—if they fuck at all."

"Your husband died when?"

Shawnee Viar looked down into her drink, thought for a moment, looked up at him and said, "A year and three weeks ago tomorrow."

"And you live with your father now."

She nodded.

"In Georgetown?"

"Maybe, but I'm not giving you my name, address or phone number till I find out if you're a weirdo or not."

"Then let's find out," he said, went over to her, put his drink on the desk, did the same with hers, gently pulled her to her feet and started unbuttoning her man's white shirt.

"You want me to keep the boots on?" she asked.

He looked down at the heavy black leather boots with their bulbous toes. "Sure," he said. "They might add a kink or two to what we've got in mind."

When the sex ended thirty-six minutes later, Shawnee Viar lay nude on the bed except for her boots. Colonel Millwed was also nude save for a corner of a sheet that covered his groin, not out of modesty, but because that was how the tangled sheet, blanket and counterpane wound up after the final variation.

Once his breath was back to normal, the Colonel said, "You must've memorized a couple of shelves of sex manuals."

"Any complaints?"

"None. You're exactly what you claim to be—a first-class weirdo."

"I had this funny feeling," she said.

"When?"

"During it. The fucking. I had this feeling somebody was watching us."

"Some people like being watched—or to pretend they're being watched. What about you?"

She seemed to think about it. "I guess it did sort of spice things up."

"If somebody'd made a tape of us," the Colonel said, "would you want to see it?"

"Sure. Who wouldn't?"

Millwed rose, went over to the TV set, pushed the eject button on the built-in VCR without switching the set on, and a videotape slid out. Shawnee Viar sat up. He turned, handed her the tape and said, "Be sure to rewind it first."

She looked down at it, then up at him. "But this isn't the original, is it?"

"No, that's next door," he said, using an over-the-shoulder thumb to indicate the room behind the TV set. He then picked up his Jockey shorts, pulled them on, sat down on a chair and reached for his black cashmere socks.

"What's this supposed to buy you?" she said, moving the videocassette back and forth a little.

"An in-house live monitor on your daddy, Hank Viar," he said, slipping his feet into his loafers. "We need to know where he goes, when he goes and who he talks to—either in person or by phone or fax." By then, the Colonel had his pants on and was buttoning his shirt. "We'll want two daily reports," he continued, "one at noon, the other at midnight."

"Or what?" she said. "You'll send him this tape?"

"It won't be sent to him," he said, pulling the sleeveless sweater down over his head. "It'll be sent to his friends and enemies."

"With your face and little-bitty cock prominently on display?"

The Colonel smiled. "Electronic magic will white out my face. As for my cock, it's just average. No birthmarks. No tattoos. Just your run-of-the-mill circumcised prick."

"Where do I call you?"

"Nice try. Somebody'll call you."

She was again studying the featureless videotape cassette when she said, "A full report will go something like this: 'Dear old Dad awoke at nine, saw no one, talked to no one and passed out dead drunk at eleven thirty-five P.M. right after the news.' Except there aren't going to be any reports."

"Fine," the Colonel said. "Then copies'll be sent to his three friends and his host of enemies—a lot of 'em still with the agency. They'll have a giggle over it. Pass it around. Old Hank Viar's kid, they'll say, fucking and sucking the mystery man."

"He won't care."

"But you will."

"Not really," she said, put the tape down, pulled the sheet loose from its tangle and draped it around her shoulders. When she had it the way she wanted, she looked at him again and said, "You didn't ask me much about my husband, did you, Colonel Millwed?"

There was a sudden absolute silence, the kind that ends not only noise but also time and motion. After hearing his name, Colonel Millwed froze—his right arm almost through the sleeve of his tweed jacket. Then time, motion and noise started again and the Colonel put his left arm through the other sleeve, tugged at the jacket's lapels, buttoned its center button and resisted the temptation to look at himself in the mirror.

"Hank talked to you about me," he said. "Probably when he was shitfaced. Even showed you a photo or two."

"Only one photo," she said. "Of you and him and the then Colonel—now General—Walker Hudson. There was one other guy in the photo. A Major Partain. Edd-with-two-ds Partain. For some reason, Twodees Partain gnaws at my old man a lot."

"I believe all that except the gnawing part," he said. "Nothing ever gnawed at Hank Viar. Not Partain. Not even the suicide of his wife. Your mother."

She continued to stare at him without expression until he nodded and said, "Okay. It's a standoff. You won't make any reports and I won't pass out any copies of the tape."

She continued to look at him without expression, neither accepting nor rejecting the offer.

"You recognized me this morning, didn't you?" he said. "From that photo."

"Why else would I be here?"

The Colonel looked unsure for a moment, as if he really didn't want to know the answer. He held out his right hand and, using his harshest command tone, barked an order. "Gimme the fucking tape."

She shook her head. "That's not part of the deal."

"What deal?"

"When I saw you this morning in that dumb convertible, I went back and pretended to lock my car and make sure it was you—one of the two guys my daddy warned me about. When you popped up at the frozen pizzas, the deal sort of popped into my mind."

"What fucking deal, goddamnit?"

"Know what killed my husband, Colonel?"

"I heard pneumonia."

She shook her head. "AIDS. And for more than a year now I've had myself checked weekly. Day before yesterday, my test turned out to be HIV positive even though I'm still asymptomatic."

He shook his head. "That doesn't mean you gave it to me."

"No, but under certain circumstances I might consider it my civic duty to report all of my recent sexual partners. And that means you. Just wonderful you."

Millwed gave her a bleak stare, then a nod of dismissal, and headed for the motel room door. Just before reaching it, he turned back and said, "Don't show that tape to anyone."

"I won't, unless there're certain circumstances."

"There won't be," he said, opened the door and was gone.

24

Emory Kite's glass of bourbon and ginger ale stopped halfway to his mouth when he saw them heading toward his preferred table at Le Dôme. In the lead was Ione Gamble, the actress-director. Following in her wake of admiring glances and gathering his own share, which he acknowledged with the charming loopy grin that helped him earn six or seven million dollars a picture, was her escort, Niles Brand.

"Jesus Christ," Kite said, "they're coming right over here."

"So they are," General Winfield said and rose.

"General," the smiling Ione Gamble said, offering her left cheek, which Winfield's lips intentionally missed by a sixteenth of an inch. "You remember Niles."

"Certainly," Winfield said, turning to shake the actor's hand. "The three of us sat together—or rather stood, I suppose—through Cuomo's keynote in '84."

"In New York," Brand said, in case Winfield couldn't recall the site of that year's Democratic convention. "Helluva speech," Niles Brand continued. "Immigrant parents. Wretched refuse. All that."

After introducing them to Edd Partain, who said it was nice

to meet them, the General introduced them to Emory Kite, who shook their hands, gave them both a dazed smile but said nothing at all.

On their way out of the restaurant, Brand asked Gamble, "Why the hell'd Millie Altford want us to shake hands with some mute midget?"

"Beats me."

"How'd I do?" he said, anxious as always for her approval.

"Wretched refuse?" she said. "Cuomo didn't say anything about wretched refuse."

"Yeah, well, if he didn't, he should've."

The General had the trout, Partain the sea bass and Emory Kite a filet mignon, which he ate noisily while giving detailed accounts of the sexual peccadilloes of various actors and actresses he had read about in an impressive number of supermarket tabloids. After the last bite of steak was chewed and swallowed, he turned to Partain and said, "What about this shooting you saw?"

"Someone shot and killed a doorman at the Eden apartment building on Wilshire."

"When?"

"Last night."

"He a friend of yours?"

"No."

"Then what d'you care?"

"I work for a woman who lives in the building."

"So?"

"My client's being considered for a top-level job in the new administration. A few nights ago, someone dumped a dead body in the driveway of the apartment building—the body of a man her daughter'd been living with in Mexico. What my client wants to know—"

Kite interrupted. "Lemme take it from here. She wants to

know if there's any connection between the dead doorman and the guy who was shacked up with her daughter."

"Any *embarrassing* connection," General Winfield said.

"She's also had several threats," Partain said.

"What kind of threats?"

"On her life. She's hired me as her security adviser."

"Sounds like bodyguard to me," Kite said.

"I'm responsible for advising her on what security precautions she should take."

"But if a shooter comes along while you're there giving her all this good advice, he'd have to go through you to get to her, right?"

Partain nodded.

"Then you're a bodyguard," Kite said. "No reason to be ashamed of it. Christ, that's what the Secret Service does. Ask those guys what they do, they'll tell you their job is to protect the President. I mean the guys on the White House detail."

"Let me spell out what I want from you," Partain said.

"Maybe you'd better."

"I don't know anything about the doorman who got shot."

"How about the other guy, the one who was fucking her daughter down in Mexico?"

"I know about him, but not about the doorman."

"I hope to Christ you at least know his name."

"He said his name was Jack. For the moment, we'll call him that. All I know about Jack is that he was a doorman and a none too successful actor. I know nothing about his friends, family or the people he owed money to."

"What makes you think he owed money?"

"Because everybody does."

"Then what you want is an A to Z background check on Jack the doorman-actor."

Partain nodded.

"Why come to me?"

"Because I recommended you," General Winfield said.

"Well, I don't know," Kite said. "I got a lot of other business out here to take care of. Besides, background checks take lots of time and cost lots of money."

"I don't know how much you charge," Partain said. "But I do know how much time they take. First, you check the guy's credit rating, if any, through TRW. Second, you find out if he's got a local police sheet. And third, you find out if the FBI's keeping tabs on him. That's three phone calls—if you know your way around. An hour's work. Maybe two."

"You're making it sound awful fucking easy," Kite said.

"That's because it is."

Kite leaned back in the chair and studied the man who wanted to hire him. "You've done this kinda shit before, haven't you?"

"Not like this."

"Where?"

"In the Army."

"CID?"

"Let's just say in the Army and let it go at that."

Kite nodded, more to himself than to either the General or the ex-Major, and said, "It'll cost you three thousand. One thousand in advance. Cash."

"You want it now or when we get outside?"

Kite looked around, as if to see who was watching, then shrugged. "Outside'll do. After you pay me, maybe you'll even remember Jack's last name."

"Thomson," Partain said. "With no 'p.'"

25

At first she thought her father had passed out from too much vodka. He was in the living room of the small Georgetown house on Volta Place, sprawled in the chair he liked to use for drinking and writing. It was a big leather and oak chair with wide flat arms. On one arm was a bottle of Smirnoff 80-proof vodka, three-quarters empty. On the other arm were a pack of cigarettes, a full ashtray and an empty glass. In front of him on a coffee table was his old black Smith-Corona portable typewriter with a sheet of white bond in it.

Shawnee Viar carried the sack of groceries through the living room, the dining area and on into the kitchen, where she put them away, all except the carton of Pall Malls. She took the carton with her when she returned to the living room and went back into the foyer. There she removed her blue overcoat with the missing ivory-colored button and hung it on the government-issue coatrack. Back in the living room again, still carrying the carton of Pall Malls, she went over to inspect her father. It was then she saw the gun on the floor beside Henry Viar's dangling right hand.

She dropped the carton of cigarettes and used both hands to cover her mouth but the long low moan escaped anyway.

After four deep breaths, she edged toward him until she could feel for a pulse in his neck, certain there would be none. She found herself wondering when they had last touched, not hugs or kisses, but just the brush of a hand. She decided it had been at least ten years, maybe even fifteen.

The gun was a semiautomatic pistol and looked to her like the one kept in the drawer of his bedside table. It was a small weapon that could be concealed in a man's hip pocket or a woman's purse. She knelt beside him to look up at his face. The eyes were slightly open and staring at his lap. The mouth, too, was slightly open.

After discovering he hadn't shot himself in the head, she noticed the small black hole in his black sweater. The hole was almost in the center of his chest and she reasoned that he must have shot himself in the heart.

Still kneeling, she turned to look at the page of bond paper in the typewriter. There was only one line on it. She read the line silently, moving her lips, then rose, went to the telephone, looked up a number in a red address book and called it. While it rang she looked at her watch and saw that it was 4:52 P.M.

The phone call was answered on the second ring by a man's voice reciting the last four digits she had dialed. She said, "I'd like to speak to General Winfield, please. This is Shawnee Viar."

"General Winfield's out of town, Ms. Viar. I'm Nick Patrokis. Maybe I can help."

"Is there a number where General Winfield can be reached?"

"I'm sorry, there isn't. But the General and I work closely together and I'm sure he'd want me to help, if I can."

"You know my father?"

"We've never met but I know who he is," Patrokis said. "And I know the General's known him for years."

"He's dead. My father, I mean."

"I'm very sorry," Patrokis said. "When did he—when did it happen?"

"I don't know. I just got here. He was kind of slumped over in a chair in the living room. I thought he was asleep. No, I didn't. I thought he was passed out. He drank a lot. Too much."

"I understand."

"He killed himself."

"How?"

"With a gun. A small one. He shot himself in the chest, the heart, I guess, and the gun's lying on the floor beside him."

"Not in his lap?"

"No. It's not in his lap. Is it supposed to be?" She didn't wait for Patrokis's answer. "He left a note. It's still in his typewriter."

"Then it's not signed, is it?"

"It's not signed."

"Can you see the note from where you are?"

"No, but I remember it. It's only one line: 'Had enough? Try suicide. I did.' "

"Have you called the police?" Patrokis said.

"Not yet. I guess I should call them, shouldn't I? But that's why I was calling General Winfield. Because I couldn't think of anybody else who'd give a damn if he's dead or not. The General dropped by the other night. They had a long talk and, well, I thought maybe the General could tell me what I should do now."

"You live in Georgetown, don't you?"

"Yes," she said and gave him the Volta Place address.

"I'll be there in fifteen minutes."

"I really don't want to trouble you—"

"It's no trouble," Patrokis said.

"What about the police?" she asked.

There was a long pause of several seconds before Patrokis answered. "I'll call them when I get there."

26

The house at 3219 Volta Place in Georgetown was just where Nick Patrokis, a native Washingtonian, knew it would be—directly across the street from where the old Second Precinct police station had been before being torn down long ago to make room for houses large enough to suit assorted Federal judges, an occasional cabinet member, the odd New York multimillionaire and even, years back, a President's mother-in-law.

The helmetless Patrokis rode his eleven-year-old Harley up over the curb and onto the sidewalk, cut the engine, removed his goggles and stuffed them into a pocket of his down-filled jacket. At shortly past 5 P.M. it was almost dark, the temperature was two degrees below freezing and street-lights had just come on, allowing Patrokis to inspect 3219, which was a small two-story brick house painted pale yellow with white trim. It sat on a twenty-foot-wide lot and he guessed it had been built sometime between 1840 and 1870. The front door was enamelled dark green.

Patrokis rang the bell and the green door was opened seconds later by Shawnee Viar, still wearing her denim skirt, man's white shirt and speed-lace boots. She stared at him silently, taking in the jagged scar, the bandana and the ring in his ear.

She said, "I like the ring. Come in."

Once in the foyer, Patrokis removed his jacket, looked around, saw the government-issue hat rack, got a nod from Shawnee Viar and hung the jacket next to her old blue coat.

"In here," she said, turned and led the way into the living room. Patrokis followed but stopped when he was no more than two steps inside it. He looked around carefully, taking his time, noting the fireless fireplace, the eclectic furniture, the jammed bookcases and, finally, the dead man in the old oak and leather chair with its wide wooden arms.

"Touch anything?" he said.

"I touched him for the first time in, I don't know, ten years—fifteen? I felt for a pulse in his throat. There wasn't any."

Patrokis went slowly over to the body of Henry Viar, stared down at it and at the semiautomatic that lay on the floor close to the dead man's dangling right hand. He then turned to read the one line on the sheet of bond paper in the portable typewriter. With his back still to Shawnee Viar, he asked, "He have insurance?"

"I guess so. My mother did."

Patrokis turned. "Your mother?"

"I found her after she shot and killed herself. But she was upstairs in the bedroom. It was, I don't know, almost twenty-five years ago—1968. I was ten and I'd just come home from school. She shot herself right here." Shawnee Viar used a forefinger to tap her right temple. She turned, looked down at the gun on the rug, then up at Patrokis. "I think they may've used the same gun. Wouldn't that be strange?"

"Very," Patrokis said, squatting to inspect the dead man. "Would you like it better if he hadn't killed himself and somebody else'd shot him?"

"I get a choice?"

"Maybe," he said. "When people shoot themselves in the heart like this they almost always pull the trigger with their thumbs. They don't have to but most of them do. And once they've shot themselves that way, the weapon'll usually drop into their laps or between their knees to the floor." He paused. "Unless they're wearing skirts."

"You're an expert?" she said. "Some kind of authority?"

"I once investigated eight guys who did it to themselves in the heart, and twenty-two others who stuck their pieces in their mouths and did it the messy way."

"What were you—a detective?"

He shook his head. "I was just somebody they sent around in Vietnam to investigate suicides. It was a kind of punishment duty. I investigated thirty-six of them."

"Twenty-two and eight add up to thirty," she said. "Not thirty-six."

"The other six were homicides," Patrokis said and turned to read the suicide note again.

"What'd you do to make them punish you?" she said.

His back was still to her when he said, "I tried to kill myself. I was going for a temple shot, like your mother, but somebody walked through the door, saw what I was up to and threw his Zippo at me."

"What happened?"

"I still pulled the trigger but my aim was off." He turned and tapped the right side of his head a few inches above and beyond his ear. "The round zipped in and out. They put a metal plate in."

"Ever try it again?" she said.

"I found a cure."

"What?"

"I discovered I had an overwhelming curiosity about what happens next." He studied her for several moments. "You ever think about suicide?"

"Only when I'm awake."

He nodded, then asked, "Well, what d'you want your father to be—a homicide victim or a suicide?"

She closed her eyes, swayed slightly, opened them and the swaying stopped. "I really do get a choice?"

Patrokis nodded again.

"Which is simpler?"

"For you? Suicide."

"But you think somebody killed him, don't you?"

"Yes. And if I think that, so will the cops. But I can pick up the piece with a pencil and lay it on his lap, or maybe let it fall between his legs to the rug and the cops'll probably call it suicide. His prints'll be all over it and they won't find anyone else's—unless you fooled around with it."

"I didn't touch it," she said.

"When they find out he's ex-CIA," Patrokis said, "they'll make a courtesy call to Langley, who'll be relieved that Henry Viar died by his own hand and not by somebody else's. A murdered CIA guy, even a retired one, always raises the specter of scandal, old grudges, treachery and nameless foreign powers. On the other hand, CIA suicides are usually regarded as regrettable but neat, logical and fitting."

"Why was he killed?" she said.

"I don't know, but if I don't fix things, the cops might wonder why there's no blowback on his right hand and how come the piece is lying where it is. Then they'll ask you a lot of questions about where you were today and where you went and what you did and who you saw while poor Dad here was being murdered. If they think it's suicide, they'll ask you all that anyway but won't pay much attention to your answers."

"What else will they ask, if they think it's suicide?"

"They'll want to know if he had any money worries, health problems, or disappointments."

"That's all he did have," she said.

The next question was as casual as Patrokis could make it. "You think he killed himself?"

"No."

"You going to tell the cops that?"

"No."

"Then I'd better call them," Patrokis said and headed for the phone.

The last Metropolitan Police homicide detective left shortly after 11 P.M. and at 11:17 P.M. a very junior CIA employee dropped by to offer the agency's condolences. Shawnee Viar listened to him in the foyer, thanked him and sent him off into the night.

"They used to send them out in pairs," Patrokis said after she returned to the living room, where the only trace of her dead father was a half-empty pack of Pall Malls. "Condolence teams. One old guy and one young guy. I don't think they have that many old guys left now."

"You ever work for them?" she said.

"Not really."

"Either you did or you didn't."

"I handled the occasional chore for them. In Vietnam."

"What about Central America?"

"I was out of it by then."

"Of what?"

"Special activities."

She turned and went to a small secretary desk. "I'd better show you something," she said, lowered the desk's lid and began opening drawers.

Patrokis waited, then said, "Show me what?"

"A picture of my dad and three guys in Central America. In El Salvador." She searched the last drawer, closed it, turned and said, "It was here yesterday because he'd showed it to me the night before. Now it's gone."

"Who were they—the three guys?"

She stared at him, chewing on her lower lip. "I can show you one of them."

"How?"

Instead of replying, she went to her large purse, took out the videocassette, examined it briefly and said, "I'll have to rewind it." She then switched on the TV set, slid the cassette into the VCR and pressed rewind. "Like a beer or something?" she said.

"I don't think so," Patrokis said.

They sat side by side in easy chairs and silence, waiting for the tape to rewind. She then used the remote to press "Play." A wide static shot of the motel bedroom came on the screen. There was no sound and the camera didn't move. Then Shawnee Viar and Colonel Ralph Millwed tumbled onto the bed naked except for her boots. The two-person audience watched the tape in silence. After it ended, she used the remote to switch off the set, then turned to Patrokis and asked, "Know him?"

"Colonel Ralph Waldo Millwed. Who picked who up?"

"It was a kind of mutual selection by the frozen pizzas in the Georgetown Safeway. On Wisconsin. He didn't think I knew who he was but I did from that photo my dad'd showed me. He sure knew who I was all right."

"How'd it play out?"

"After the sex stuff? He threatened to send a copy of the tape to Langley with his face whited out somehow."

"Unless you did what?"

"Monitor everyone Hank saw, called, wrote or faxed and make two phone reports a day—one at noon, one at midnight."

"What'd you say?"

"I called him by name, let him know my husband'd died of AIDS, which is true, and that I'm HIV positive, which isn't true. I told him to stay away from Hank and me or I'd send the tape to the Army along with proof I'm HIV positive."

Patrokis stared at her for a long time before he said, "You're lucky."

She frowned. "Lucky?"

"That you're still alive," he said.

27

The next morning at 5:23 A.M., as if on schedule, Edd Partain heard the faint clink from the kitchen of cup against saucer. He again rose silently from the sleeping Jessica Carver's bed, pulled on his pants and plaid robe and went barefoot into the kitchen where the Braun coffeemaker was at work and General Winfield already had set out two cups and saucers.

They muttered their good mornings and silently watched the machine dribble coffee into the glass pot. When there was enough for two cups, the General filled one, handed it to Partain, then filled his own. They took seats at the old scarred breakfast table and neither spoke until after their first few sips.

The General said, "Patrokis called me around midnight at the hospital. Three A.M. his time. Henry Viar is dead. The Washington police think it was suicide. Patrokis disagrees—privately. He thinks someone shot Viar through the heart, using Henry's own weapon. A thirty-two semiautomatic."

"I'm sorry," Partain said, surprised that he really was. "Who found him?"

"His daughter. Shawnee."

"When?"

"Around four-thirty P.M. East Coast time. One-thirty Pacific time. She must've discovered him while we were at lunch with Mr. Kite."

"The daughter called you at VOMIT and got Nick instead?" The General nodded.

"Well, Nick's certainly the expert on suicide."

The General nodded again, sipped more coffee and said, "Henry left a brief unsigned note in his typewriter. It read, 'Had enough? Try suicide. I did.'"

Partain shook his head. "Sounds like somebody trying to sound like Viar."

"So it does," the General said, rose, went to the coffeemaker, poured himself a fresh cup, warmed up Partain's, resumed his seat at the table and said, "There's more. It involves Shawnee Viar and Colonel Millwed."

Partain started to say something, decided not to and listened silently for four minutes to the General's report, which was a concise, dispassionate tale of motel sex in the afternoon, including an account of how Shawnee Viar obtained a copy of the tape.

When he finished, Partain asked, "She went straight home from the motel?"

"Yes."

"Then Millwed couldn't've—"

"No," the General said, interrupting, "he couldn't've. Patrokis suspects that whoever was operating the camera in the next motel room gave Millwed a ride back to his car. The Colonel had left it at the Last Call, according to Shawnee. That's a bar almost in Bethesda. Know it?"

Partain shook his head. "I don't know Washington that well."

"Patrokis says the distance would've made it impossible for Millwed to have killed Viar."

"Why the hell would Millwed want to kill him? Hank was

probably their errand boy, their gofer, their on-call dissembler. If Millwed'd wanted to kill somebody, it'd be Shawnee Viar so he could get his tape back."

"Patrokis thinks it may have been whoever stole the photograph."

"What photograph?"

"Of Viar, Millwed, Colonel Walker Hudson and you. In El Salvador."

"What does a photograph prove?"

Winfield sighed. "That's what I asked Patrokis."

At 8 A.M. the telephone in Millicent Altford's living room rang. General Winfield, Jessica Carver and Partain were all in the room, sharing various sections of the *Los Angeles Times* and *The New York Times*. Because Partain was closest, he answered the phone with a hello.

"This is Emory Kite," the deep growling voice said. "I got a report on Jack, the dead doorman. You want it by phone or in person?"

"How do we pay you over the phone?"

Kite chuckled. "You'll pay me. That's my business. Making people pay up."

"We'd like it in person."

"Okay," Kite said. "How 'bout right away?"

"Right away's fine," Partain said.

Kite sat in an easy chair with the glass of orange juice he'd accepted after turning down an offer of coffee. Seated on a couch were Partain and Jessica Carver. General Winfield occupied an easy chair opposite Emory Kite.

The short detective drank half of his orange juice, put the glass down on a table and addressed General Winfield. "I don't know if the lady's supposed to hear all this."

"She is," the General said.

"Okay, then. Here we go: John Byford Thomson with no

'p.' Born January 31, 1960, Boulder, Colorado. Son of Mr. and Mrs. Richard Clark Thomson; he, insurance salesman; she, housewife. One younger brother, one older sister, both married. Jack had two years at the University of Colorado, majored in speech, whatever that is, and minored in Spanish. Quit college to take a staff radio announcer's job at KOA in Denver. That was in 1981. Fired, 1983, NRG."

"What's NRG?" Jessica Carver said.

"No reason given," said Kite and went on with his no-notes report. "Hired by Golden Assets, Inc., a boiler room outfit that peddled penny stocks by phone. Jack apparently gave good phone because he stayed with Golden Assets till the state closed 'em down eighteen months later. Thomson mustt've saved a few bucks because he went to Mexico, lived mostly in Guadalajara and claimed to be an independent travel consultant, whatever that is, until the Mexicans kicked him out in 1989. By 1990 he's here in L.A., where he hooks up with a woman agent who gets him a little acting work, mostly two- and three-line stuff in TV pilots that never went anywhere.

"She also gets him some radio commercials and TV voiceovers, but never enough to live on. But Jack joins the Screen Actors Guild and then, in 1990, a little over two years ago, goes to work here as night doorman. He never had any bank accounts or credit cards, but he did join the SAG credit union. His salary here at the Eden was fourteen hundred a month, plus tips.

"Well, he starts depositing one hundred, two hundred, and once or twice even three hundred in his credit union account every month. I figure it's his tips or maybe radio money. All this time he's living in this crummy studio apartment just off Pico in west L.A. Drives an '81 Honda Civic. But on November fifth last year he deposits five thousand cash in his credit union account.

"Jack's got no steady girlfriends, no boyfriends, no priors, but he still gets shot dead two nights ago just outside here down by the front entrance. Thirty-caliber round. Cops think it's some kind of sporting rifle. His folks in Boulder want him cremated and his ashes shipped home to them. I guess the only thing really interesting about Jack was his time in Guadalajara, but that'll cost you an extra two-fifty because that's what I hadda wire a private cop down there that speaks English. The interesting stuff is that our friend Jack wasn't just running a travel consultant business. He was also running a stud service and blackmail game on his mostly middle-aged women clients. After the Mexican cops listen to a few of the girls' complaints, they tell Jack to take the next flight out. He catches the bus instead."

Emory Kite stopped talking, looked around the room and said, "Any questions?"

"What do the L.A. cops think?" Partain asked.

"Well, they don't exactly confide in me, but a guy they do talk to told me, for two hundred bucks, that they've almost decided to write it off as another random drive-by shooting. But an upscale drive-by, what with that limo and all."

"Just another homicide, then," the General said.

"Doesn't mean the homicide guys aren't gonna work on it," Kite said. "But it's not way up on their must-solve list."

"What do you think, Mr. Kite?" Jessica Carver said.

He looked at her thoughtfully. "Well, if it was me looking into it, I'd try and find out where that five thousand cash money came from. Your friend Jack lived sorta like a hermit—except for his making the rounds looking for acting work. He seemed to do his job here okay. No complaints from management. He saved his money. Drove an old clunker. Didn't do dope. Didn't drink a lot. Went to the pictures in the afternoon when they're cheap. Didn't spend a lot on clothes, but out here you don't have to. Pair of jeans and a nice clean T-shirt out here and you're all dressed up. So where does the five thousand cash money come from? About the only thing I could think of is maybe he made a porn picture."

"That wouldn't have done his career any good," she said.

"What career?" Kite said, finished his orange juice, stood up, looked at the General and said, "Anything else?"

Winfield rose, produced a plain white envelope from his breast pocket, added a $50 and four $100 bills to it, walked over and handed it to the detective. "Thank you, Mr. Kite. You were very efficient. We appreciate it."

"Glad to be of help."

The General asked, "Are you going back to Washington now?"

"Haven't decided yet. All depends on how things work out." He nodded goodbye to Carver and Partain, turned, left the room and, from the foyer, called, "See you back in Washington, General."

There was a silence after Kite's departure that lasted until Jessica Carver said, "Four years in Guadalajara?"

"How long'd your friend Dave Laney been going down there?" Partain said.

"Five or six years."

General Winfield sighed. "Guadalajara is a very, very large city with an extraordinarily large North American population. There is no evidence whatever that the doorman and your friend ever met there."

"But it sure makes things neat, doesn't it?" she said. "First Dave is dumped out dead on the driveway here. Then a day later, somebody waits in a limo across the street and takes out Jack. Drive-by shooting—like hell. A witness removal program is what it looks like."

"Witnesses to what, Jessica?" the General said.

"To whatever the fuck's going on here," she said, then turned to Partain. "To whatever the fuck it is Ma hired you to find out."

"She hired me to provide her with security."

"From what? I mean, who're the danger guys?"

"I don't know," Partain said.

They stared at each other for a long moment, then Partain turned and left the room, heading for the kitchen.

Jessica Carver turned back to the General. "Is he really as good as you and Millie seem to think he is?"

"He may even be better than that," the General said.

28

Partain entered Millicent Altford's hospital room and found her sitting in an armchair, wearing a smoke-gray silk suit, her long legs tucked back to the left and crossed at the ankles. On her feet were black suede pumps with two-inch heels that matched her purse. Next to her feet was a worn black leather suitcase with silver fittings that looked both old and expensive.

Before Partain could say anything, she said, "I called you five minutes ago but Jessie said you were on your way."

He nodded at the suitcase. "Leaving for good?"

"Leaving for Washington."

"Why?"

"Because around seven-thirty this morning I got a call from the counsel of a three-man House subcommittee that's been looking into campaign financing and paying particular attention to soft money and bundling—my specialties. This guy said I could chat now or be subpoenaed later."

"I thought your guy won," Partain said.

"He did but some of my congressional friends didn't. One of them used to be chairman of this same subcommittee. He was an old CIO leftie out of the Packinghouse Workers when he first got elected in '54 during the Eisenhower years."

"Christ. How old is he anyway?"

"Seventy-seven. But he wanted one last term. Well, they all want that, but he had stiff competition in the primary. An ex-flower child turned New Democrat and middle-aged twit. So I sent my old pal a small bundle."

"How big's a small bundle?" Partain said.

"A hundred thousand. My guy loses by three hundred and twenty-six votes. So guess who's on this campaign finance subcommittee?"

"The middle-aged twit," Partain said. "What's he want—revenge?"

She shrugged. "That—or maybe he just wants to get on C-Span. The car downstairs?"

"You want me to drive you to the airport?"

She stared at him. "We're not too swift this morning, are we? Hard night?" Without waiting for answers, she rose and said, "I'll use real short sentences. You and I're driving to the airport. LAX. There we'll stick the car into long-term parking. Don't worry about the fifteen bucks a day or whatever it is they charge. Then we'll get on a plane. Please note the 'we.' We then fly nonstop first-class to Dulles. There we rent a car, drive into Washington and check into the Mayflower."

"I'm not packed," Partain said, just to watch her reaction.

"What's to pack? You've got on a nice blue suit, a clean white shirt and a navy and maroon tie. You look a little like some Secret Service agent with six kids to feed. When we get to Washington, we'll buy you a topcoat and a suit that fits. That one looks a couple of sizes too small."

"Maybe I'd better let the General know," he said.

"Don't bother," she said. "He and Jessie are flying into Washington tonight. Coach."

* * *

Millicent Altford came out of the hospital, followed by Partain, who carried her suitcase. The Lexus coupe was parked just west of the entrance. Partain unlocked both doors with a touch of the electronic key. Altford got in on the passenger side, which was nearer the hospital entrance. Partain went around the car's front, opened the driver's door and flicked the button that unlocked the trunk.

Partain had almost reached the trunk when a Yellow Cab pulled into the drive and slowed to a crawl. Partain's back was to the cab when the semiautomatic's silencer nosed out of the car's lowered rear window. It coughed twice, almost apologetically, and two rounds slammed into Partain's back just between his shoulder blades. The cab sped off down the circular drive, turned right onto Olympic Boulevard and raced west.

Partain dropped the suitcase first, then fell forward, landing on his hands and knees. Millicent Altford, looking into the rearview mirror, saw him fall. She was out of the car and kneeling beside him in seconds, but by then he was down on his elbows.

"How bad?" she said.

"Shot . . . twice."

"I'll get a doctor."

"No," he said and slowly got back up on his hands and knees. He took a deep breath. "In Wyoming," he said, then stopped to suck in more air. "In Wyoming . . . I sold . . . guns and ammo."

"You need a doctor," she said.

He took another deep breath and used it to say, "And bulletproof vests."

She grinned suddenly. "You're wearing one, aren't you?"

Partain only nodded.

Her grin went away. "Then where the hell's mine?"

* * *

The Yellow Cab turned right at the Avenue of the Stars in Century City and several blocks later descended into an underground garage. The cabdriver was the same Mexican who had driven the getaway limousine, and his accent was still just as thick when he said, "You don't miss this time."

"I never miss," said Emory Kite.

The Mexican parked the Yellow Cab three levels down in what apparently was a permanently reserved slot. Next to it was the Lincoln limousine. The Mexican got out, opened the left rear door of the cab for Kite, led him around the rear of it to the Lincoln, then unlocked and opened the limo's rear passenger door. As Kite climbed in, the driver asked, "Where to, *jefe?*"

"LAX."

"What airline?"

"United."

"Back to Washington, huh?"

"New York," Kite lied.

The Mexican driver opened his door, got in, buckled up, started the engine, then asked one more question. "Why the fuck anybody ever want to go to New York?"

"For the money," said Emory Kite.

The Lexus coupe was parked on the second level of the long-term-parking lot across from United Airlines. Partain, leaning forward slightly, sat in the passenger seat, bare to the waist. His coat, shirt, tie and Kevlar vest were in his lap. He examined the two holes in his jacket, poking his little finger through both of them. He removed the two .25-caliber rounds from the car's flip-open cup holder, noted their slightly blunted tips and put them away in his right pants pocket.

Partain had started wearing the vest the day after the drive-by shooting of Jack the doorman. The manufacturer called it the "Executive Protector" and cautioned that it protected only the chest, stomach, back and waist, leaving vulnerable the head, neck and throat. Both groin and buttocks were also defenseless. Kneecaps were equally expendable.

Only Jessica Carver knew that Partain had begun wearing the vest. The first night they had gone to bed, she had watched him take it off without comment. The second time she'd asked him to leave it on.

Partain heard the clicking high heels to his right, turned and saw Millicent Altford approaching the car, carrying a large plastic sack. "Your new outfit," she announced.

Partain pulled the long-sleeve gray sweatshirt down over his head and the refastened Executive Protector vest. The front of the sweatshirt read, "I Love L.A." The hieroglyphic for "love" was the standard red heart. The second garment she handed him was a blue and gold UCLA warm-up jacket.

"I suppose there was nothing less—"

"Cute?"

"I was going to say embarrassing."

"Put it on," she said. "They're about to call our flight."

As she watched him slip on the UCLA jacket, she said, "You've got a nice build."

He ignored the compliment and asked, "What do I do with my shirt, tie and coat?"

"I'll take care of 'em," she said. He handed them over and watched with dismay as she dropped all three into a nearby trash container.

"That coat could've been rewoven," he said when she returned.

"I told you we'll buy you new stuff in Washington. A nice topcoat from Burberrys. Some suits and a couple of jackets and pants from Brooks Brothers or Neiman's."

"You ever been inside a J. C. Penney's?"

"Not in forty-two years," she said.

* * *

They were almost the last to board the United 747 and were seated in the front two seats on the port side of the first-class cabin. Altford said she preferred the window seat. Partain didn't care where he sat. He had buckled his seat belt and was glancing through an airline magazine when Altford nudged his elbow and said, "Somebody you know?"

Partain looked up and found Emory Kite standing in the aisle, staring down at him, wide-eyed and openmouthed. Then the mouth snapped shut and the eyes narrowed.

"You feel all right?" Partain asked, unable to put any real concern into his question.

"Flying," the small man said. "Flying always puts me off my feed." He turned toward his seat across from Partain, then turned back. "Washington, huh?"

"Just for the night," Partain said. "After that, it's on to either Paris or London."

Kite nodded, sat down in the window seat and buckled himself in automatically, staring all the while at Partain, who eventually noticed it and replied with a small smile and a slightly raised eyebrow, as if to say, "Okay, what now?"

"I've never been to Paris," Kite said.

"You'll love it," Partain said and returned to his magazine.

Kite nodded glumly, then leaned back in his seat and closed his eyes. That's where I'll go when all this crap's over, he decided. I'll go to Paris and check into some fancy hotel, eat me some fancy French food and fuck me some fancy French whores. He was still leaning back in his seat with his eyes closed and a slight smile on his lips when the flight attendant asked if he would like something to drink.

"Champagne," Emory Kite said, opening his eyes. "French champagne."

29

They obviously knew Millicent Altford at the Mayflower Hotel. The doorman welcomed her by name and he himself whisked her rented Chrysler sedan away. An assistant manager checked her in, offering a two-room suite for the price of a single and also a special reduced rate for the room of what he called her "companion."

"Mr. Partain's my security executive," Altford said, her tone icy, "and I want his room right next to mine."

"Certainly, Mrs. Altford," the assistant manager said.

Because Altford said she needed an hour to herself and because Partain had nothing to unpack, he inspected her rooms first, then his own, washed his face and hands and went down to the lobby, where he bought toothpaste, a toothbrush, a razor, blades, shaving cream and what the salesclerk swore was an odorless aftershave lotion.

He had just turned from the drugs and sundries counter when the male voice behind him said, "For somebody in the back-watching trade, Twodees, you sure don't give a damn about your own."

Partain turned and said, "Ever hear of the shoemaker's barefoot children, Colonel?"

"Yeah, but now that I've bumped into you—"

"You didn't bump into me."

Colonel Ralph Waldo Millwed shrugged and smiled, displaying most of his remarkably even gray teeth. "Let's call it an unexpected coincidence."

"All coincidences are unexpected," Partain said.

"Then let's go and have a drink in the T and C and discuss it some more."

"Why would I want to do that?"

"Because there's a possibility, maybe even a probability, that we need to discuss."

"The last thing we discussed was why the sun shouldn't set on my head in Sheridan."

"Ancient history, Twodees. Olden times. Let's talk."

"All right," Partain said. "Why not?"

In the Mayflower's Town and Country bar they sat at a table at a decent remove from a pair of middle-aged lobbyists who were carrying on a desultory debate about whether they should go home or call up a couple of whores. When the drinks came, vodka on the rocks for the Colonel and bourbon and water for Partain, Millwed leaned forward and rested his tweed elbows on the small round table. "I'm not gonna beat around the bush, Twodees."

"Sure you are. But since I'm a slow drinker, take all the time you need."

The Colonel leaned back to give Partain a cool thoughtful inspection. Along with his brownish-green tweed jacket, Millwed now wore a black suede vest with brass buttons, a very pale yellow shirt, striped green and brown tie and brown flannel pants. He looked prosperous, natty and, in Partain's judgment, as duplicitous as ever.

"I like your UCLA jacket," the Colonel said.

"No, you don't."

"How's L.A. been treating you?"

"I was born there."

"I thought Bakersfield."

Partain shrugged. "A suburb."

"Grew up poor like me, I expect."

"Not like you, Ralph. My old man drove a truck."

"Mine was a bookkeeper."

"I guess you could call a CPA a bookkeeper."

"Let me ask you something."

"Is this the pitch?"

"This is the pitch," Millwed said. "How'd you like to have your record expunged, go back on active duty as a light-colonel and retire on a full twenty-year pension after a year of soft duty at, say, Fort Sam?"

"I'd like it."

"Thought so. And as sort of a hardship bonus there'd be a quarter of a million in the bank of your choice anywhere in the world."

"I'd like that, too."

"Knew you would."

Partain glanced at his watch. "You said we wouldn't beat around the bush."

Millwed spread his hands, palms up. "I've made my presentation."

"Not quite. You forgot the quid pro quo—the stuff you expect me to do."

Millwed produced a fresh smile, broader and merrier than before. He leaned toward Partain, still smiling, and said, "You don't have to do one fucking thing, Twodees. Not one."

"Nothing at all?"

"Nothing—except quit your job."

"That's it?"

"That's it. Quit your job and go lie on some beach for a month until the paperwork's done. Then go back in as a light-colonel, finish out your year down at Fort Sam doing PR for the polo team or some such shit and then retire on your pension plus the tax-free quarter mil."

"You can fix all that, Ralphie?"

This time the Colonel's smile was a thin one. "A two-star general can."

"When do you have to know?"

"Twenty-four hours."

"I need forty-eight."

"Why?"

"I have to think up an excuse for quitting that'll satisfy everybody. Something that won't leave them wondering."

"Tell 'em the truth. Tell 'em you've been asked to re-up as a light-colonel."

Partain smiled slightly. "You really want me to tell General Winfield that?"

The Colonel's expression turned thoughtful. "Yeah, well, maybe you'd better not. Maybe you'd better come up with something more—palatable."

"You mean lie to them?"

Millwed's wide smile reappeared. "Exactly."

An hour later, in the parlor of the small century-old house on Fourth Street, S.E., Colonel Millwed was sitting on the ornate but remarkably preserved Victorian couch and listening to Emory Kite's third and final version of the botched murder of Edd Partain.

"Take the silencer I used," Kite was saying. "I make my own, you know, right here in the basement, and I'd never use one on anything bigger than a twenty-five caliber. You use one on a thirty-eight, a nine millimeter or a forty-five semiautomatic and you almost gotta use a bipod to steady the fucker. But with a twenty-five you got concealability, portability, silence and accuracy. And with accuracy you got your stopping power. And this thing wasn't no rolling shot either. Manny pulls the cab to a stop just when Partain turns to put a suitcase in the trunk. I had time. Plenty of time. I squeezed off two rounds that take him right between the shoulder blades. It was a kill shot if I ever saw one."

"He must've been wearing Kevlar," the Colonel said for the third time.

"Well, how the fuck was I to know that?"

"Wouldn't a head shot've been almost as easy and far more certain?" the Colonel said, trying to put some curiosity into his tone.

"A head shot, huh? Well, the human head is about one-fourth or maybe one-fifth the size of the human torso—waist to neck. It's also, I don't know, ten times as hard. I know a shooter once who went for a head shot, and the guy who's supposed to get it moves his head just a hair. He got hit all right, but his skull's so fucking hard the slug ricocheted off and hit his wife in the mouth and killed her and she was the one paying for the hit."

"Well, it was a nice try, Emory," the Colonel said.

"But nice tries don't pay off, do they?"

"No, they don't."

"What nice tries do," Kite said, "is give you a heart attack. I get on the plane and head for my seat up there in first class, looking forward to a few belts and maybe a halfway decent meal and a nice long snooze and who do I see? The fucking ghost of Twodees Partain, alive as you and me."

"Let's hear about the doorman," the Colonel said.

"Jack Thomson, with no 'p.' Well, Jack wasn't any problem. I had a real nice piece I borrowed from Manny, a scope and good light from the building. It was a simple pop. Almost a gimme. Fact is, Partain was only a few feet away and I could've had him, too, but I thought that might screw things up. Manny—you know Manny?"

"We've never met but we talked on the phone once."

"That's right. Then you know that accent he's got. We're

driving away in the limo and Manny said, 'Chew meesed.' He means I missed. He thought I was going for Partain but hit Jack the doorman by mistake."

The Colonel nodded and said, "I need to know something else. How did Manny take care of the General's nephew?"

"Well, first of all you gotta realize Manny don't know Dave Laney was the General's nephew because Manny don't know there's any General Hudson."

"Good."

"I talk to you and then call Manny and tell him there's this guy who's giving some friends of mine a hard time. We settle on a price. Then Manny locates Dave Laney and sticks with him when he goes into the hospital. Laney ducks into the men's john and comes out dressed up like a doctor. This interests Manny and he follows Laney into the elevator, gets off a floor below the one Laney punches, then runs up the stairs, peeks around a door and watches Laney trying to smother the Altford woman up there in her private room. But Altford puts up a hell of a fight, rolls off the bed and starts screaming and Dave Laney bugs out. So Manny follows him down and out of the hospital and sees him hightailing it up Olympic, still wearing his doctor clothes. Manny and his guys snatch Dave and toss him into the van. Three of 'em hold him down, Manny drives and another guy smothers him— Dave, I mean."

"How?"

"They stuff a T-shirt into Dave's mouth and pinch his nose so he can't breathe. Pretty soon Dave's dead. Then they drive over to Wilshire and dump him out on the Eden's drive."

"Why there?"

"They thought it might be kinda cute."

"Cute?"

"Yeah. Dave's been done and they're driving along Wilshire when Manny sees the Altford lady and Partain get out of her car. Manny stops, backs up, they dump Dave in the driveway and take off. Who knows what's cute to Mexicans?"

The Colonel sighed. "Anything else?"

"Yeah, one thing," Kite said. "Uh—what'd the General, you know, *say* when he told you to get rid of his nephew?"

"You want the exact words?"

Kite shrugged, then nodded.

"He said, 'Lose him.'"

Kite smiled, then said, "Lose him," shook his head in admiration and added, "His own kinfolk."

The Colonel rose. "By the way, Emory, Partain has been granted a temporary reprieve."

The corners of Kite's thin mouth curled down in disappointment. "That mean you want your money back?"

"I said *temporary*," the Colonel replied.

30

Partain glanced up from the *Washington Post* as Millicent Altford glided into the hotel suite's living room, spun around with practiced grace and asked, "How do I look?"

"How do you want to look?"

"Like a bunch of money."

"Pretty ladies in black dresses that cost that much always look like money to me."

"How much do you think it cost?"

He shrugged. "A thousand?"

"Two-sixty-five on sale at Saks."

Partain put the paper down and looked at his watch. "When do you meet these guys?"

"Nine-thirty."

"Then we'd better go."

After he followed Millicent Altford into the rear of the independent taxicab, the hotel doorman closed the door and Altford introduced Partain to the driver. "Jerry . . . Edd."

The driver had turned to study Partain and his UCLA jacket. He was a slim black in his mid-thirties with the calm intimidating gaze that most cops and some cons try to acquire. "You the shotgun?"

"I'm the shotgun."

"And just what might we be expecting?"

"The unexpected."

"The usual, then," Jerry said, turned back to the wheel and was pulling away from the curb when Altford asked, "How's the family, Jerry?"

"Wife's working. Daughter's doing fine at Howard. And I'm still a GS-9. How you been, Millie?"

"I've been better."

"Now why'd I suspect that?"

Partain hoped the Occidental Grill just down from the Treasury Building on Pennsylvania wasn't as old as it tried to look. Inside, its walls were lined with photographs and perhaps even a few daguerreotypes of politicians, scalawags, statesmen, civil servants and mountebanks from the past—many of them a century dead. As he followed Altford, and she followed the maîtresse d', Partain raked the room but saw nothing that bothered him except the photographs.

Two men rose from a table at Altford's approach. One was short, tubby, blond and not more than 30, who for some reason reminded Partain of an ill-tempered puppy. The other was tall, fit, dark-haired and a smiler with pretty blue eyes. Both wore dark suits and ugly red ties and tried not to stare at Partain's warm-up jacket.

Altford stuck out her hand at the older and taller of the two and said, "Congressman Finch, I'm Millicent Altford."

"My pleasure, Mrs. Altford," the Congressman said, indicated the tubby man and added, "This is—"

"We spoke on the phone," Altford said, offering her hand to the shorter man and not letting the Congressman finish. "You're Willy MacArthur."

"*Will* MacArthur," he insisted, released her hand and looked past her at Partain, whose eyes were quartering the room.

Altford noticed MacArthur's curiosity. "Mr. Partain, this is Congressman Finch and Mr. MacArthur, who's counsel to the subcommittee."

Partain gave them a collective nod and went back to reading the room.

"Mr. Partain won't be joining us," Altford said as she sat down at the table and accepted a menu from the maîtresse d'.

When the Congressman and the counsel were seated, MacArthur asked, "He your bodyguard?"

Partain didn't let her answer. "I'll be back at ten-thirty, Ms. Altford."

"Thank you, Mr. Partain."

As Partain turned away, he heard MacArthur ask Altford why she needed a bodyguard. Partain lingered just long enough to give the restaurant one last inspection and hear her say, "I think I'd very much like a drink and I do so hope you both'll join me."

At K Street the cab turned right onto Connecticut Avenue and it was then that Jerry, the driver, asked Partain, "How long've you been shotgun?"

"Why?"

"Because I don't want nothing to happen to Millie."

"Known her long?"

"Long as I can remember."

"Nothing's going to happen to her."

"Not over your dead body, right?"

"Close," Partain said.

Partain rang the bell to the entrance of the narrow four-story building whose ground floor housed the Greek restaurant.

Seconds later, the irritating unlocking buzzer sounded. Partain pushed the door open, climbed four flights of stairs and found a grinning Nick Patrokis waiting on the fourth-floor landing.

Partain stopped on the next to the last step and examined Patrokis. "You grew a beard and an earring."

Still grinning, Patrokis grabbed Partain in a bear hug and lifted him up to the landing, where he lost the grin, abruptly let Partain go, stepped back and said, "That's not blubber I felt. That's Kevlar."

Partain poked a finger into Patrokis's ample gut and said, "Blubber."

Patrokis led the way into VOMIT headquarters, where, for the first time, Partain took in the long narrow room, the partitioned space for Emory Kite's office and the woman with gray eyes and the long auburn hair who rose from a chair beside a huge old golden oak desk.

Patrokis said, "Shawnee Viar, Edd Partain."

"We've already met," she said. "Sort of."

"Where?" said Partain.

"In a photograph. There were four guys in it. You and three others."

"Who were the other three?"

She answered his question with one of her own. "You didn't happen to shoot my old dad in the heart yesterday afternoon, did you?"

"I was in L.A. yesterday afternoon and I'm sorry Hank's dead."

"Are you?" she said, studied him for a moment and nodded. "Yes, I think you almost are. It was Hank who showed me the photograph a day or two before he died. He was in it. You were in it. So was Colonel Millwed, except he was a captain then."

"Who else?"

"Was in it? Colonel Walker Hudson—now Major General Hudson."

"What'd Hank say about us?"

"That the three of you were real mean bastards. Was he right?"

"He was about two of us," Partain said. "The other one's a pussy."

"But you're not the other one, are you?"

Before Partain could reply, Patrokis said, "After Shawnee found her father, she called General Winfield here but got me instead. I've been doing what I can but she's still a little shook."

"Am I?" she said, studied Patrokis for a while, turned back to Partain and studied him, then turned again to Patrokis and asked, "You two met in Vietnam?"

Patrokis nodded. "He's the one who threw the Zippo at me."

They ate at the card table. They ate the Greek dishes that had been dispatched by the uncle from his ground-floor restaurant. There were only the three of them but the uncle had sent enough for four, more than enough really, and all of it had been lugged up the four flights of stairs by a teenage Nicaraguan busboy. Partain tipped him $10 and wrote it down in his expense notebook.

After dinner, Patrokis cleaned everything up and was storing away the folding card table when Partain asked him, "How's business?"

"We got nineteen new members last month, lost four to death and disgruntlement and our newsletter circulation's holding at about a ninety-six percent renewal rate."

"You put out a newsletter?" Shawnee Viar asked.

"Seven or eight times a year."

"What's it called—*The Vomitorium?*"

"*The VOMIT Verifier.*"

"What's it verify?"

"Deceit and bullshit."

"Who writes it?"

"I write about a third," Patrokis said. "Members contribute the rest."

"I once edited a now-and-again eight-page newsletter for a hospital," she said. "We called it *Cries from the Locked Ward.* I did the whole thing on a computer."

Patrokis sighed. "We have a computer but I still don't know how to use it."

She smiled at him. "And you don't want to learn either, do you?" She didn't wait for an answer. "Tell you what. I'll come down here and use it to store all your records and files and do the mailing list and even put out your newsletter. Probably save you a bundle. How much'll you pay me to save you a bundle?"

Patrokis looked at Partain for guidance. Partain gave him none. Nick Patrokis bit his lower lip, cleared his throat and said, "This is embarrassing as hell but I suppose we might just possibly pay you a thousand a month."

"That much?" she said. "I'll take it. When do I start?"

"Tomorrow?"

"Tomorrow I have to bury dear old Dad, but that's in the morning. I could be here by one—or one-thirty?"

Patrokis turned away from her to look slowly around VOMIT headquarters as if for the last time, turned back to Shawnee Viar and said, "One or one-thirty's fine."

"Where're the services?" Partain asked her.

She named an undertaker on Wisconsin Avenue and said, "Eleven o'clock, and there won't be any formal eulogy although I did get somebody to say a few words."

"Who?" Partain said.

"General Hudson."

"You called him or did he call you?"

"I called him," she said. "At the Pentagon. He said he'd be honored."

"Why not someone from the agency?"

"Who?" she said. "Besides, wouldn't it be neat if it's the murderer who eulogizes the victim?"

31

Harold Finch, the newly elected U.S. Representative from a safe Democratic district in Ohio, railed throughout dinner at the enormous cost of running for public office. Millicent Altford listened, mostly in silence, and ate her crab cakes. When she was done she pushed her plate an inch away, leaned slightly forward and interrupted the Congressman to ask, "Would you really like to know why you're here in Washington and Joey Sizemore's not?"

Sensing a trap, the Congressman frowned and said, "I like to think it's because I ran the better campaign."

"What d'you two guys really know about Sizemore?"

"He was about the last of the big-band Congressmen," Will MacArthur said and looked surprised when no one chuckled.

"Yeah, right," she said. "Hell, Joey's so old he can remember Herbert Hoover, and the Depression to him is just like day before yesterday. When he first got elected way back in 1954 he'd been director of organization for the CIO's Packinghouse Workers. Ask your average guy today what CIO stands for and he'll probably tell you Chief Information Officer."

"What does it stand for?" MacArthur said. "I forget."

"Look it up," she said.

"We're all well aware of Joey's glorious record," the Congressman said. "God knows we heard about it enough. But the truth is he simply got old and out of touch. It happens."

"He wasn't out of touch," she said. "He was out of money. You outspent him three to one in the primary and coasted through the general. And maybe we'll get back to that, but first I'm going to tell you about me and Joey Sizemore before he ever went to Congress."

MacArthur looked at his watch, making no effort to sneak a glance.

Altford grinned at him. "Ever hear of *Liberty* magazine, Will?"

"Of course."

"I doubt it. Well, *Liberty* used to run a little time schedule just above each article. Reading time: three minutes twenty-two seconds—or seven minutes fourteen seconds. The listening time for the story about Joey Sizemore and me'll take six minutes nineteen seconds, so you might as well stop squirming."

"I've always been interested in political history," MacArthur said.

"No, you haven't," she said. "You got a little interested after you hired on with the Congressman here, but before that you were primarily interested in wills, escrows, insurance, mortgages and estate planning."

The Congressman grinned. "Did her research, Will."

"You betcha," Altford said. "Anyway, in 1952 I was fresh out of college and working at Foote, Cone and Belding in Chicago. I'd decided the country was going straight to hell unless it elected Adlai Stevenson President. So I went down to Stevenson headquarters in Chicago and volunteered my services. I finally got in to see what may've been a deputy assistant campaign manager. It was a typical campaign office for the times. One big room. Lots of desks. Typewriters. Ringing phones. Hot as hell. Noisy. And then there was this fifty-year-old slob sitting behind one of the desks.

"Sitting to one side of him was a smooth redheaded guy of about thirty or thirty-one. I tell the slob my name and that I want to help out in the campaign and he tells me they aren't hiring. I tell him I'm volunteering part-time and he tells me I don't talk like I'm from around there. I tell him that's because I'm not, I'm from Dallas, but I work at Foote, Cone.

"Then the slob asks who sent me and I'm about to tell him no one sent me when the redheaded guy says, 'I sent her.'

"The slob says, 'Well, if you sent her, you find her a slot.'

"The redhead, of course, is Joey Sizemore and he takes me outside where we catch a cab and head for the old Morrison Hotel that they tore down years ago. We ride up to the eleventh floor and go into a big room that has two desks, two phones on each desk, a secretary called Norma, who's at least sixty, and nothing else.

"Joey introduces me to Norma, tells me she used to be a senior long-distance telephone operator with Southwestern Bell, uses a key to open a desk drawer and hands me a typewritten list of names with addresses and phone numbers that's about an inch thick. It was the Fat Cat List. Every Democrat in the country who had an estimated net worth of one hundred thousand or more, which'd be about a million today."

Altford paused, sipped some water, and went on. "All I had to do was call each name and talk whoever answered into contributing a minimum of one thousand dollars to the Stevenson campaign. Norma had this sexy contralto voice and placed each call person-to-person, working east to west. All operator-assisted then. No Touch-Tone. No direct-dialing. Ancient times.

"I asked Sizemore what to say. He said since I was in the ad business, I'd think up something. There were almost two thousand names on that list and we called every damn one of them. A lot of them twice."

"What was your batting average?" the Congressman asked.

"Point five ninety-three."

"Good Lord."

"That's when I learned what makes people give money to politicians."

The Congressman smiled. "Is it a secret?"

She shook her head. "Fear and flattery."

Still smiling, Congressman Finch said, "What about hope for a better tomorrow?"

"Forget hope," she said.

There was a silence until MacArthur said, "But Stevenson lost."

The Congressman sighed long and deeply and after it ended Altford asked, "How much did it cost you to beat Joey Sizemore in the primary—nine hundred thousand, a million?"

"Close."

"Your money?"

"I don't have that kind of money," he said.

"Well, not many congressional candidates do until they get reelected a few times and build up their war chests. I sent Joey a bundle of one hundred thousand and he spent it smart. If I'd've sent him another hundred thousand, he'd've whipped your butt."

The Congressman smiled again. "Why didn't you?"

"Because I knew he'd be vulnerable in the general election. Joey Sizemore's not quite Little Rock's type. The Republicans sensed this and were all set to spend a ton of money, if Joey'd won the primary. But he didn't, you did and the GOP backed off."

There was another silence until MacArthur said, "I'm sorry, Mrs. Altford, but I'm still not sure I get the point of all this."

"Then you weren't listening," the Congressman said. "The point is that there's a primary every two years."

"So?"

The Congressman ignored him and spoke to Millicent Altford instead. "How much could you raise if . . ." He let the question trail off.

"If I'm still pissed off enough two years from now?"

Finch nodded.

"A million or so, but I'd have to call in every last one of my markers."

The Congressman put all of his considerable charm into a smile. "We didn't invite you here to antagonize you, Mrs. Altford. We asked you here to give us advice and counsel on how to reform campaign financing."

"Simple," she said. "Outlaw bundling. Do away with soft money. Provide Federal financing. Establish campaign spending limits—proportional ones, of course—so somebody running for the Senate in New York can spend more than somebody running for it in South Dakota. You know all the cures. It's just that most of you guys don't want to take them."

The Congressman nodded thoughtfully, then turned to MacArthur, who was staring at Millicent Altford, his mouth slightly open. "I see no need for Mrs. Altford to appear in person before the subcommittee, do you, Will?"

MacArthur closed his mouth, swallowed, then opened it to say, "Maybe she could just write a letter instead, setting forth her views."

"Would you be willing to do that—write us a letter? It needn't be long."

"Happy to," she said.

"One last question?" the Congressman said.

"Certainly."

"Would you accept me as a—well, as a client?"

"In a general election? No question."

The Congressman twinkled at her. "I may get in touch with you later in the year."

"That'll be too late," she said.

"I just got sworn in."

"And four men and at least two women are already thinking about running against you in the primary."

Before the Congressman could respond, MacArthur said, "Your bodyguard's here."

She looked up, saw Partain approaching, then smiled at MacArthur. "Who says he's my bodyguard, Willy?"

32

After Jerry, the driver, turned his cab off Connecticut Avenue and into Kalorama Circle, Partain asked Millicent Altford if they were lost.

"I heard that," Jerry said.

"Well?"

"We picked up a tail."

"That I know," Partain said. "But what I don't know is why you'd head for a circle drive to lose it."

"Don't wanta lose him. What I wanta do is let you all out, then do me a drop-behind, get on his butt and stick there till I find out where he lives and who he is."

"What's he driving?" Altford asked.

"He's not," Jerry said. "Got himself an old black '70s Caddy limo with a driver. Thinks it makes him invisible."

The cab slowed, then stopped, and Altford said, "We're here. The littlest house on the circle."

Looking to his right, Partain saw a four-story gray stone house that was tall enough to need an elevator and large enough to serve as an embassy for either Hungary, Portugal or the erstwhile Yugoslavia.

As if anticipating his question, Altford said, "The General's second wife died and left it to him along with a few million dollars that kept company with the one and a half million his folks left him."

"What happened to the first wife?"

"She broke her neck and left leg skiing Aspen in '67 while he was in Vietnam. She left him another million or so and her house in Aspen. He never quite got over her."

"Or you," Partain said.

"Or me," she admitted. "Or Hank Viar's wife for that matter, who also had a few bucks."

"You all ever gonna get out?" Jerry said.

"You have Vernon's number?" she asked.

"Sure."

"When you find out who's following us, call me."

"Right."

"Where's the old Caddy now?" Partain said.

"Three houses back, peeping around the curve. Lights off. Still invisible."

Once out of the cab, Partain took her left arm and felt it stiffen through her thick dark gray cashmere coat. There was just enough street and security lighting for him to inspect the house that had a black slate roof, a lot of black or dark gray shutters and a deeply recessed entryway.

When they reached the front door he let her ring the bell while he turned to watch Jerry's cab pull away. Seconds later the old black Cadillac limousine, its rear windows tinted, its lights off, drifted slowly by the General's house.

The thick carved door was opened by Winfield, who smiled and said, "Come in and let me take your coats, or coat, since I notice Mr. Partain's not wearing one."

Once they were inside, Altford turned, let the General have her coat and said, "There's something you could do for me tomorrow, sugar."

"Anything."

"Take Twodees in hand and buy him a couple of decent suits, a jacket, some pants and a nice but not too heavy topcoat he can wear in California on the nine days of the year he'll need it. Throw in some shirts, ties, socks and underwear. Charge everything, give me the receipts and I'll write you a check."

With Altford's coat now over his arm, the General turned to Partain and said, "I don't wish to impose."

"What I wear embarrasses her," Partain said. "Maybe you can pick out something that won't."

"What time?" the General said.

"Around noon—right after Hank Viar's funeral?"

"It's at eleven, I'm told, so why don't I pick you up at the Mayflower at, say, ten-fifteen and we'll go to the funeral together. May I lend you a shirt, tie and jacket?"

Partain agreed with thanks and the General turned back to Millicent Altford. "Are you planning to go?"

"I liked Violet a lot, but I despised him and can't think of any reason why I ought to be at his funeral."

The General nodded his understanding. "I remember what good friends you and Violet were."

"You should," she said. "You introduced us."

Partain guessed that the General's library on the second floor contained at least 9,000 volumes. It was about the size of Partain's high school library in Bakersfield but smelled pleasantly of leather and furniture polish instead of library paste and janitor. Partain wanted to spend months in it.

There were a number of high-back upholstered chairs and just-so floor lamps. There were also a big carved desk and a black walnut magazine table and a couple of rolling ladders to reach the top three or four shelves.

Two big leather chairs were drawn up in front of the fireplace. Curled up in the left one, her hands wrapped around a mug of hot chocolate, was Jessica Carver, who rose, put the mug down, kissed her mother on the cheek, patted Partain's and announced that there was a pot of just-made hot chocolate in a Pullman kitchen behind the folding doors.

Her mother said she wanted a stiff drink, not chocolate, but Partain chose chocolate and the General served everyone, not forgetting a whiskey for himself. After they were settled around the fire, General Winfield asked, "How did it go with the Congressman?"

"I lectured him and the subcommittee's new counsel on ancient history and then discoursed briefly on the primacy of money in politics. By the time I'd finished, they were pleading with me not to appear before them, but write 'em a letter instead. A short one."

"Were they—competent?" the General asked.

"They were young. The Congressman was a smart-enough forty-two or -three. The counsel was thirty, if that, and tiresome. He may've been the one who set me up. I'll nose around town tomorrow and try and find out if any of those Little Rock kiddy snots put him up to it. If so, I'll do something about it."

"What?" Partain asked.

"Explain the rule."

Partain smiled. "Which is?"

"Don't fuck with Millie Altford."

"How far back did the ancient history lecture go?" the General asked, but before Altford could reply, the telephone rang. The General murmured an apology, rose and crossed the room to answer it.

Partain looked at Jessica Carver and said, "Want to go to Henry Viar's funeral tomorrow?"

"Why should I?"

"There're a couple of people I'd like you to meet. Nick Patrokis and Viar's daughter, Shawnee."

She looked at him for a moment and said, "You want a second opinion on her, don't you?"

It was then that the General said the call was for Altford. She gave him an inquiring look before reaching for the phone, and the General, his hand over its mouthpiece, murmured, "Sylvia."

"Aw, shit," Altford said, took the phone, put it to her ear and said, "What's wrong, honey?"

She listened, then shuddered visibly, sucked in a deep breath and used it to say, "I'm so sorry, Sylvia, so very, very sorry. Where is he?" She listened, nodded and said, "I'll be there in ten minutes."

Back at the fireplace, the General at her side, Altford took another deep breath and said, "Jerry's been shot. He's in intensive care at Sibley and they don't know if he'll make it. That was Sylvia. His wife. I have to be there."

"I'll drive you, if the General will lend us his car," Partain said.

"Of course," Winfield said.

Millicent Altford studied Partain for a second or two, then nodded and said with great formality, "That's very kind of you, Mr. Partain."

33

Sibley Memorial Hospital was out on Loughboro Road in northwest Washington and after Partain found himself on Massachusetts Avenue, heading more or less northwest, he increased the speed of the borrowed BMW convertible to 60 miles per hour until he was stopped by a red light.

While they waited for the green he asked Altford, "Who is he? Jerry?"

Staring straight ahead she said, "He's my first husband's bastard son."

"The husband who didn't finish the inside loop?"

She turned, examined him indifferently and said, "Jessie already told you, didn't she?"

"Not about Jerry."

"He was born in 1957, the son of Harry Montague, my future husband, and the young black maid who worked for Harry's folks. Harry and I were engaged when I found out about it and I told him the wedding was off unless he acknowledged the kid legally and did something for the mother financially. The son of a bitch laughed at me."

"Not much of a civil libertarian, Harry," Partain said.

She shrugged. "In Dallas then who was? So I went to Texarkana the next weekend and talked to my former Congressman, the sainted Wright Patman. He told me there wasn't anything he could do since Harry didn't even live in his district, but then he grinned and said he had an idea but couldn't tell me about it."

"You asked a U.S. Representative to involve himself in a domestic squabble?"

"Maybe it sounds like a domestic squabble to you, but to me it was a civil rights issue and back then I was the biggest mouth in Dallas on that."

"I still don't see why a Congressman—"

She interrupted. "Because the Montague family was in the airplane parts business and the Federal government was their biggest customer. And because in Texas you damn well mess with whatever gets you elected and my kinfolks had lots of votes and lots of friends in Patman's district."

"Anything happen?" he asked.

"The light's green," she said and after a silence of two blocks, looked at Partain and said, "What do you care, anyway?"

"Somebody just shot one of your baby-sitters and I care just one hell of a lot about who and what he was."

"Okay," she said. "Harry and I were still arguing about the baby and his mother and we still weren't married but sleeping together almost every night at this place his folks had out at the lake. That's where we were when the phone rang one morning and Senator Lyndon B. Johnson's on the line."

"No kidding?"

"No kidding. Johnson was talking so loud I could hear snatches of what he was telling Harry. Stuff like 'doing right by that little nigger baby' and how Harry'd also better do 'something nice for that baby's mama.' It went on and on and Harry Montague, the Korean War Marine pilot and almost ace, shivered and shriveled and damn near wet his drawers."

"So you got married."

"Yeah, we got married but not until Harry agreed that 'H. Montague' would go where it said 'father' on Jerry's birth certificate."

"Did his mother come to work for you and Harry then?"

Again, she turned to stare at him. "You sure like soupy endings, don't you? No, she didn't come to work for us. All Harry ever did was mail her ten ten-dollar bills the first of every month, if he didn't forget and I had to remind him. Most months he forgot. But the money stopped when Harry went up in his old biplane and failed to make the loop."

"What happened to Jerry and his mother?" Partain said.

"I'm coming to that. Right after I married Dr. Carver, I told him about Jerry and his mama, and the doctor—devout secular humanist that he was—suggested she become our live-in housekeeper and bring the kid with her."

"A happy ending after all," Partain said.

"It was for a while. Then Jessica came along and Jerry sort of looked after her some. After the doctor died in '69, I managed to keep us all together 'til Jerry got out of high school. After that he sort of scuffled around for a while, dealing dope mostly, but then he straightened out, went to Denver and got on as an undercover narcotics cop. That lasted nine years until he got shot, retired on a small disability, moved to Washington, landed a job at the National Archives, bought himself a cab and moonlighted whenever he could."

"He ever change his last name?" Partain said.

"No. Why?"

"I don't know," he said. "I think I would've."

By the time they reached Sibley Memorial, Jerry Montague was dead from a bullet wound in his head. Altford tried to comfort Jerry's handsome wife and pretty young daughter while Partain talked to a pair of bored homicide detectives.

To them it was another in a long string of random Washington cabdriver shootings. The only thing unusual about it, they said, was the eyewitness testimony of a homeless man they called "Billy the Bum," who claimed to have seen it all happen.

The older of the detectives described what Billy the Bum claimed to have seen. "There's this old black Caddy limo rolling along Mass Ave about seven blocks west of Wisconsin, okay?" the detective said.

Partain nodded.

"And not far behind it, according to Billy, comes this indy cab with the owner-victim behind the wheel. Got the picture?"

Partain said he did.

"Well, the old limo starts to buck and snort and backfire like it's got engine trouble, then stops dead. The cab, it stops maybe fifty feet behind it."

"Now comes the funny part," said the second detective. "The limo driver keeps turning the engine over trying to start it, but it won't fire up. So finally the limo's left rear door opens and out gets this real short guy, I mean short, who starts walking back to the cab, spreading his hands out like, you know, he's helpless and what the hell can he do? The cabdriver just sits there behind the wheel, staring at him."

The first detective again took over. "When the short guy reaches the cab, the cabbie won't roll down his window. The short guy taps on it politely and says something Billy the Bum can't hear and that's when the cabbie lowers the window. When he does, the short guy comes up with a small semiautomatic of some kind, sticks it in the cabbie's ear and blows him away. Then he looks around, the short guy, I mean, strolls back to the limo, gets in and away they go."

"How short is short?"

The first detective nodded his appreciation of Partain's question. "Yeah, I know what you mean. Billy the Bum's six-two or -three and skinny as a pole. So short to him might mean five-five or -six. But we pressed him on it pretty good and he swears the shooter was no more'n five even. Maybe less."

"Did Billy the Bum call it in?" Partain asked.

"Nah," the second detective said. "He just waited for us to show up. Right after a shot's heard in that neighborhood, you probably got nineteen different houses dialing 911."

"We figure it was a busted drug deal."

Partain nodded as if he liked the notion and asked, "I don't suppose Billy the Bum got the license number of the old limo?"

"Billy don't think that's way up there on his list of civic responsibilities," the detective said.

Just after midnight Partain let himself out through the General's front door and started walking toward Connecticut Avenue in search of a taxi. The temperature had dropped into the low twenties and he felt the cold immediately. He had gone less than a hundred feet when he heard the rapid clicking footsteps. He turned to find Jessica Carver hurrying toward him, a blue airline bag slung over her right shoulder.

"It's turned into sort of an Irish wake back there," she said.

"That's why I left."

"Millie's getting nostalgic and a little bombed and she and Vernon'll probably wind up in bed."

He nodded.

"So I thought tonight I'd sleep in her room at the hotel."

"Or mine," he said.

"Right," she said. "Or yours."

34

The Memory Room of the funeral home on Wisconsin Avenue seemed to have been designed for those who died without leaving more than a dozen mourners, for that was the number of chairs that had been set out, four wide and three deep.

Seven of the twelve chairs were occupied. Partain and Jessica Carver sat in the second row on the right just behind the kid from the CIA, who had delivered the agency's condolences the night of Henry Viar's death. Next to Partain and Carver were General Winfield and Nick Patrokis. In the back row by himself was Colonel Ralph Millwed in dress uniform. In the front row, seated together, were Shawnee Viar and Major General Walker L. Hudson.

A closed wood casket, painted to look like old silver, rested on two trestles draped in dark blue velvet. Four mourners had sent flowers. Partain had sent the roses and suspected that the three other floral tributes were from Vernon Winfield, General Hudson and the CIA.

The muted CD strings ended promptly at 11 A.M. Shawnee Viar, wearing no makeup and a black dress that came to mid-calf, rose, turned and said, "Thank you for coming. General Walker Hudson has offered to say a few words. General Hudson."

She sat down and General Hudson rose, turning to face his audience of six, including Shawnee Viar. Hudson was also in dress uniform but the only medal he wore was the long blue and silver badge of the combat infantryman. He looked grave, if not particularly sad, as he inspected each member of his audience, then snapped open his purselike mouth and said, "We're here to mourn the passing of an old friend, Henry Viar, and to offer our sympathy and condolences to his daughter, Shawnee."

There was a practiced pause before he continued: "I knew and admired Hank Viar for more than twenty-five years as a patriot, a father, a husband and a shrewd judge of men. We served together twice, once in Vietnam and again in Central America. He was a man who deeply loved his country and dedicated his life to it. He was also one of those unsung anonymous heroes who helped win the Cold War and we should all be grateful for his untiring efforts. Henry Viar was one of this nation's great patriots and I'm proud to have served with him and to have been his friend."

The General did a smart about-face, threw the casket a snappy salute, held it for a long beat, ended it, backed up exactly two paces and sat down without even looking. Shawnee Viar leaned over to whisper something in his ear before she rose and again turned to the mourners.

"My father may have been all the things the General said, but he was also a cruel, uncaring, spiteful man and I'm not in the least sorry he's dead."

She turned and hurried through a side door. Patrokis rose and went after her, leaving behind a silence not of the stunned variety, but rather the kind that didn't quite know how to end itself because the remaining mourners, except for Partain and Carver, were too far apart to lean over and whisper "May God forgive her" or perhaps "She sure nailed old Hank, didn't she?"

Partain ended the silence when he rose, walked over to General Hudson, who had also risen, and said, "Great eulogy, General. A lot of truth in it, especially the part about Hank being a father and a husband."

"What the fuck're you doing here, Twodees?"

"Paying my respects to a gallant Cold Warrior."

"The silly shit went and shot himself. Not much gallantry in that."

"What about your offer?" Partain said. "The one where you get me reinstated as a light-colonel."

"It stands—providing."

"Providing what?"

"Providing you say nothing, do nothing."

"For how long?"

"Not long."

"Sure you can swing it?"

"They reinstated MacArthur after they fired him for shacking up with that Eurasian mistress of his. So there's plenty of precedent, although you're not exactly a MacArthur."

"Don't wait too long," Partain said.

"Don't get too eager."

Partain returned to Jessica Carver, who was listening to the young CIA representative. He was telling her that the agency tried to be represented at the funerals or memorial services of most of its senior employees, even those who'd served long ago in the Office of Strategic Services during World War Two.

"Some of those old OSS guys, a few anyway, are way up in their nineties. I had to be at one service last week at this fancy estate out on the Eastern Shore—in Maryland? The deceased was a real old guy of about eighty. He had this funny-strange name, Minor Jackson, and the only mourners were this ancient dwarf and the two pretty young French girls he'd brought. The girls said they'd all flown in from Paris on the Concorde. You should've seen the place this guy had. But nobody else came, no neighbors, no household help, no minister. Nobody. Just the two girls and the dwarf and me."

"What was the dwarf's name?" Partain asked.

"Nick something."

"Ploscaru?"

The young CIA man nodded. "Right. Ploscaru. He had to be ninety at least. You knew him?"

"I'd heard he was dead," Partain said.

In the haphazardly furnished living room of the house on Volta Place in Georgetown, Patrokis had arranged for a caterer, not his uncle, to lay on some finger food and wine. The invitations had been verbal. Colonel Millwed hadn't been invited but General Hudson had and had declined with regret. Partain had been asked to invite the young CIA man, who begged off because of another funeral he had to attend late that afternoon.

Partain loaded his plate with small crustless sandwiches, devilled eggs and Triscuits covered with melted cheese that he suspected was Velveeta. He then looked around for something to drink and was relieved to find twelve bottles of a sparkling California wine and two dozen glasses on a corner table.

Nick Patrokis sat with Shawnee Viar, who had nothing on her plate other than a half-eaten devilled egg. From the fingers of her right hand an empty wineglass dangled. Patrokis offered to get her more wine but she shook her head and said, "How awful was I?"

"Awful enough."

"Good."

"Why'd you invite him to speak?"

"Perversity. Or wishful thinking. I thought that if I asked

him to speak and he didn't show up, it'd prove he killed Hank. But he showed up."

Patrokis smiled. "So he's no longer a suspect."

She shook her head. "Now I suspect he's just a lot smarter than I thought he was."

Across the room Jessica Carver had finished a pair of devilled eggs and was biting cautiously into one of the crustless sandwiches when Partain said, "How do you read her—Shawnee?"

She put the sandwich back on her plate, studied Shawnee Viar across the room for a moment or two, then said, "Probably a chronic mood-swinger and I like her."

"Why?"

"Because she probably feels just the way I do when I wake up each morning. But I've learned to shovel out the bullshit and by ten, noon at the latest, I'm more or less functional."

"Think she could kill her father?"

"Sure," she said, "if sufficiently provoked. But she'd think about it for a long, long time. The pleasure'd be in the planning."

"How d'you know?"

"Because that's how I'd do it."

Partain removed the Kevlar vest before trying on a topcoat at the men's store just north of the Mayflower Hotel. He chose an eggshell-white single-breasted coat with a plaid zip-out lining, ignoring the recommendation from Jessica Carver and Vernon Winfield that the belted double-breasted model offered more swagger.

"When I need swagger, I'll buy a stick," Partain said.

"A scarf would be nice," the General suggested. "I strongly recommend a scarf."

"The only thing easier to lose than a scarf is an umbrella," Partain said.

* * *

At another men's store on Connecticut, purchases were made just as quickly. Partain chose two suits, one a plain dark blue, the other gray with a faint stripe. Shirts were next. Partain picked out six identical white ones, specifying no button-down collars or French cuffs. While choosing the shirts, he asked Jessica Carver to choose two ties. When she showed him her choices, he said, "They need a box."

She then insisted he buy a jacket and they agreed on a lightweight brown herringbone. They also agreed on two pairs of slacks, one chocolate gabardine, the other tan whipcord. A dozen pairs of Jockey shorts with 32-inch waistbands completed the shopping and everything was billed to General Winfield's gold American Express card.

Three minutes later the clerk who had sold Partain the clothing returned, wearing an embarrassed somber face. After reaching General Winfield, he said, "I'm awfully sorry, General, but your Amex card's been cancelled."

The General was stunned. "That's impossible," he said. "I used it no more than thirty minutes ago."

"It could be an inadvertent cancellation," the salesman said. "I'm terribly sorry but—"

Jessica Carver didn't let him finish. She whipped out her VISA card and thrust it at the salesman. "Put it all on this."

The salesman accepted the VISA card, checked its expiration date, returned the Amex card to the General, made more apologetic sounds and hurried away.

"I don't understand it," the General said. "And I'm terribly embarrassed."

"Maybe you just forgot to pay your bill," she said.

"I never forget."

Jessica Carver turned to Partain. "What about shoes? Millie wanted you to buy some new shoes."

"I'll buy my own shoes," Partain said.

* * *

After the trio broke up, Partain stopped at the first shoe store he came to and bought a pair of plain cordovan oxfords and a pair of brown Weejuns. For another $10 the clerk promised to drop them off himself at the Mayflower's front desk.

Partain then asked to use the store's telephone book. The clerk led him into the rear storeroom and left him alone. Partain looked under "Attorneys" in the Yellow Pages until he came to one whose display advertisement read:

BANKRUPTCY?
Business Reorganization?
Specialist In
Liquidation & Chapter 11's
Also
Debtors & Creditors

The attorney's office was in a building on the northwest corner of 14th and K and Partain decided to walk. Twenty minutes later he was seated in front of the gray metal desk of Ransom Leeds, who seemed to be two parts bonhomie and one part bile.

"You want me to run a credit check on this guy, right?"

Partain nodded.

"Why not have your company do it?"

"Because I don't have a company," Partain said. "Yet."

"You say he's a retired Army brigadier general. How long was he in?"

"Twenty years."

"What do they retire on—half pay?"

"I'm not sure. Maybe."

"Let's be cautious and say half." Leeds reached into a desk drawer, brought out a well-thumbed copy of *The World Almanac* and turned to page 702. "Okay. It says here a brigadier general with twenty years drags down $6,052.50 a month.

Half of that'd be three thousand and change. A little over thirty-six thousand a year and not bad, considering all the perks those guys get." He studied Partain for a moment before asking, "What is it you don't like about this deal—whatever the deal is?"

"That he can't carry his end."

"How old is he?"

"Sixty-seven, I think."

"Address?"

Partain recited the address on Kalorama Circle and Leeds whistled. "He may be busted now, but he sure was flush once."

"A wife left it to him. The house."

"How much is involved in your deal—roughly?"

"One-point-two million."

"Half and half?"

Partain nodded.

"It'll cost you five hundred bucks—cash."

Partain removed five $100 bills from his wallet, placed them on the desk and covered them with his palm. "First, the report."

Leeds shrugged, picked up his phone, punched one button and, after it was immediately answered, said, "Betsy. Gimme the once-over-lightly on a retired Army brigadier general, Vernon NMI Winfield who lives on Kalorama Circle with the rest of the unhappy rich."

While waiting for Betsy's computer to reveal General Winfield's financial situation, Leeds whistled "Mi chiamano Mimi" and was a third of the way through it when Betsy came back on the line.

"Shoot," Leeds said, picked up a ballpoint pen and poised it over a yellow legal pad.

He listened and made notes for several minutes in a kind of private shorthand. Partain tried to read the shorthand upside down but quickly gave up. A few minutes later, Leeds thanked

Betsy, hung up and stared at Partain. "You don't want to do a deal with this guy," he said.

"Why?"

"His sole income's his pension, as far as I can tell. His VISA card's filthy, so's his MasterCard, and Amex just cut him off completely. His checking account at Riggs is one thousand and change. His BMW's leased and he's two months behind on his payments. And two months ago he re-fied that Kalorama Circle house of his to the max."

"How much?" Partain said.

"Did he borrow? One-point-two million. That means his equity's now about two or three hundred K."

"What'd he do with the one-point-two million?" Partain said.

"Better ask him," Leeds said, "because there's no record of his depositing the check in Washington, Virginia or Maryland. Maybe he's using it as a bookmark. Maybe it's on hold in Vegas or Atlantic City. Maybe he drank it up."

"Drinking's not his problem," Partain said, removed his hand from the five $100 bills, rose, nodded goodbye and left.

35

At dusk that same day, General Walker Hudson stood at a sixth-floor window of the Marriott Hotel just across Key Bridge from Georgetown. He stood, cigar in one hand, a drink in the other, staring across the Potomac as Washington's lights came on in what was to him their usual illogical pattern.

The General now wore a dark gray tweed suit, white shirt and a tie striped with crimson and yellow. In his left hand was a drink of Wild Turkey, chilled and diluted by a single ice cube. In his right hand was a cigar that boasted three-quarters of an inch of firm ash.

Seated in a chair behind him, staring at the room's taupe carpet, was Colonel Ralph Millwed—elbows on spread knees, both hands clutching a glass that was empty save for two ice cubes. The Colonel now wore a gray worsted suit, blue shirt and a blue and crimson tie.

Without looking up, Millwed said, "Go on."

"Where was I?" the General asked.

"Sneaking down the alley."

"Right. I'd parked two blocks away—but I told you that, didn't I?"

"Right."

"The alley was fenced on both sides and when I came to the gate I opened it and found myself in the garden, which was an absolute mess."

"What'd you wear?"

"Coveralls. The green ones with 'L&D Restorations' across the back. Pity about the garden, though. All dead grass and leaves. Then I opened the screen door and tried the kitchen door knob. It turned as expected and I was inside by eleven-seventeen—"

"Looked at your watch, did you?"

"Right. Where were you then?"

"Where I was supposed to be," Millwed said, not looking up from his inspection of the carpet. "At the Safeway on Wisconsin, putting a move on the woman."

The General nodded, studied the lights across the river again and said, "He was in the living room. Sitting in a chair—his favorite, I suspect. He was a little hunched over, studying the floor, holding a glass and having himself a morning drink. Not, I think, the first of the day."

"What'd he do?" the Colonel said to the floor.

"You mean was he surprised, shocked, any of that?"

"Yes."

"He heard me, looked up, saw my weapon and said, 'What the fuck d'you want?' So I told him."

"What'd he say then?"

The General drank some whiskey, admired the ash on the cigar, drew in some smoke, blew it out and said, "That he needed to piss."

"You let him?"

"Why not? The bathroom was upstairs anyway. So upstairs we went. He pissed. I watched. And after that he handed them over."

"Just like that?"

"He had no choice, Ralph."

"It was loaded—his piece?"

"Fully loaded."

"And the other stuff?"

"They were nicely hidden, but all there. The photograph of the four of us. And the thirty-two red spiral notebooks. By that I mean their covers were red."

"Where'd he hide 'em?"

"The weapon wasn't really hidden. It was in the drawer of a bedside table. The notebooks and the photo were behind the baseboard behind a bed. We had to move the bed out a couple of feet to get to it."

"You helped him, huh?"

"The bed's legs were on casters."

"Funny kind of bed."

"It was more of a studio couch really. After he handed it all over I got down and took a look just to make sure he hadn't squirrelled away something else. After the bed was back in place, I told him to lie facedown on it with his hands behind him. He called me some names, then did what I said."

"You read them then? The nasty parts?"

"Every word."

"It all there?"

"Every last detail. You. Me. The Atlacatl battalion. Names. The money. The Mickey Mouse seal. And Twodees. All of it."

"What about Twodees's wife?"

"That, too. In detail."

"Shit. He wasn't supposed to know about that."

"He was a spy, for God's sake," the General said. "And a competent one when he got around to it. He wrote it all in black ink with a real fountain pen and no cross-outs. His penmanship was pure Palmer method, which they still must've taught when he was in grade school."

"And after you read it?" Millwed asked.

"We went back downstairs. He sat down in the same chair.

Poured himself a drink but didn't offer me one. Lit a Pall Mall. Had a big gulp of booze. Put the glass down and took a drag on his cigarette and I shot him right after he blew the smoke out."

"With his own weapon," Millwed said.

The General nodded.

"And left it on the floor near his right hand like I told you."

"Precisely as you told me."

The Colonel finally looked up. "Somebody moved it. The weapon."

"Yes," the General said, still staring out into the Washington night. "Somebody did."

"Patrokis probably," the Colonel said. "They had him on some shit detail in Vietnam, investigating suicides. He probably moved the piece to Viar's lap or to the floor between his legs or wherever it was that made 'em rule it suicide." Colonel Millwed grunted. "I wasn't expecting that fucking Patrokis."

The General turned from the window, went over to an ashtray, tapped off his inch and a quarter of ash and examined the Colonel. "Just as I wasn't expecting the woman to con you out of that tape."

"She knew who I was, for Christ sake," Millwed said. "She wasn't supposed to know that."

"Forget the tape," the General said.

"*Forget* it?"

"Certainly. Now that Viar's killed himself, what does it prove? That an unmarried colonel on extended temporary duty took time off to bed the attractive daughter of an old friend and, being the soul of discretion, used an out-of-the-way motel. If the tape should surface somewhere, I might have to place a naughty-naughty letter in your file. But what the hell, they'll say. At least it wasn't some fifteen-year-old boy."

"I don't want any letter," Millwed said.

"Forget the letter. It hasn't happened, it probably won't and we have something else to decide."

"Twodees," the Colonel said.

"Twodees," the General agreed.

Millwed turned to reach for the bottle of Wild Turkey and poured an inch of whiskey into his glass. He raised the bottle questioningly at the General, who shook his head. The Colonel replaced the bottle, tasted his drink and said, "You know what I really want?"

"Sure, Ralph. You want your own personal copies of Hank Viar's little red notebooks."

"Yes, sir. Exactly, sir."

"You'll get copies."

"When?"

"After Kite does Twodees."

"I want them now, General," Millwed said, not quite making it an order.

The General nodded patiently, as if dealing with a fool. "I didn't quite finish, Colonel."

"Then finish."

"You'll have your very own Xeroxed copies of Viar's journals as soon as Kite does Twodees—and you do Kite."

The Colonel leaned back in his chair, nodding contentedly. "I wouldn't mind doing Kite. With him and Twodees both gone, that'd leave who?"

"Nobody."

"What about the Altford woman, Patrokis and General Winfield?"

"They weren't in El Salvador."

"Neither was Kite."

"We'll just have to pretend he was," General Hudson said.

36

The four of them ate a late dinner at the Kudzu Cafe on upper 14th Street in northwest Washington. The cafe featured what some call soul food and others southern cooking. Everything was served family style in large dishes and bowls that offered fried chicken, country ham, mashed potatoes, chicken gravy, redeye gravy, corn bread, biscuits, turnip greens, okra fried and boiled, sliced tomatoes, black-eyed peas and, for dessert, a choice of pecan or lemon meringue pie or both.

Shawnee Viar ate little. Jessica Carver ate a little of almost everything, passing on what she called the "slime okra." Partain sampled nearly everything and Patrokis ate large quantities of everything, especially the fried chicken, then leaned back in his chair and announced, "God, I love stuff cooked in lard."

The bill came with the coffee. Partain paid it, added a 20 percent tip and wrote the total into his expense notebook. Shawnee Viar watched him curiously.

"This a business expense?" she said.

He nodded.

"And here I was thinking my newest and dearest friends

had gathered to feast and reminisce about the late Henry Viar, bad husband, worse father, aged spy and, late in his career, the disappearer's failed apprentice."

"The what?" Jessica Carver said.

"In Central America," Shawnee said, "in San Salvador, to be precise, old Hank sort of apprenticed himself to those who made people disappear. But he really wasn't any good at it. 'The mind accepts,' he wrote, 'but the stomach rejects.'"

"He wrote that or said it?" Partain asked.

"Wrote it. Up until almost the very end he'd pound out his daily pensées on the old Smith-Corona, then copy them into red spiral notebooks with a Mont Blanc pen that some shit gave him. The Shah's sister, I think, just after the Kurds got dished."

"You read them—these journals?" Partain said.

"Sure. Sometimes I'd read the wadded-up typewritten pages in the wastebasket and sometimes I'd read the notebooks themselves. All thirty-two of them. One for each year." She paused, still staring at Partain, then said, "You had a wife, I think. In fact, I know you did because old Hank always referred to her as Señora Partain."

Partain thought he felt the blood drain from his face. It prickled. Then his face turned hot and he wondered if his color had gone from flour white to Valentine red. When he saw them all staring at him, he sucked in air, held it, let it out slowly, then smiled what he knew must be a ghastly smile at Shawnee Viar and asked, "What else did he say about her?"

"Your wife?"

"Yes."

"You want it verbatim?" she said. "I have this trick memory that recalls stuff like that verbatim—well, almost verbatim. It's how I made Phi Beta Kappa, fat lot of good it did me."

"As close as you can," Partain said, his voice cracking on "can."

"Okay," she said. "About your wife my old dad wrote

something like this, but remember, it's not exactly word for word."

Partain made himself nod. Shawnee Viar closed her eyes for a moment, as if trying to visualize the words, then opened her eyes, stared at something that seemed to hover a foot above Partain's head and began to recite:

" 'Colonel H. and Captain M. dropped by to discuss the wife of Major P. Seems they're getting pressure from our hosts to do something or other about the lovely Señora Partain. What, pray? I ask. My two militarists suggest she might disappear—at least for a while. How long is a while? I ask. Just arrange it, Hank, says my Colonel. Put it in writing, say I. They refuse, brave lads, and I think of calling Major P., but such a call could be self-incriminating and, after all, perhaps nothing will happen. Still, something probably should be done and I must think more about it. It's now three days later and I apparently thought too long. Yesterday, Señora Partain disappeared one hundred meters from her house. Perhaps I should try to buy her back. Or is it too late? I'll talk to Colonel H. about it. And Captain M., of course. Later. I've talked to them and it is, alas, far too late.' "

Shawnee Viar stopped talking, lowered her gaze to Partain's face, saw what was there, said, "Christ!" and shrank away from it. The others were also staring at Partain, whose eyes glittered and whose lips were twisted into a snarl. The color in his face had again deepened into a dark dangerous-looking red. He closed his eyes then, willing them back to normal. The snarl went away and the dark red face changed quickly to bright pink and then, more slowly, to normal.

Partain opened his eyes and very softly said, "I'd like to read that one journal, Shawnee."

She gave her head a single slow shake. "It's gone. They're all gone. The day Hank was killed I looked for them. They were behind a baseboard that was behind his couch upstairs.

The photo's gone, too." She looked at Patrokis, as if for corroboration. "Remember when I went upstairs to pee?"

He nodded, still watching Partain.

"That's when I looked for them," she said. "Maybe that's why they killed him. For the journals. I'm very sorry, Major."

"I'm not a major."

"I'm still sorry," she said and turned to Patrokis. "I can't go back to Volta Place tonight."

"Stay with me," he said.

"At VOMIT?"

"I don't really live there. I've got an apartment on Nineteenth." He paused. "You can have the couch or the bed."

Shawnee's glance toured the table and stopped at Jessica Carver. "What d'you think?"

"I think you might be a little spacey right now and if you don't take Nick up on his offer, I'll know you are."

"What if he wants to fuck?"

Carver shrugged. "Think of it as therapy."

Shawnee Viar turned to Patrokis and said, "Let's go."

They both rose. Partain, still seated, looked up at Shawnee Viar and asked, "Was that really what the journal said?"

"Not word for word," she said. "But close. Very close."

After they left, Partain and Jessica Carver sat in silence for what seemed to her an interminable three minutes until she ended it with a question. "You going to sit and brood all night?"

He shook his head. "Of course not. I'll get you a cab."

"What about you?"

"I'll walk back."

"Walk?"

He ignored the question. "Tell your mother I need to see her. Tonight. Late. After eleven."

"Should I mention General Winfield and his dirty plastic?"

"Not yet."

She leaned forward to examine him carefully, even critically, as if for character fissures or crumbling resolve. "I don't want anything to happen to Millie," she said. "A little mild excitement and adventure, fine. But nothing bad."

He nodded.

"As for you, you've just had a rotten shock. How rotten I can't even imagine. After you see Millie, I'll sit up with you all night. Get drunk with you. Listen to you." She paused. "Come as you are. Anytime. No reservation needed."

He wanted to smile at her and felt his lips stretch into something that he hoped resembled one. He then tried to make his eyes crinkle, although he wasn't at all sure what muscles to use.

"Does it hurt?" she asked.

"What?"

"You look like you're in pain."

"I am," he said, rose and went around the table. "Let's get you a cab."

Partain walked south down the east side of 14th Street to L, then turned west and went the rest of the way to Connecticut Avenue and the Mayflower Hotel. He was propositioned by no whores. Importuned by no beggars. Threatened by no jackrollers. A patrol car slowed beside him near 14th and T. The near cop gave him a long speculative look and, in return, received a savage smile. The cop car rolled on.

As he walked he wondered why he hadn't suspected long ago that his dead wife's lack of politics would've been interpreted as a disguise. A Salvadoran intellectual marries a mustang major in the U.S. Army assigned to intelligence, but claims she has no interest in the politics of her own country. That'd bother them all right—enough to make them go to the Major's superiors, to that fucking Hudson, and maybe that equally fucking Millwed, and say this woman of Major Partain's is a cleverly disguised spy and something must be done about her either by you or us. So those two fuckers, Hudson and Millwed, hand the problem off to the Great Ditherer, Hank Viar, the Pepys of El Salvador, who says nothing to me, does nothing, as those two fuckers knew he wouldn't. But tells dear diary he maybe ought to do something. But doesn't. And they, whoever they are or were, make her disappear. And isn't it awful that Viar is dead and you can't ask him what really happened to her and then kill him no matter what his reply.

Partain's rage had diminished, if not vanished, by the time he knocked on the door of Millicent Altford's suite. She asked who it was through the door. He replied. The door opened. He went in and she said, "Who ran over your puppy?"

"Let's talk about something else," Partain said. "Let's talk about that keeper of the guttering flame, General Vernon Winfield, because he's onto you, lady."

"You drunk?" she said.

"No."

"Wanta be?"

"Maybe."

"Sit down."

Partain sat down on a couch and waited for her to hand him a drink. He didn't care what it was and she, sensing this, handed him two ounces of iced Scotch. He remembered to thank her and noticed she was wearing a suit he hadn't seen, a Hershey-brown one with cream piping. "New suit?" he said.

She sat down in an armchair with her own drink and crossed her legs. "I bought it just before I checked into the hospital," she said.

"Shows off your legs."

"Well, you advertise whatever's left," she said, sipped her drink and then asked, "What d'you mean Vernon's onto me?"

"He knows your sun-dried one-point-two million's missing."

"Does he, now?"

Partain nodded. "He really must have a yen for you."

"A yen? You could've said he longs for me. Yearns for me. Even has the hots for me. But yen sounds like diluted desire."

"He's broke," Partain said.

She started to giggle, tried to stop but couldn't until Partain said, "You don't believe me."

"I didn't say that. I asked you a question, then giggled at your answer. So how d'you know he's broke?"

"His American Express card's cancelled. His VISA card's maxed out. He's two, maybe three months behind on his BMW lease."

"You call that broke?"

Partain ignored the question and said, "He also did something else. He refinanced that chateau of his on Kalorama Circle for one-point-two million exactly. The same amount that was stolen from your safe and the same amount you've got squirrelled away in that safe-deposit box in Santa Paula."

"Ran a check on him, did you?" she said.

"I had somebody run one."

"Here in Washington?"

He nodded.

"I reckon it didn't quite stretch to Aspen, did it? Thought not. You see, dear heart, Vernon's been buying up Aspen since 1958. Must own half of it now. Well, maybe three or four percent anyway. Check out his total net worth and you'll find it's between fifteen and twenty million."

"So why the bad plastic?"

She sighed. "It's somebody to talk to. Once in a while, he gets lonely. So he lets his car lease ride and gets a call from the BMW store and that's good for a fifteen-minute chat. Amex uses mostly girls and they can be a lot of fun, if you're sixty-seven or so. Same goes for VISA. Then he'll pay up, although usually he overpays, and the girls'll call back all aflutter about his new credit balance."

She paused, frowned and said, "One-point-two million, huh? Not in cash, I hope."

"I don't know," Partain said.

"He must've got a whiff from somewhere."

"That it was stolen?"

She nodded. "He probably thinks that's why I checked into the hospital—because I let it be stolen and didn't know what to do about it. He may even have it all planned out that when he and I meet to tot up the books next month, I'll 'fess up that all the money's gone for good and then ask, Sweet Jesus, whatever can I do? And Vernon maybe hopes to snap open a big new shiny black attaché case, plumb full of hundred-dollar bills, and say, 'Don't worry, little darlin', everything's gonna be just fine.'"

"You don't believe that."

"No, sir. I don't."

Partain finished his drink and said, "How'd he find out?"

"Somebody told him," she said. "Not me. Not you. That leaves the thief."

"Or somebody the thief told," Partain said, placed his glass on a table and rose. He stood there for a moment, looking as if he had forgotten something and uncertain about whether he really wanted to remember it.

She leaned forward and looked up to examine him more closely. "What's eating you, Twodees?" she said, her voice gentle, almost coaxing.

"I found out what caused the disappearance of my wife," he said.

She closed her eyes for several seconds, then opened them and asked, "What're you going to do about it?"

"Right now, I'm going to go get drunk with your daughter."

"I couldn't suggest anything better," said Millicent Altford.

37

General Vernon Winfield left his house the next morning at 7:15 A.M., carrying a black leather overnight bag. He walked briskly to Connecticut Avenue, turned south and continued the pace that was now aided by a mostly downhill grade.

The January weather, for a change, was fair but cold with little wind. The General wore his camel hair topcoat, his Borsalino hat and fur-lined leather gloves. He had settled into the rhythm of his pace and, without a glance, passed the narrow four-story building that housed the Acropolis Restaurant and VOMIT.

After reaching the Dupont Circle Metro station, he hurried down into a waiting red-line car, congratulating himself on either phenomenal or lucky timing. Winfield resurfaced near Union Station, soon reached and crossed the Capitol grounds, waited patiently for a green light at Second and Pennsylvania Avenue, then headed east until he came to Fourth Street, where he turned south again, ignoring the modest birthplace of J. Edgar Hoover.

Two and a half blocks later, on the east side of Fourth, he climbed five concrete steps, opened and went through a three-foot-high wrought-iron gate and six paces later reached a door that he guessed to be one hundred years old. He shifted the black overnight bag to his left hand, set it down, stripped off his right glove and used bare knuckles to knock on the old door.

It was opened almost immediately by an exceptionally pretty young brown-haired woman who obviously was just leaving. She wore a sheared beaver coat, pink mittens and a large brown leather purse slung over her right shoulder.

"You here to see Kitey?" she said.

The General nodded, smiling slightly.

"Well, he's upstairs in the shower and I've gotta beat it so why don't you just go in and sit down and make yourself uncomfortable on anything you pick." She examined him more carefully, as if pricing his topcoat and hat. "You like fun?"

"Fun?" the General said.

"You know. Fun and games." She used her teeth to yank off her right pink mitten, plunged the bare hand into her oversized purse, came up with a business card and handed it to Winfield. He looked down and saw that the card read "Connie." Underneath that was a telephone number.

"Anytime," she said, tugging on the mitten, "after six."

Then she was gone, hurrying through the wrought-iron gate and bounding down the five steps. The General put her card in a topcoat pocket, picked up the overnight bag and entered the front parlor of Emory Kite.

He removed his hat, topcoat and remaining glove, placing them all on what he decided was a remarkably ugly love seat. After glancing around the rest of the Victorian room, the General grimaced slightly and sat down on the red velvet sofa, the black overnight case on his knees.

Winfield didn't rise when he heard someone clatter down the stairs. Emory Kite entered the parlor, wearing pants, shirt and leather-heeled loafers. He started at the sight of the General, recovered nicely and asked, "Connie gone?"

"She said she couldn't wait."

"Uh-huh," Kite said with a suspicious frown that he quickly erased with a grin. "Gave you her card, I bet."

The General smiled slightly and nodded.

"I don't mean to step out of line, General, but if you're ever in the mood for a little of the strange, you can't do any better'n Connie. Five hundred a night and cheap at the price. Nice girl, too. Went to college, got herself a pretty fair job at Interior, doesn't do drugs and loves to travel."

"Interesting," the General said.

"Want some coffee? I told her to make a pot."

"Yes, I would, thank you, Mr. Kite."

"Be right back."

Kite returned from the kitchen in less than two minutes with two mugs of coffee. He handed one mug to the General, then held his own with both hands as he sat down in a big armchair that was low enough for his feet to rest on the floor. Kite noisily sipped his coffee, peering over the mug's rim at Winfield. "This ain't no social call, is it?"

"No, Mr. Kite, it's not. I'm in need of your services yet again."

Kite's left hand gave his earlobe a tug that seemed to make the corners of his mouth curl down. "Whatcha got in mind?"

"I'd like you to replace what you once removed—or had removed."

Kite gave the left earlobe another tug and this time his eyes widened in either real or pretended surprise. "You mean in L.A.?"

"In Los Angeles, yes."

"And you want it put back exactly where it was?"

"That's not necessary. Once inside, you can leave it almost anywhere."

"I'm not going in if anybody's there."

"I assure you no one will be there."

"And my end?"

"The same as before. And as before, you'll take care of your own expenses."

"Why?" Kite said with what Winfield took to be an honestly puzzled frown. "I mean, you needed it then but now you don't. How come?"

"I needed it desperately then," Winfield said. "But I no longer do. I now consider it a loan that must be repaid anonymously. But this time no one is to be injured and, above all, no one is to be killed."

Kite pointed his sharp chin at the black overnight bag that still rested on the General's knees. "That it?" Kite asked.

The General nodded.

Kite put his mug down and rose. "Then maybe we oughta count it."

"Yes, I think we should."

The General rose, holding the overnight bag by its handle, and looked around the room. He noticed a marble-top table that was placed against the far wall. The marble's color was mauve streaked by cream and each of the table's six ornately carved mahogany legs ended in the inevitable ball and claw.

"That table do?" the General asked.

Kite looked. "Sure. I'll just move the lamp over some."

He crossed to the table and moved a shaded brass lamp to the rear left side. The General went over to place the overnight bag on the marble. "It's unlocked," he said.

"All hundreds?"

"Of course."

"One-point-two million?"

"Exactly, Mr. Kite."

Kite nodded, unsnapped the bag's fasteners and lifted the lid, revealing neat, tightly packed rows of banded $100 bills. Kite stared at the money fondly, perhaps even lovingly, and was still staring at it when General Winfield cleared his throat and said, "Emory."

"Yeah?"

"Close the lid."

Kite froze, then thawed quickly enough to ask, "Why?" But he didn't really wait for an answer. Instead, he slammed down the lid, spun around and lunged at the General, but slowed, then stopped altogether after Winfield shot him in the forehead with a .22-caliber revolver.

38

The rented two-bedroom third-floor apartment of Nick Patrokis was at 1911 R Street, N.W., and only a two-minute walk from VOMIT, providing the Connecticut Avenue lights were with him. The apartment had once been occupied by his uncle, the restaurateur, who years ago had moved to the farther reaches of Maryland out Massachusetts Avenue just beyond the District line.

After moving, the uncle had continued to pay the rent on the apartment because it was cheaper than paying the hotel and motel bills of his extended family, whose members dropped in on him with alarming regularity from Athens and London and Sydney and Rome and Brussels. With the founding of VOMIT, the uncle subleased the apartment to his nephew, Nicholas, and by letter, telephone, fax and word of mouth, informed members of his family that if they were planning to visit him in Washington, he could recommend a Holiday Inn out on New York Avenue that was cheap, clean and only a bit dangerous.

At 8:08 that morning, shortly after General Winfield shot Emory Kite, Nick Patrokis awoke in his bedroom, looked left and found a naked Shawnee Viar sitting cross-legged on the bed, studying him with what he thought looked suspiciously like adoration.

"Let's get married," she said.

"When?"

"Next year. The year after. Ten years from now."

"That's an idea," Patrokis said, rose naked from the bed and hurried into the bathroom. Even with the bathroom door closed he heard the loud ring of the black nineteen-year-old Touch-Tone phone that had yet to need repair and whose twin models fetched $100 to $150 at the swap meets where Patrokis had acquired much of his clothing and all of the furniture for the apartment and VOMIT.

After the second ring the phone went silent. When Patrokis, still naked, came out of the bathroom, Shawnee Viar offered him the instrument and said, "It's Partain."

Patrokis said hello and Partain said, "I just got a call from General Hudson."

"Why?"

"He wants me to meet with him and Colonel Millwed."

"Again—why?"

"So we can talk about my going back in the Army as a lieutenant colonel, serving out my twentieth year and retiring on a well-deserved pension."

"Tell him to go ahead and put in the papers."

"I did, but he still wants to talk."

"Where?"

"He'll call back with time and place."

"Why is it," Patrokis asked, "that I suspect the three of you will meet by moonlight at some lonely crossroads in Rappahannock County?"

"Think I should take along a weapon?"

"You have one?"

"No."

"The gun seller has no gun?"

"Do you?"

"What would I do with a gun?" Patrokis said.

"He wants a gun?" Shawnee Viar asked.

"Hold on," Patrokis said, put a hand over the mouthpiece, turned to Shawnee and said, "Why d'you ask?"

"He can have Hank's," she said.

"I thought the cops took it."

"They did, but he has a couple of others stashed around the house."

"Would you lend one to Partain?"

"What's he want with it?"

"I don't know," Patrokis said. "Maybe he wants to shoot Colonel Millwed. Or General Hudson. Or both."

"Tell him I'll bring it to him wherever he is," she said.

At 8:59 A.M. the telephone rang in Edd Partain's hotel room. After he answered it, Millicent Altford said, "My daughter back in her own bed yet?"

"She's not here."

"You dressed?"

"Yes."

"Then get your butt over here right now without anybody seeing you. Think you can handle that?"

"I can try."

Partain opened his hotel room door, glanced up and down the corridor, saw no one, closed his door, went four quick steps to the door next to his, opened it and slipped inside.

"Lock it up good," Millicent Altford said.

Partain shot the bolt, fastened the chain and turned to look first at Altford, who was sitting in a chair, wearing her cashmere robe, then at General Vernon Winfield, who sat at attention in a straight-back chair, hat and gloves off but topcoat still on, the black overnight bag on his knees.

"Sugar here just killed himself a private detective," Millicent Altford said. "The one you all had lunch with at the Dôme."

"Emory Kite," Partain said, merely to be saying something.

"Kite," she agreed, rose, went over to where the whisky was, poured herself an ounce and a half of Scotch and tossed most of it down. "Sugar here's turning me into a morning drinker."

"I take it he's not here to kill you," Partain said.

"I find that extremely offensive, Mr. Partain," the General said.

"He's got a gun," Altford said.

"Want me to take it away from him?"

Before Altford could reply, the General removed the short-barrelled revolver from his topcoat pocket and looked at it thoughtfully. "It fires five twenty-two-caliber long rounds with hollow points. They do tremendous damage but are effective at only very short range. This particular weapon shoots high and right and is virtually useless unless fired by an expert marksman. I shot Mr. Kite just above the bridge of his nose from a distance of perhaps six feet. He was in motion at the time."

Partain walked over to the General, held out his right hand and said, "Mind?"

"Not at all," Winfield said and handed the revolver butt-first to Partain, who examined it, sniffed its two-inch barrel, nodded and tucked the weapon away in his right hip pocket.

"Now show him what's in the bag, sugar," Millicent Altford said.

The General thought about it first, then opened the black overnight bag to reveal the tightly packed banded bundles of $100 bills.

"How much?" Partain said.

"He says one-point-two million but I didn't count it," she said, turned to the General, studied him briefly, drank the rest of her Scotch, sighed and said, "Better tell Twodees how you shorted the yen, optioned all that raw land in Arizona, went in with that wildcatter up in North Dakota and then dumped your Chrysler to buy Apple Computer."

"Yes, perhaps I should," the General said and looked at Partain. "Over the past several years I made some extremely unwise investments. I had to cover my short position on the yen; sold some stocks I should have kept and kept those I should've sold. There were several other, well, desperate ventures, gambles really, and last October I was virtually bankrupt and in dire need of one million dollars. The magic figure. Not a great amount of money, if inflation is taken into account, but—"

Partain interrupted. "What about the property you own in Aspen?"

"It's all leveraged to the limit with first, second and third mortgages. I can't raise a dime on it." He sighed. "Which is why I engaged Mr. Kite's services."

Partain looked at Altford. "Kite stole your one-point-two million?"

"Kite farmed it out, according to sugar here," she said. "Remember poor Dave Laney? Well, he and Kite hooked up together somehow, maybe through General Hudson, who was Dave's uncle. Anyway, Dave flew up to L.A. from Guadalajara on election day last year at Kite's request. For a sixty-thousand-dollar cut Dave went up to my apartment, worked my safe's combination, which he probably got from Jessica without her knowledge, put the money into a bag or something and was escorted in and out of the building by dear dead Jack Thomson, night doorman and sometime actor, who got five thousand dollars cash money and a bullet in the back of his head for his bit part."

"Shot by Mr. Kite, I believe," the General said.

"Why didn't you mortgage your house?"

The General stared straight ahead. "The house was to go to the organization."

"To VOMIT?"

Winfield nodded. "The money from Millicent I thought of as a loan."

"Who really recommended me to you?" Partain asked Altford.

"I already told you, Nick Patrokis."

"Not him?" Partain said, nodding at the General.

"I concurred when Nick told me," the General said. "Millicent was extremely vague as to why she wanted a bodyguard. I of course knew it was because of the stolen money. She was frightened and understandably so."

Partain said, "How'd you approach him—Kite?"

"Nick and I long ago discovered Kite'd been planted on us by General Hudson and Colonel Millwed. We'd had some of our people follow Kite several times and that led us to his meetings with Millwed at out-of-the-way places. After them, Millwed would usually rendezvous with General Hudson at this very hotel. They preferred small rooms on the fourth or fifth floor."

"That doesn't tell me how you approached Kite."

"I simply went over to him in his office one day when no one else was around and asked if he knew of anyone who'd like to steal one million two hundred thousand dollars from a safe for which I had the combination."

"*You* had it?" Altford said.

"The last time we audited the books, Millicent, I'm afraid I peered over your shoulder."

"Christ."

"What'd he say?" Partain asked. "Kite?"

"He wanted details, of course. And there was the matter of the commission. I offered two hundred thousand and refused to bargain. He eventually accepted." The General paused. "It was all rather businesslike."

"Let's you and me do some business," she said. "Tell me

why they had to go and kill my first husband's son, Jerry Montague?"

"Mr. Kite again," the General said. "I think he was following his prime target, Mr. Partain. Not you, Millicent. Jerry Montague simply got in Mr. Kite's way. I'm very sorry."

"Who'd pay Kite to kill me?" Partain said. "Hudson and Millwed?"

"I suspect so. Because of all their unsavory activities in El Salvador. From a hint or two that I got from Mr. Kite, they seem to have inexhaustible funds."

"You say you paid Kite a flat two hundred thousand to steal Mrs. Altford's one-point-two million. No expenses?"

"None. When I was on my way to see him this morning, I had the notion of paying him the same amount to replace the stolen money. Not in Millicent's safe, of course. But somewhere in her apartment. As a surprise."

"What changed your mind?" Partain said.

The General frowned at the question, then nodded his understanding and said, "You mean why did I kill him instead?"

Partain said nothing. Neither did Millicent Altford.

"It simply had to end," the General said. "It had gone on too long. Far too long."

"Did you like it?" Partain said.

Mild shock spread across Winfield's face, and he blushed slightly. "Shooting Mr. Kite? No, sir, I did not."

"I mean all the other stuff—the deceit and the plotting and the betrayal?"

"The treachery, you mean?"

Partain nodded.

"I regret to say I found it—stimulating."

The General put the still-open black overnight bag on the floor and rose. "It's all there, Millicent," he said, gathering up his hat and gloves. "One million two hundred thousand dollars. When we—I mean you, of course—audit the books next month, you'll be able to strike a balance."

Millicent stared at him, then shook her head and said, "I'm so sorry for you. I really am."

He seemed not to hear. "I think I'll walk home. Have some tea. Write a few letters." He looked at Altford, then at Partain. "Goodbye, Millicent. Mr. Partain."

Partain looked a question at Altford, who shook her head.

The General crossed slowly to the door, turned back and said, "Call them in an hour or so and tell them I'll be at home."

"The police?"

"Who else?" he said, turned again, opened the door and was gone.

39

Edd Partain lay fully dressed on the hotel room bed, staring at the ceiling and thinking about his dead wife, about General Winfield and about whether he wanted any lunch when the telephone rang at 12:33 P.M.

He took the phone off the bedside table without rising, brought it down to his left ear and said hello. A woman's voice said, "Mr. Partain? This is Captain Lake, General Hudson's aide? The General deeply regrets the short notice but hopes you'll be able to join him for dinner tonight at his home in Arlington? Would that be possible, sir?"

"I think so," Partain said, guessing she was from Virginia, probably from down around Lynchburg.

"Oh, good. Dinner'll be around eight and the General can send a car for you. But if you prefer to drive yourself, I'll see that a map to his house is left in your hotel box."

"I'll drive myself," Partain said, relieved that the rising inflections had ended.

"He'll be pleased to hear you've accepted."

"Could I bring someone?" Partain said.

There was no hesitation when she said, "General Hudson was hoping you might."

Connie Weeks, the Department of Interior statistician and after-six call girl, was wearing only a Cartier watch when she turned to General Hudson and said, "You were right. He's bringing somebody."

The General nodded and leaned back in the pale brown suede club chair to light a cigar. He wore only a pair of gray worsted pants.

"Probably bringing Patrokis," said Colonel Millwed, who was sprawled on the long couch that was the color of rich cream. The Colonel wore only an unbuttoned white shirt.

"I didn't think it proper to ask who," Connie Weeks said and glanced at her watch. "Now if one of you wants a quickie, I've just got time. But no threesie."

The General waved his cigar in polite refusal and said, "I'll pass, but maybe Colonel Long Dong over there's interested."

Millwed, now gazing at the ceiling, shook his head and said, "Colonel Dong's done been sucked dry."

"Here you go, Connie," the General said, reached into a hip pocket and produced a small plain white envelope. "You'll find a little extra in there."

She smiled, accepted the envelope and said, "Thank you, gentlemen," turned and headed for her apartment's one bedroom, only to stop and turn around when the General said, "Heard about Emory?"

"No," she said. "What?"

"Somebody shot and killed him this morning," he said, then waited for her reaction, which turned out to be one of surprise, if not shock, and of sadness, if not grief. "Emory *Kite*?"

"I hope to Christ he's the only Emory I know," Colonel Millwed said as he swung his feet to the floor and sat up.

"What time'd you leave him this morning?" the General said.

"Eight. Close to eight."

"Notice anything different?"

"Sure. As I went out the front door some old guy wanted in. Middle sixties, I guess, about six feet tall, gray hair—what I could see of it—blue eyes, no beard, no glasses, no fat. He was carrying a black overnight bag and wearing a camel hair topcoat and a fancy hat and walked the way you guys walk, like you're always in a parade."

"He say anything?"

"He said, 'Fun.' "

"Fun?"

"He looked like a possible client so I asked him if he liked fun. And he said 'fun' the way you just said it—as if he didn't know what I was talking about. So I gave him my business card, the one with only my first name and phone number, and told him to call me anytime after six."

"What'd he say?"

"Nothing. He just smiled a little and put my card in his pocket."

General Hudson sighed, then nodded at Colonel Millwed, who rose behind Connie Weeks, grabbed her chin with one hand, the back of her head with the other, pulled hard right, pushed hard left and broke her neck.

Ten minutes later, Colonel Millwed was wearing a suit and tie and holding a roll of Bounty paper towels as he looked around Connie Weeks's living room for something else to wipe down or mop up. The dead woman still lay on the polished hardwood floor near the cream couch.

"Any suggestions?" the Colonel said, carefully stepping over her body.

General Hudson, now in blue blazer, white shirt, tie and gray slacks, glanced around the room and said, "Just the semen in her vagina."

"That's yours. She swallowed mine."

"Let's go," the General said and they left, taking with them Connie Weeks's Cartier watch, her other jewelry, her cash and her credit cards.

They hurried along the apartment house corridor, met no one, took the stairs down one floor, caught an empty elevator, rode it to the basement garage and walked out separately, ten minutes apart. Colonel Millwed kept the cash and later threw the watch, the jewelry and the credit cards into the Potomac.

It was Nick Patrokis who officially identified General Vernon Winfield after the Metropolitan Police found him dead of a self-inflicted gunshot wound. The body lay not far from the large ornate desk in the library, which Partain had guessed contained 9,000 books.

The homicide sergeant was Frank Tine, a tall light brown man of at least 40 who wore a handsome shockproof face and clothing chosen for comfort and warmth by someone, perhaps himself, perhaps his wife, who didn't want him to go around looking all that handsome.

"Know how it looks to me?" Tine asked Patrokis, who stared at the General's body as a police photographer shot frame after frame of 35mm film. "Looks to me like the General sat down at his desk and wrote it all out, then got up and walked over here and shot himself so he wouldn't splatter anything on that new will of his that leaves everything to"—Tine looked down at his notes—"the Victims of Military Intelligence Treachery, whatever the fuck that might be."

"VOMIT," Patrokis said. "He was one of its two founders. I'm the other one."

"He also wrote something else."

Patrokis didn't ask what and looked around the huge room

to see whether anything looked different. He decided that it looked as if somebody had died.

"Want to know what else he wrote?" Tine said.

"Sure."

"A confession."

"That he killed Emory Kite? Yeah, I heard that."

"How the hell'd you hear he wrote a confession?"

"I didn't. I heard he admitted he'd killed Kite. Mrs. Altford called me. After she called you."

Sergeant Tine nodded and turned slowly all the way around, as if inspecting, maybe even appraising, the library. "Think he'd read all these books?"

"Most of them probably."

"How much you think he was worth?"

"I think he was damn near broke and had been for some time."

"Big house like this?"

"It's got a maximum mortgage on it."

"That mean you VOMIT folks aren't gonna get much?"

"Probably nothing," Patrokis said.

"Why d'you think he killed Kite?" the Sergeant asked, his tone lacking all curiosity.

"I don't know," Patrokis said.

"Think he was sick?"

"Who—Kite?"

"The General."

"No. He wasn't sick."

"Kite blackmailing him?"

"I doubt it."

"But that'd give the General a motive, wouldn't it?" Sergeant Tine said. "Say some pissant private cop's threatening to ruin your life. That makes you mad enough to go do something about it. But you don't think it through. And the glow from getting even lasts about two minutes, maybe less, before it hits you what you've really gone and done. So you go tell somebody about it, maybe your oldest friend, maybe this Altford lady, and then you go home, write some stuff, think if there's anything else you ought to do, decide there isn't except one last thing and you go ahead and do it."

The Sergeant gave the big room another appreciative examination before he asked, "How many books in here, you think?"

"About six thousand."

"That many?" he said, looked around some more, then turned back to Patrokis and said, "And the dumb funny thing about all this is that it happened to somebody who, from the looks of things, had it all, all his life."

"He did have it all," Patrokis said. "It's just that he was never quite sure what to do with it."

"Like we would," Tine said.

Patrokis smiled slightly. "Like we would."

<u>40</u>

The only item not packed and ready for travel was the black leather overnight case that contained the one-point-two million dollars. It lay on the bed in Millicent Altford's hotel bedroom, its top flung carelessly back, its suspect contents indecently exposed.

Partain watched as Altford, wearing tailored jeans, a thick white silk pullover and her dark gray cashmere topcoat, picked up two of the bound packets of $100 bills that contained $5,000 each, hesitated, picked up another one, turned, went over to Partain, grabbed his right hand and slapped the three packets into his palm.

"Too much," he said.

"That's for me to decide," she said, picked up a bottle on the room's dresser, poured its remaining two and a half ounces of Scotch into a pair of glasses, handed him one and asked, "You going back to L.A.?"

"In a day or two."

"Well, you've got a first-class ticket with an open return, so take your time."

"Jessica around?" he asked.

"Somewhere," she said, finished her drink, put the glass down, went over to the bed, lowered the lid on the money case and zipped it closed. She wanted to lock it but had no key and asked Partain, "What d'you think? Carry-on or check it through?"

"Check it through unless you want some security X-ray taking a peek inside."

There was a firm knock at the door of the suite's sitting room followed by the voice of a bellman announcing his presence. Altford hurried into the sitting room and opened the corridor door. The bellman was a young Latino, who smiled winningly and said, "Luggage?"

"In the bedroom."

He nodded, hurried into the bedroom, grinned at Partain, picked up Altford's suitcase, then indicated the black overnight case on the bed and asked, "This too?"

"That too," she said.

He picked it up, sagged to one side because of its unexpected weight, said, "Heavy, no?" and was gone.

After the corridor door closed, Millicent Altford examined Partain briefly. "You wanta work for me steady?"

"Doing what?" he said, finished his drink and put the glass down.

"Who knows?"

"What's it pay?"

"The same as a light-colonel'd make."

He grinned. "I'll let you know."

She nodded and left him with a smile and a conspiratorial wink. After he heard the corridor door in the sitting room close, Partain picked up the bedroom phone and dialed a number that was answered on the third ring.

"It's Edd Partain, Shawnee. What'd you decide about dinner?"

"Wouldn't miss it for the world," said Shawnee Viar.

* * *

Partain was wearing his new blue suit, a new white shirt, one of his two new ties and the Kevlar vest when Shawnee Viar picked him up in her gray Volvo station wagon at 7 P.M., just north of the Mayflower entrance.

Partain handed her the nicely drawn Xeroxed copy of a map to General Walker Hudson's house that someone had left in his hotel box. Shawnee looked at it for a long moment with the aid of the dashboard lights, nodded and said, "Yeah, I know where it is. Out there it's half-acre lots, pools, pine trees, dogs and not quite enough room for a horse."

After going through Georgetown they crossed Key Bridge, turned onto the George Washington Memorial Parkway and eventually turned left onto a twisting blacktop that went on for 1.7 miles until they came to the promised curb mailbox with a coxcomb of wooden letters that spelled "Hudson."

A fairly long paving-block drive led up to a sprawling one-story stone house with an immense chimney and extremely wide eaves. The builder had left as many pines as possible and there was only a trace of a proper yard.

"What if—" she said.

"I don't know," Partain said, not letting her finish.

She stopped the Volvo at the top of the drive in front of the entrance, then switched off the engine and the headlights. Two lanternlike fixtures glowed on either side of the entrance door, which appeared to be made from thick slabs of oak.

Partain got out first. Shawnee came out more slowly, wearing a long tan raincoat that almost met the tops of her speed-lace boots. Partain had no idea what was beneath the buttoned-up raincoat. Maybe shorts and a tank top. Maybe even a dress.

"Is there a Mrs. General Hudson?" she asked.

"There were three of them but they all left," Partain said as he reached the oak door and pressed an inset ivory-colored button. Chimes rang inside. Partain counted to five and the door was opened on six by Colonel Ralph Millwed, wearing a false smile, a dress uniform and all of his ribbons.

"Ms. Shawnee Viar!" the Colonel said, raising his voice and making a mock announcement of the guests' names. "And Mr. Twodees Partain!"

He opened the door wide and Shawnee Viar brushed past him. Partain followed her into the room and stopped, waiting for Millwed to close the door. It was a large oblong room with too much expensive furniture. At its far end, General Walker Hudson, also in dress uniform, was rising from a burgundy leather couch, wearing a wide smile.

Partain heard the front door close, took two fast steps backward, used his right elbow as a piston and twice drove it deeply into Colonel Millwed's solar plexus, torturing its ganglia of sympathetic nerves.

Partain spun around and waited, seemingly forever, until Millwed doubled over, clutching his midsection. It was then that Partain brought up his right knee and broke Millwed's nose.

After the Colonel collapsed on the polished random-width pine floor, Partain knelt, searched him quickly and removed a small Beretta semiautomatic from the right hip pocket. It was just after he had the Beretta in his hand that Partain heard Shawnee Viar snarl her command. "Back down, asshole."

He turned to look. General Hudson was slowly lowering himself into the burgundy leather couch. Shawnee stood no more than four feet from him, both hands aiming a .38 Colt revolver at the General's chest. The barrel of the pistol wavered scarcely at all.

Partain turned back to Colonel Millwed, who still lay curled up on the pine floor and was now making mewling noises interrupted by an occasional series of harsh grunts. Partain took out a handkerchief, thoroughly wiped the Colonel's Beretta, wrapped the handkerchief around the barrel and placed the weapon in the Colonel's right hand.

"I'll break all the fingers of your right hand if you don't do exactly what I say," Partain murmured. "I'm now going to aim the Beretta and you're going to pull the trigger. When I say fire, you fire."

Partain aimed the weapon in Millwed's hand at a nearby overstuffed armchair and said, "Fire." The gun went off and a round hole appeared in the chair's back.

"Let go the gun," Partain said.

The weapon fell a few inches to the floor. Partain rose, kicked it six feet away, then turned and walked past it until he was a yard away from the General.

"You two are in deep, deep shit," General Hudson said in a pleased and confident voice, then leaned back on the couch and crossed his legs.

"Both hands on that top knee after you put out your cigar," Partain said.

The General did as told and said, "Now what?"

"You okay, Shawnee?" Partain asked.

"Never better."

"We want two things," Partain said to the General. "We want Hank Viar's thirty-two notebooks. That's first."

The General's eyes danced from Partain to Shawnee Viar and back. "What if I don't have them?"

"I get to shoot you," Shawnee said.

"And if I do have them?"

"Then you live," Partain said.

"And the catch?"

"We'll get to that."

The General nodded at a cherrywood cabinet to Partain's left. "See that cabinet over there?"

Partain looked, nodded and turned back.

"Well, it's not exactly a cabinet, although it's got that nice Tiffany lamp on it. It's a safe. Viar's stuff's inside it."

"Is there an alarm?"

"No alarm."

"If it's a silent one, you won't finish the night."

"No alarm."

"What's the combination?"

The General rattled it off. Partain went over to the cabinet, knelt, cautiously opened the wood door, revealing a sturdy gray steel safe. Partain worked the combination, waited, pulled down the safe's handle, tugged at it and opened the safe.

There were two steel shelves. The bottom one held the thirty-two red spiral notebooks of Henry Viar. The top shelf was packed almost solid with currency, mostly banded $50 and $100 bills. Partain guessed there was nearly $400,000.

Partain removed the spiral notebooks, closed the safe's door and rose.

"Let's make him read us the part where they tried to make Hank disappear your wife," Shawnee said.

"We might," Partain said and put the spiral notebooks on a table.

"Not taking the cash?" the General said.

"It's not mine," Partain said, then turned to look at Colonel Millwed, who now lay on his left side and was inching his way toward the Beretta that still lay five feet away.

"No closer, Ralph," Partain said, "or I'll have to bust something else."

The Colonel whimpered and lay still.

"Now comes the catch," the General said.

Partain agreed with a nod and took a small .22-caliber revolver from his jacket pocket. "This is the same weapon that General Winfield used to kill Emory Kite this morning. You heard about Kite, of course."

"I heard."

"Well, you get to use it on Colonel Millwed."

"Kill him?"

Partain nodded.

"No," the General said, snapping the word out. "Never."

"Think about it," Partain said. "He's already shot at you

and missed with his Beretta. This was after your argument that ended in a brief brutal fight that'll explain Ralphie's bumps and bruises."

"You broke his fucking nose, mister."

"And you put up a great fight. But to save your own life, you eventually had to shoot him and you regret it very, very much."

"Let's hear the rest of it," General Hudson said.

"If you don't shoot him, Shawnee here shoots you."

"Then she dies in jail."

"I've already spent a year in a locked ward, dickhead," Shawnee said. "The most I'll get is six months and I'll be out in two. I'm Hank Viar's loony grief-crazed daughter, remember? You murdered my daddy and I went bonkers."

The General cleared his throat and said, "And if I shoot him?"

"You fuck!" the Colonel screamed.

"It'll probably end your Army career but you'll be alive."

"Let's get it over with, then," the General said.

"GODDAMN YOU, WALKER!" the Colonel yelled.

The three of them ignored him as Partain took the .38-caliber revolver from Shawnee Viar, aimed it at the General and said, "Let's go see Millwed. That's when I hand you the twenty-two and you shoot him. I'd suggest the temple but you might have your own preference."

"Partain, you fuck," Millwed said, not bothering to scream or yell.

As the General and Partain went slowly over to the prostrate Colonel, Shawnee Viar gathered up the thirty-two red spiral notebooks, pressed them to her chest and followed the two men. Her eyes were wide and bright and amused.

When the two men reached him, the Colonel looked up and begged. "Please, Walker. Don't kill me. For God's sake, don't."

"Let's do it," the General said to Partain.

Partain used his right hand to stick the barrel of the .38-caliber revolver into the General's right ear. "Insurance," Partain said, then handed over the .22.

"I'M GODDAMN BEGGING YOU, YOU FUCK!" the Colonel roared and then squeezed his eyes shut.

"Sorry, pal," the General said, squatted, held the small revolver two inches away from Millwed's temple and pulled the trigger. There was a loud snap and a click.

The General turned pale. The Colonel began to weep. Partain bent over, removed the .22 from the General's hand, straightened, put the small gun away and said, "Let's go, Shawnee."

The General rose slowly, staring at Partain. Fear had settled on his face for the first time. His voice sounded old and scratchy when he asked, "What happens to Viar's diaries?"

"The Army gets them," Partain said. "You guys can work out a defense between you. I suspect the Colonel's will be that he was only following orders, right, Ralph?"

"Fuck you, Partain," the Colonel whispered.

"Can I kick him just once in the balls?" Shawnee Viar said.

"If you really want to," Partain said.

"No," she said. "I guess I don't."

41

When the United 747 was forty miles west of Dulles, Edd Partain stopped a passing flight attendant in the first-class section and said, "There's a Ms. J. Carver back in steerage who needs to upgrade her seat." He indicated the vacant aisle seat next to his. "This one's empty. Can you arrange it?"

"Who's buying?" the attendant asked.

"I am."

"She have a cheapo ticket?"

"Probably."

"It'll cost you a bundle."

Partain reached into a pocket of his new brown herringbone jacket, came up with some folded-over $100 bills and said, "Here's a thousand. If it's more, let me know."

The flight attendant, a handsome 50, fussed over Jessica Carver for almost five minutes, urging her to have another breakfast, which was refused, or a drink, which was accepted. Carver swallowed some of her Bloody Mary and asked Partain, "Where were you last night?"

"With Patrokis and Shawnee. Most of the time."

"And earlier?"

"Shawnee and I put on a recital for General Hudson and Colonel Millwed."

"You going to tell me about it?"

Partain turned to stare down at the cloud layer 15,000 feet below, then turned back and said, "Sure. Why not? But Shawnee comes out as the heroine."

"Good."

It took Partain twenty minutes to tell her and when he was done, she asked, "Who else knows?"

"Just Patrokis—and you."

"When's it all coming out?"

Partain smiled. "On the first real slow news day."

Over the Grand Canyon, Partain said, "Your mother wants me to go to work for her."

"Doing what?"

"Probably apprentice rainmaker."

"You going to?"

"Maybe."

"That means we'll both have jobs," she said. "I got an offer from the transition team yesterday."

"What kind of offer?"

"They're looking for the best baby-talk writer in the country and a guy who has this hot ad agency in Venice recommended me."

"What's a baby-talk writer?"

"Someone who can boil a one-hundred-page position paper down into three words. Maybe four."

"Like a billboard?"

"Exactly."

"Did you take it?"

"It's a five-hundred-a-day consultant's job. I told them I'd have to work out of L.A., not Washington, and that made them antsy until I described how wonderful modern telecommunications are. Fast, too."

"Then you'll have to find a place to live," Partain said.

"We both will," she said.

Their welcoming committee at LAX consisted only of the LAPD homicide Detective Sergeant Ovid Knox, as resplendent as ever in cashmere and gabardine. Both Partain and Carver had only carry-on luggage. Knox took it away from them, piled it on a cart he had rented, and offered them a ride into town.

When they were on the 405 in Knox's plain brown Chevrolet sedan and heading for Wilshire, he said, "I busted a guy called Manny Rosales on an old felony rap three days ago, squeezed him some and he gave up a Washington private cop called Emory Kite. Ever hear of him?"

"He's dead," Partain said.

"So I found out. But it seems Kite was the one who took out your ex-boyfriend, Dave Laney, and also Jack Thomson, the doorman."

"Why?" Jessica Carver said.

Knox ignored the question and said, "So that about wraps up Manny, Kite, Laney and Thomson. But the Washington cops tell me a retired brigadier general did Kite yesterday, then went home, wrote a confession, and did himself."

"General Winfield was an old friend of my mother's," Carver said.

There was a long silence until Sergeant Knox said, "Got any questions? Because if you don't, I do."

"One," Partain said. "You wouldn't happen to know where we could rent a nice two-bedroom apartment, would you?"

Knox thought about it, then asked, "Brentwood okay?"